THE NEIGHBORS

THE
NEIGHBORS

JANE ABBOTT

PEOPLES BOOK CLUB, CHICAGO

This is a special edition published exclusively for the members of the Peoples Book Club, P.O. Box 6570 A, Chicago 80, Illinois, and 228 Bloor Street West, Toronto 5, Ontario, Canada. It was originally published by J. B. Lippincott Company, Philadelphia and New York.

Library of Congress catalog card number 52-5095

THE NEIGHBORS

CHAPTER I

IT HAD BEEN Will Brent's habit for years to wait a half-hour after closing time to leave his plant and to pause, on his way out, and run his eyes over the place to assure himself that everything was as it should be. At such moments, along with his concern, he invariably enjoyed an agreeable satisfaction in his enterprise.

It was far from an impressive plant—three old low planked buildings built around a smaller one of such antiquity that its roof sagged low in the middle. No high wire fence enclosed it. No railroad sidings flanked it. Over the door of the very old building hung a painted sign: "W. Brent, Smithy 1810." It had remained where it was even after a Brent of a later generation turned the smithy into a factory for the manufacturing of nails. The Will Brent of the present day would have seen it sacrilege to take it down. In his eyes it was the outward sign of his family's deep roots in the soil of New England industry.

That it never had brought wealth to any succeeding generation of Brents did not matter—it brought enough to raise and educate children, live in modest comfort—its greatest profit was in the knowledge that Brent nails were known for their superior quality the length and breadth of New England. And little existed for a Brent beyond New England.

He always walked the distance to and from the plant. The exercise kept him in good physical condition and he considered that was important as it set a good example for the men he employed. "Look at me—I can't remember when I've had a sick day," he could say to any

7

absentee. If they looked, they saw a tall, lean man, nearing sixty, but straight-shouldered, strong of limb.

But on this particular day, a day in June, he left the plant without so much as a glance at it and his shoulders sagged a little with the weight that was on his mind. A letter had come during the day from his half-sister Deborah, in which she had written that she was returning to Sweethome.

"In heaven's name, *why?*"

She had not shown her face in the village since she had run off with Paul Bouvais, almost forty years ago. And why come now? Will Brent knew well that the story of conduct such as hers was not forgotten even in forty years in a community like Sweethome.

In that time she had lived here, there and everywhere, or so he had gathered from the cards she sent him from time to time. He never had written to her in answer, for two reasons—one, he had grown to feel that she was no longer one of the family; the other, he was never certain by what surname to address her, should he write. After Bouvais it had been Curtis—there might be others. . . . She had signed this last letter "Deborah Brent," and he frowned over that.

She had written, "I heard from Clare that no one is living now in the old house. I'd like to go there. I suppose the old furniture is still in it. . . ."

If Deborah had not known the old house was untenanted she might not have planned to come. Will Brent rarely used profanity but he damned Clare Hersey now with some explosiveness. She and Deborah had been girlhood chums and apparently had written back and forth through these years—Deborah probably knew as much of everything that had happened in Sweethome as he did. And Sweethome would know from Clare everything about Debbie.

The "old" house was their father's house, where he and Deborah had grown up. It had been occupied by Doctor Pryor and his wife until a year ago when the Doctor retired and went to Florida to live. The old furniture was still in it. He could think of no reason to give

8

Deborah why she could not settle there. "And pay rent," he said, aloud. By his father's will the old house—as had the plant—had come to him.

The worrisome part of it was that it was next to his own which had belonged to his mother's family, the Merritts. It had seemed practical to move into it after he married because the older house was the larger of the two and would bring in a higher rental. Deborah, when she came, would be only a stone's throw away—a well-worn path led from his back door across his side yard, through a trellised arbor and on to the back door of the other house. And that was too close for his liking! He did not want his girls exposed to Debbie's doubtful influence. Nell, particularly, at her age, near nineteen. Of late he had noticed signs of restlessness in her, of small rebellions. Susan was too steady-headed to be affected by any unconventional ideas; Bill, his boy, and fifteen, was too young.

A quarter of a mile from the plant the road joined the highway through the village. This skirted the Sequag River which divided the sheep and goats of the valley as definitely as any traditional railroad tracks. On one side, the solid citizens of Sweethome had their homes, their churches, their stores, their graded school. Most lived, as had the Brents, in houses built generations ago, one like the other, white-painted, traces of their original salt-box architecture still apparent, with fanlighted doors, generous yards and old trees. All of which, with the hillside back of it, combined to give the village a look of secure living.

On the other side of the river was a stretch of treeless flat land, often, in the past, flooded during the spring thaws. In Will Brent's boyhood there had been only a few homes there, "shanties," Sweethome had called them, though some were a little better than that, occupied by a drift of French-Canadians and Italians, who looked to the rich soil of the valley bottom to yield them a living with a minimum of investment. The Bouvais family had been one of these. Eventually the state had constructed a reservoir at the upper flow

9

of the river, minimizing the likelihood of floods; a knitting mill had been built near the dam below the bridge that connected the Flats and Sweethome; a spur of the Pittsfield line of the New Haven and Hartford Railroad had been run in; flimsy bungalows, a church, a few stores, had appeared seemingly overnight along the dirt roads that zigzagged over the Flats, giving it a look of thriving occupation.

Then a realty firm in Canaan had bought up the land not already owned, had called it "Park Meadows." It had enough political influence to have a state highway built across the valley so that the natives of Sweethome were obliged to drive through the Flats when their destination was to the north or the west, or else follow circuitous roads over the hills. A huge billboard at the edge of the river, neon-lighted at night, informed Sweethome that exclusive building lots were still available. But Sweethome turned a cold shoulder to it. It had to use the new highway and the flag-stop railway station, but live in the Flats—no! It was very well satisfied with its own exclusiveness.

Now, as conspicuous as the sign across the river, stood the recently built plant of the Rudolph Petersen Co. Bolts, Screws, Nails: buildings of yellow brick with generous plots of newly sodded grass separating them, young trees outlining the roads that wound about the buildings. Stretching off to right and left were homes for the workers and their families, each of yellow brick, but each a little different in its architecture, each with its trees and grass. A modern plant—it was said in Sweethome that everything in it from the machines to the plumbing in the houses was of the very latest invention. It was said, too, that a television set had been installed in each home.

On any other evening Will Brent, reaching the River Road, would have looked over at the new plant, as he had since the day, over a year ago, when men began to dig up ground for the concrete supports. The outrage he and the others of Sweethome had felt then at this Rudolph Petersen for moving his works from New Jersey to this valley in Connecticut, had worn down to a fine scorn, fostered by his secure entrenchment in the reputation of his products for superlative quality. Scorn for the man himself . . . Will Brent never had met him but he had frequently seen him driving through Sweethome in his big convertible car, top down, wearing no hat even in cold weather, broad-shouldered, red-faced. A type Will Brent did not like. But tonight he threw no thought even of scorn across to this foreigner and his plant—he walked along, frowning into the space ahead, pondering on how much he was going to tell the girls about Deborah.

"We will not speak of Deborah Brent, ever again," his mother had said. It was breakfast time: She had gone up to Debbie's room, then come down. "She climbed out the window last night—down the cherry tree. She's gone with that fellow. We're through with her. She's made her bed, she can lie in it."

The way she said it, the look on her face, had made it a law. For his father to obey as well as himself. He had realized, young as he was, that the look of sadness sometimes on his father's face, came from some yearning to defend his daughter but never, to his knowledge, had his father had the courage to put it into words.

As the years went ahead it had come to seem as if Debbie had dropped out of existence, except at those times when cards had come to him from her, jarring him to the knowledge that she was very much alive. He never spoke of her before the children. They never had seen her, so she could have little reality for them. Now he must tell them something about her. . . .

Not of her frequent marriages—if they *were* marriages. Bouvais had died, he knew, but he knew nothing of the others. He did not know anything about her financial circumstances. He felt a sudden prickle of sweat on his brow and mopped it with the back of his hand. Why, she might be coming back for him to support her!

Then, as suddenly as this thought thrust itself into his mind, came another. . . . In those cards she had sent to him she had addressed him as "Dear Willie." No one had called him that since he had grown to manhood. Could it be—could it be that Debbie had kept through these years a feeling of fondness, of kinship toward him? And might look to him for a return of it? This, oddly, was as disquieting to him as the possibility of having to support her.

He found Susan talking on the telephone when he walked in the side door. "Yes. Yes, indeed, I'll be very glad to do it for you. Tomorrow? I'll come about half-past two."

She put the receiver on the hook. "Hello, Father." There was a little lift of excitement in her voice. "That was John Wendell—he's asked me to do some typing for him. I told him one day last week that I'd be glad to help him anyway I could."

"You don't think the village will say you're running after this young minister?"

Susan gave a shaky laugh. "Sitting at a typewriter isn't running after him! That's silly, Father!"

He patted her shoulder. "Yes, it is. I know I don't have to worry about you doing anything that would make tongues wag. Dinner ready? Where's Nell?"

"I don't know. But we can't wait for her. Bill has to be back at Higgins' at seven—it's Monday evening. Go and wash up, Father, and I'll put things on the table."

As Will Brent went up the stairs he wondered as he had many times before what he would have done after Mary died without this dependable girl of his to take over. She had been in her first year of teaching in the grade school in New Hartford but she had turned in her resignation at once. "You need me here, Father," she had said over his protest. And she had met the responsibilities of the home and the two younger children so willingly, so competently, that there had seemed no break—he had to admit that she really was a better housekeeper than Mary had been. More saving.

This young minister, Wendell—Susan had appeared quite set up because he'd asked her to do something for him. Unless the fellow was blind he'd see her a perfect wife for a man in his kind of work. She was, as well, very pleasing to look at, with her brown hair and brown eyes which she had inherited from Mary, the gentleness in her face that was like Mary's, too. As he sloshed soapy water over his face he reflected on this possibility and on the change it would bring here at home—though, of course, he told himself, he wanted Susan to marry sometime, when she met the right man. He had felt a prick of concern now and then because, tied down as she was, she was not meeting any right men. This Wendell was a personable young chap—though, coming to that in his thoughts, Will Brent made some reservations. Wendell was too unconventional in his sermons for his liking, too—unpredictable. He'd been given a D.S.C. for something he had done in the war but that did not guarantee he had the makings of the kind of minister they wanted—a minister like Winfield Marcy, his predecessor. As one of the deacons of the church, it was within Will Brent's province to watch this new man.

Down in the kitchen, dishing up the supper, Susan was thinking, happily, "He didn't ask Judith Sears or Libby White—and they *have* been really running after him!" Telling him that day that she would be glad to do some typing for him—it was after he had remarked that he needed a half-dozen extra pairs of hands to get through the clerical work that had piled up—was not the same as contriving opportunities to meet him, the way Judith and Libby were doing. Often, after Sunday service, she slipped out of the side door instead of going through the vestibule, telling herself she was saving John Wendell *one* handshake, while Judith and Libby, dolled up as they never before had dolled up for church, hung around him there in the vestibule, keeping him from his dinner. . . .

Yet he had noticed her—he had called on her to help him! He had asked her to come to his office. . . .

Young Bill came into the dining room from the kitchen as his father entered it from the hall.

"Good evening, son."

"H'lo." But Bill looked at the steaming dishes on the table instead

13

of at his father. He slid into his chair without pulling it out.

"Have you washed, Bill?" asked Susan.

"Oh, cripes!" But he got to his feet awkwardly, started toward the kitchen.

"Upstairs, Bill!"

Bill growled something inarticulate but he did Susan's bidding. Susan's smile, following him, was indulgent. She was too inwardly aglow with expectancy even to think of how she had to tell Bill every night to go upstairs, and not to the kitchen, to wash.

"Has he done his homework?" asked Will Brent.

"He said he didn't have any to do."

"It would not hurt him to review his studies—examinations are coming soon. His marks have been lower than ever this term."

"He's growing so fast, Father. That accounts for it."

Bill came back, his thin face pink from lathering, his thick fair hair dripping with the water with which he had hastily tried to smooth it to some tidiness. He sat down, looked down at his plate. "Don't we ever have anything but meatloaf?"

His father answered. "When I was your age, son, I ate what was put before me without any comment. We have been waiting for you to come to say grace."

He bent his head. "We thank Thee, our Heavenly Father, for this food and ask Your Blessing on it and on our home. Amen."

"Well, you could put more *meat* in it," continued Bill, at the same time lifting a loaded forkful to his mouth.

"I don't like Nell coming in late like this so often," observed Will Brent. "She ought to tell you where she goes—telephone to you, at least."

Bill's head jerked up, his lips opened, then closed.

Susan said, "It might occur to her that it'd be nice to get the dishes cleared away early so as to do something else."

She had spoken mildly but her father took it as reproach.

Nell had graduated last June from the Winsted High School but

14

she had not been interested in further study at the State Normal, as Susan had been. She had told her father that she wanted to go somewhere and take voice training. And what would she do with that, he had demanded. There had been prolonged argument over it which had ended with his dictum that until she could make up her mind to take some study that would fit her to earn a sensible livelihood she could stay home and help Susan. But it was evident she was not helping Susan much. "I'll speak to her when she comes in." At the same moment he thought, a little wearily, "I will not speak of Debbie until she comes—tell the two girls at the same time." Wait until Bill had gone to Higgins' General Store where he worked afternoons and Monday evenings behind a soda bar which recently had been installed.

Susan was bringing in the dessert when Nell ran into the house. A gust of breeze seemed to come with her. "The late Nellie Brent!" she cried gaily from the door. "And am I hungry! What's to eat?"

Will Brent did not speak the rebuke he had planned, mainly because he saw that she was in no mood to listen to it. Her face was aglow, her blue eyes had little sparks of light in them, her mouth its upward curve. She was not a pretty girl—her nose was too short, her chin too pointed for the wideness of her mouth, her eyes, sometimes blue, sometimes green, had an odd upward slant toward the temples—but so alive and warm were the changing expressions on her face that it attracted where mere prettiness did not. Above it her hair grew brush-like, thick and wavy, from brow and temples, a sheen of copper. At times, especially since she had grown older, Will Brent had felt faintly disturbed when he looked at this younger daughter who did not take after anyone in his family or in her mother's. He told himself that he never knew what was going on under that blaze of hair. He was disturbed now, and silenced.

"Your dinner's on a plate in the oven," said Susan.

"Thanks, darling." Nell went to the kitchen, humming a snatch of a song, her step as light, and came back with her plate. "What do

15

you think, Sue—I am going to sing in that chorus for the Commemoration. Mrs. Peely asked me to. Seems they need sopranos."

"So that's where you have been," said Will Brent, his smile on her quick in his relief.

"Huh," muttered Bill over his last mouthful of pie.

Susan said nothing. She was struggling with a little stab of jealousy. This chorus which Mrs. Peely was getting together would take part in the Commemoration in July of the two-hundredth anniversary of the laying of the cornerstone of the Congregational Church. Later, John Wendell would direct it. But immediately she told herself that what she was going to do for him tomorrow was worth much more than singing with a dozen or so others.

"I'll have to buy a white dress—I've nothing from last summer. . . ."

"Your mother used to make her dresses."

"Oh, yes, my grandmother did too and my great-grandmother. They spun the cloth. And they churned their own butter and made their own soap and the men folks went out and killed deer and wild pigs and turkeys, for their food!" Nell's warm voice, her dancing eyes, added to the impudence of her retort. "I've heard it all before. Tell me something new! If there ever *is* anything new in these parts!"

"There is," thought Will Brent with some grimness.

Bill got up from his chair. "See y'later." He went out through the kitchen, banging the screen door after him.

Will Brent cleared his throat. "I had quite a surprise today—a letter from my half-sister Deborah. Your Aunt Deborah, I suppose you could call her. I had not heard from her for years. Even more surprising—she wrote that she is coming back to Sweethome. She'll live in the house next door."

He stopped there. Perhaps it might not be necessary to say more. He waited for their reaction.

Both of the girls were staring at him in utter surprise.

"Aunt Deborah! I'd forgotten her!" cried Susan. "It's been ages since you've spoken of her, Father."

"It's been so long since I've seen her—she's lived in so many places in the West—that I've known little about her to say," explained Will Brent guardedly.

"I wonder what she'll be like," said Nell but with no great interest. She added, "She must be awfully old!"

"She is three years older than I am—am I awfully old in your eyes, daughter?"

"Well . . ." Nell gave her careless laugh. "When you get stuffy you do, Daddy!"

Will Brent allowed himself to relax. The girls did not appear overly curious about Deborah.

He said to Susan, "I suppose we ought to get Abby Boyd in to go over the other house. . . ."

"When is she coming?" asked Susan.

"As soon as she can settle some affairs in San Francisco—that is where she has been living, I take it, for a time. It could be in a week or in a month, I can't say."

"I'll see Abby tomorrow," said Susan. She got up a little quickly, carried her dessert plate to the kitchen, to hide what might be betrayed on her face. For she was thinking, "Aunt Deborah here— Father wouldn't need me—I could—I could . . ."

"Dad!" Nell cried and now the high pitch of her voice took Susan back to the dining room as quickly as she had left it. Now Nell was on the edge of her chair, plainly excited. "Dad, it was Aunt Deborah, wasn't it, who eloped with a man from the Flats? Climbed out of her bedroom window and down a tree? Your mother had locked her in her room; I remember, Jeanie Wilson told me all about it, way back in grade school. She'd heard her mother telling it all to someone. I remember Jeanie said her mother said Aunt Deborah was fast and I slapped her for it. Slapped her *hard!* She didn't speak

17

to me for weeks afterwards. Funny, my forgetting anything in the family as divinely Victorian as that! And she's been married a lot since, hasn't she?"

Will Brent felt a chill at the back of his neck. "That elopement of hers had far better be forgotten, Nell. I've no doubt but that she has looked back upon her conduct with considerable regret. Self-respect is the most valuable thing we can possess through life."

He broke off because he saw a sudden darkening in Nell's eyes, a suggestion of defiance. "What was wrong with the boy from the Flats?" There was defiance in her voice.

"He was a foreigner, for one thing. Half French. For another, he had no steady employment, earned what money he did earn playing a fiddle at the dances around about." Will Brent got up from his chair. "Nell, I forbid you to speak of it again. Your Aunt Deborah will appreciate it, I am certain, if you put it entirely out of your mind. You'll see Abby tomorrow, Susan?"

"Yes," said Susan.

He went out on the porch to smoke the only cigar he permitted himself through a day. But he had no enjoyment in it tonight. He kept hearing that defiance in Nell's voice. He did not like it.

CHAPTER II

At HALF-PAST TWO the next afternoon Susan rang the doorbell of the parsonage of the Sweethome Congregational Church, then locked her fingers tightly together to control their trembling.

She was unfamiliar with this inner agitation. She had found herself, without knowing it, putting on her new print dress, then had realized in time that this was not an occasion to wear it and had hurriedly changed to a more appropriate, freshly laundered, yellow cotton. She had been glad Nell was in the kitchen, ironing, and not a witness to her last minute's touch of a little perfume under the lobes of her ears.

She had called, "See you later," to Nell and gone off before Nell could ask her where she was going.

She hoped Mrs. Donnell would answer her ring. Eliza Donnell had kept house for Winfield Marcy for the fifteen years after his wife died, and, after his death, had stayed on with John Wendell. It had not crossed anyone's thoughts that she would not stay. Sweethome saw her as integral a part of the parsonage as the old beams of its structure. A spare, forbidding-looking woman—one glance from her, Susan knew, would chill this excitement that was possessing her.

But the door swung back and John Wendell himself stood in it. He was putting his hand out to her with a broad smile. "I was waiting for you to come!"

His smile was very pleasant, with a sweetness in it that banished entirely the rather tense gravity usually on his face. Susan stood before it, almost tongue-tied. His appearance added to her confusion. On the occasions when she had met him he had been dressed in sober dark serge—now he was wearing old gray slacks and a much-worn plaid sports coat.

She managed to get out, "I hope I really can help you!"

He led her to a room at the side of the hall which served as the church office and his study. She had been in it often during Winfield Marcy's regime, yet now it had an unfamiliar look because it was John Wendell's. Or perhaps because of the litter it was in.

He saw her glance go over it. "I must apologize for my untidiness— Mrs. Donnell is shocked by it. But I'll have it in order as soon as I finish some shelves I am making and a set of files. Sit down, Miss Brent." He swept some magazines from a chair to the floor, drew the chair toward the desk. "Will you be comfortable here?"

"Yes, indeed. Only . . ." Susan laughed. The top of the desk was hidden by books and magazines.

John Wendell met that situation by stacking them in a pile at one end of the desk. Then he produced a battered old typewriter. "Hope it works. I haven't touched it in months. Say, I am assuming that you do type. . . ."

"I can—fairly well. I took a course in it at school."

"You could be the world's worst and still beat me at it. I'll get the stuff I need to have copied."

He found it, brought it to her, a thick sheaf of small-size sheets of paper scrawled over in lead pencil.

"These are notes I've made from time to time, over the last few years—from sermons I heard while I was in the Seminary, books I've studied—and a lot I took down after talks with a chaplain in the army. I've been putting them in alphabetical order. I've this much done. See, I bought these cards to copy them on. Think they'll do?"

"I—think so." Susan picked up a card and the top sheet of the notes. But she had trouble keeping her hands steady and the words on the paper zigzagged crazily together.

20

"I'll sit over here at the table where you can give me an s.o.s. if you can't read my handwriting. I have to finish a report to go to the State Superintendent." He sat down, his back to her.

The instructor of the business course she had taken in school had laid much emphasis on the impersonal attitude the secretary always should maintain toward her job. Susan drew her chair closer to the desk, slipped a card under the roller of the typewriter and tried to make this situation seem only business-like. The typewriter did work and after a moment's study she could read the up-slanting lines of the notes and she began to type, but at the same time she was thinking of just how John Wendell looked, there at the table behind her. Even though she held her eyes on her work she could see him—his broad shoulders and head, with its close-cut, mouse-colored hair, bent to his work, his thick, slightly crooked brows drawn into a half-frown. She knew these features about him and others—that his nose had a perceptible bump just below its bridge, as if it had been broken at some time, that his chin was square and jutted a very little, because through each Sunday service since he had come to Sweethome she had been more aware of such things than that he was preaching sermons very different from those old Winfield Marcy had given them.

The house was very still. Whatever Mrs. Donnell was doing, she was making no sound. There swept in on Susan a sudden thrilling sense of closeness to this man, enwrapped with her in the deep quiet. Crazy in her, she told herself, striking a wrong key, but just the same she felt it—as if, with these notes with which he had entrusted her and from which he would find ideas for his sermons, she were a little way inside his mind.

She thought, a little dizzily, "There are a lot of notes—it's going to take a long time to copy them! Then maybe I can help him catalogue them!'

A clock struck somewhere and John Wendell pushed back his chair. "I didn't realize it was so late! You mustn't work another minute,

Miss Brent." He went to her, gathered up the notes. "You will not want to help me again."

"But I'm not a bit tired," protested Susan. "And I'd like to help you some other afternoon."

"Will you? Say on Friday?"

"Yes, I'll come on Friday."

"How about a cup of tea to finish the afternoon off? I'll ask Mrs. Donnell to make us some." He did not wait for her to answer but went off to the kitchen. Almost at once he was back. "I'd forgotten— she's gone to Winsted this afternoon. But—any reason we can't make it for ourselves? Mind going out to the kitchen? It's really the pleasantest room in the house."

The little exciting thrill was still beating along Susan's pulses. "Of course I don't mind!"

The kitchen was pleasant and inviting with the afternoon sun filling it. John Wendell went to a cupboard, got out a squat brown teapot, looked at it in his hands, a little bewilderedly. "Do you make it in this?"

Susan said quickly, "Let me do it!" She took the pot from him, carried it to the stove, went back to the cupboard. "And we have to have some tea to put into it!" The voice with which she spoke was new to her ears, as if she were suddenly a different girl, these hands moving over the shelves of a strange cupboard were not hers, her light laugh . . .

"Now cups and saucers . . ."

"I smelled a cake baking this morning. It must be around somewhere." To Susan's ears his voice had a new sound.

They drank their tea at the round kitchen table. Mrs. Donnell had laid out a fork and knife and plate on it. Tonight, thought Susan, he'd fix his own supper.

"You keep house for your father, don't you, Miss Brent?"

"Yes. I have since my mother died—five years ago."

"You were teaching before that. . . ."

Evidently he knew quite a bit about her. A little flush spread up Susan's cheeks.

"Yes, but I didn't mind resigning—I didn't like teaching and I am not patient enough to make a good teacher."

"I'd say you have plenty of patience—to take on the responsibilities of running a house and family at your age. You must have had to lose out on a lot of good times. . . ."

She did not want him to think she saw herself a martyr, doing her duty. She never had thought of herself as such. She said with a little laugh. "There's never much going on in Sweethome to lose out on!"

John Wendell nodded his head. "I've observed that—and that the young people go outside for their amusement." He hitched forward on his chair, his brows pulling together in sudden earnestness. "I've some ideas I'd like to put across, here. Maybe you can help me—advise me, at least. One is—dances here in the village . . ."

"There's a dance at the Grange every now and then," put in Susan.

"Yes. I've heard about them. What I had in mind were dances for the younger kids. Ball games, too. I imagine there are enough boys around here to make up two teams. Girls, too. Football, in its season. What I'd like to see someday is a gymnasium that could be cleared for parties. A stage—older people could get up plays . . . A playground outside . . ."

He paused. He had been talking so fast that he found himself out of breath. Susan, too, felt her breath holding in her throat. She was certain from his manner that he was confiding to her ambitions which he had told to no one else as yet.

"There used to be a community house next to the Methodist Church—years ago. No one used it and they sold it."

"I know. I was told that. But my idea is to have one that belongs to the people—not to our church or the Methodist or any particular group." He laughed. "I daresay I'm after more than I can get—I've been here long enough to suspect that—but, just the same, I am going

23

to try for it. Try to find a few who will see the need for it—and give the money to help put it across."

It touched Susan's mind that there was not anyone in Sweethome who, even if he had the money, would spend it in such a prodigal way. But she did not say that. She said, in the voice that was new to her ears, "It would be wonderful!"

He went on, "You see, a gathering place such as I have in mind would bring this community and the people of the Flats together. Speaking of them—I'd like to see some of them in my congregation. We haven't a single communicant from across the river."

"They have a church," said Susan.

"Yes, and a good one—have you ever met Father Duffy? He's as fine as they come. But they are not all Roman Catholics over there—there must be quite a few who want to go to church yet hesitate to cross the river. It's this tradition of separation I'd like to see scrapped, a community seeing itself superior to its neighbors. . . ." He got up from the table, took up the teapot from the stove, came back, filled her cup and his own—all, Susan suspected, without any thought of what he was doing. He sat down again, took a long swallow of the hot tea.

"Maybe the war has made me feel that way—I grew up in a town in New Hampshire not much different from yours, here. If I'd come here straight from finishing at the Seminary I would probably be looking down my nose at the people of the Flats—but I didn't. I learned something in those years. . . ." He stopped with some abruptness, then he smiled. "You must forgive me for talking so much—I haven't, to anyone else here in Sweethome, and it feels good. Thanks for listening—and you said you had no patience!"

"But I'm awfully interested," protested Susan. She added, "Really I am! You're—well, so different from Dr. Marcy!"

"Am I?" John Wendell said it, a little dryly. "I'm afraid that may not take so well in Sweethome. If I were smart I'd keep my resignation all typewritten out, handy on my desk."

24

"Oh, *no!*" cried Susan. Then, confused by the warmth she had let into her voice, she got up from her chair. "I must go. Thanks for the tea and the cake. It tasted good."

"Didn't it, though? And thank *you* for helping me. Friday?"

"Yes. I'll come. . . ."

He went to the front door with her, offered her his hand, held hers for a moment in a strong clasp.

Outside, Susan was scarcely conscious of her feet touching the ground or of anything about her except sunshine all around her and in her. Then a figure took shape before her, a woman's voice said, "Why, hello, Susan!"

She stopped short. "Oh, good afternoon, Mrs. Coggin. Lovely day, isn't it?"

She saw Mrs. Coggin's eyes go from her to the door of the parsonage, saw the glint of interest that was sharpening them.

"Been having your soul doctored up, Susan? I wouldn't say it needed it." But Mrs. Coggin gave a little laugh to imply that she knew Susan had not been at the parsonage in the interest of her soul. She added, "You young girls! But I didn't think *you* were one to run after him!"

Indignation helped Susan steady her voice. "I was doing some typing for Mr. Wendell." She moved to go on, grateful that Mrs. Coggin's home was in the other direction.

But Mrs. Coggin was not ready to let her go. "What's this, Susan, about Deborah Brent coming back to Sweethome? I saw Abby this afternoon and she says you told her to get the old Brent house cleaned up for her to live in."

"Yes, she's coming very soon."

"Queer, isn't it, that she'd want to come back here after all these years she hasn't set foot in the place?"

"Perhaps it always has seemed home to her," defended Susan.

"Well, it'll be real exciting to see what she's like now."

Susan had heard the story of Aunt Debbie, years ago, from schoolmates, as Nell had, but she answered stoutly. "We—my father and the rest of us are very glad she is coming."

"Of course you are!" Though there was a slightly amused inflection of questioning in the older woman's agreement. "Well, I must go along—nice to have run into you, Susan."

There was no bright sunshine now for Susan as she walked on down the road. Instead, her indignation at Mrs. Coggin's implication was growing swiftly into horror. By night Mrs. Coggin would have told a dozen others that Susan Brent had spent the afternoon at the parsonage—and as many would know that Mrs. Donnell had gone to Winsted. They'd chitchat over it, give little meaning laughs. . . .

"If they knew what we talked about," she thought, furiously, yet at the same time frightened.

All at once she did not want to go straight home—face Nell there and the questions Nell might ask about where she had been. She turned a corner and walked toward River Road which paralleled Central Road and on which was the small shopping district. She needed some things from Higgins', she remembered. Bicarbonate for her father, cleansing tissue: "I might as well get more toothpaste while I'm there."

It steadied her to jerk her mind back into its usual routine of thought.

As she approached Higgins' she saw an open car stop a little beyond it, recognized Nell by the bright sheen of her hair as one of the occupants. The boy with her, black-haired, slim, dark, was no one from Sweethome. . . . Nell was making no move to get out of the car, instead she had drawn a little closer to her companion. Now Susan's heart knew a new sickness.

Then Nell saw her coming, waved a hand toward her, swung open the door and got out of the car, giving her companion a gay backward nod of her head.

"Hello, Sue. I thought you'd be home at this hour! It's near supper-time, isn't it?"

"I thought you were finishing the ironing. That you'd start supper." Susan's tone was sharper than she ever allowed it to be toward Nell.

"I had a date. It was too grand a day, anyway, to spend ironing."

They turned together into Higgins'. "Who was that boy?" asked Susan.

"Tony DiVito."

Susan went ahead of Nell through the door. "From the Flats, I suppose," she said, low, over her shoulder.

"Yes, he's from the Flats."

Susan nodded to Bill behind the soda bar, gave her order to Mr. Higgins. Nell perched herself on a stool at the bar.

"Aren't you coming home?" asked Susan, when her package was wrapped.

"I'll be along—I'm dying of thirst. Bill, jerk me a chocolate soda!"

Susan went on, the sick feeling heavy in her.

"She's been playing around with this young Italian—that's why she's late for supper so often. From the Flats—what everyone here is saying about it—and Father so hates talk. . . ."

She rarely went to her father with any issue between her and Nell or Bill, confident that she could straighten it out herself. But this, now, was too big a thing to meet alone.

But at home, starting supper, it came to her that she could not tell her father what Nell was up to—what right had she when she had laid her own self open to their horrid gossip this afternoon?

Suddenly she dropped the knife she had in her hand. *I haven't talked like this to anyone else here in Sweethome and it feels good.*

Their gossip could not take away from her the knowledge that he had said that to her.

CHAPTER III

Nᴇʟʟ Bʀᴇɴᴛ sɴᴜɢɢʟᴇᴅ deep under the bed covers, and listened to the sounds from downstairs.

A half-hour ago her father had put his head in her door. "Time to get up, Nell." She had answered him but she had not stirred; she was not going to, until she was certain he had left for the plant.

She had no doubt but that Susan would tell her father at breakfast that she was going around with a boy from the Flats. She had not, last night, but she had looked so troubled that Nell was certain it was very much on her mind.

She heard the screen door bang—but that was Bill, starting off in a rush to catch the bus to go to high school in Winsted. For an instant she felt a pang of envy—it had been fun, those morning bus rides, with that loon of a driver who was a ventriloquist and made the girls appear to say things to the boys and the boys to the girls. Then she remembered that she had outgrown such amusement, oh, outgrown it by a long way, since she had known Tony.

She drew her arms down from her head, curled her hands into small fists. "It isn't going to make any difference, what Father says— or Susan—or *any*body!" Tony was the divinest male who ever breathed, even if his family did live over on the Flats. She closed her eyes, to bring Tony close to her—closer, until she had the feeling of his hands on her, his mouth hard against hers. Even only thinking about it brought that heavenly sensation of dissolving into nothing.

Though he was only a little older than they, Tony made goops of

28

the other boys she knew, with their loud voices, their fumbling passes. Some of them had made love to her—Joe Coggin quite often, last summer, but, oh, not the way Tony did! With Tony it was the real thing. "I belong to Tony." He had said that she did, just the other day. They had composed a song between them. "My love is yours, through summer time and winter time and fall time and all time." They called it their theme song.

Loving Tony had met the restlessness in her of not knowing what to do when her father had refused to let her go somewhere and take singing lessons. She had thought of looking for a job in one of the stores in Winsted, or, maybe, Great Barrington, though she had made no move to find one. Now she was certain that her indecision was because part of her was waiting for love to come—for Tony! No, the *whole* of her . . .

She'd be with him again, this afternoon. "Meet me, same spot— same time, sweetness?" The time was four o'clock, the spot was the corner where River Road turned to cross the bridge. "I know a swell place to go," he had said, and she remembered something in his eyes when he said it that had made her go warm, all through her.

"Nell?" called her father, up the stairs. "Nell, aren't you coming down?"

"In a twink," she called back, making a face at the door. *Couldn't* he let her alone? No! "Early to bed, early to rise . . ."

She would have to face it out with him tonight, of course. She drew a little sigh—he'd go on and on, much more than he had when she announced that she was not going to church any more. What was the use, she had argued, when you are bored to death every minute of the service? *To set an example.* She had laughed at that. Sometimes laughing at her father silenced him. But she could not laugh if he said mean things about Tony.

She heard the screen door close again, more quietly now, so she knew it was her father going off. She got out of bed, let her nightgown slip to the floor, kicked it expertly to a chair. She need not hurry about dressing—the hours until four would be endless as it was. Though, of course, she could help Sue. . . .

She crossed to the open window, stood there letting the cool morning air wash over her bare body. She loved to be naked and feel her skin tingling and her blood running warm under it. This morning, however, she enjoyed it only with her senses and let her mind dwell on Susan's lot. She did not think Sue ever had been in love. Certainly not with that drip she had played around with when she was teaching in New Hartford. He had come to the house for supper one Sunday evening and all he had talked about was a federation of the democratic nations. Their father'd called him a radical—had said he did not like him. Sue never had invited him again. And what chance had she to meet any men she'd look at twice here in Sweethome or going shopping or to the movies in Winsted? Poor Sue . . .

The window in which she stood faced the side of the old house next door. Close to it was a cherry tree, its branches gnarled and twisted with age. Nell had looked at it times without number without seeing it. Now suddenly her eyes focused on it. It was the tree which Aunt Debbie had shinnied down! Susan's plight slipped out of her mind; Aunt Debbie came into it—Aunt Debbie would be on her side about Tony.

Then, disappointedly, she remembered that Aunt Debbie was an old woman, now—too old to have sympathy or understanding of a girl's love affairs.

Susan was assembling an icebox pudding when she went into the kitchen.

"Hi!" said Nell to her back.

Susan turned. "Hi! There's oatmeal in the double boiler if you want it."

"I'll just have some toast and milk."

Nell felt an immense relief. Susan was not wearing the severe face which she put on whenever either Bill or herself was in the doghouse

30

over something. She had an abstracted look which Nell never had seen before.

"Can you finish the ironing this morning, Nell?" But she did not ask it as if the world would come to an end if the ironing were not done by Wednesday.

"Sure. There isn't much. I'll do it as soon as I've eaten something."

This instant compliance sprang partly from the pity she had felt for Susan, upstairs, and partly from the conviction that Susan had not told her father about Tony. She sat down at the table with her milk and toast. She wished she could talk to Susan about Tony, tell her—oh, tell her . . . But Susan, like her father, persisted in thinking of her as still a child. She felt for a moment very bereft, with no one to talk to about Tony. Her girl friends, in Sweethome, whom she could count on the fingers of one hand, schoolmates since primary days, were not the kind to whom you confided your love life—in fact, this last year, she had not thought of them as friends.

Susan put the pudding in the refrigerator, went to the sink and began to rinse the breakfast dishes.

"I'll do those, Sue."

"Will you? I should go over to the other house—Abby's coming today to clean it."

"I don't see why you have to help."

"Abby's not thorough—I don't want Aunt Debbie to come and find any dirt in the corners."

"Pooh," said Nell, biting into her toast. Then, "It'll be exciting to see what she is like, won't it?"

It was what Mrs. Coggin had said. Reminded of the ready gossip, Susan turned a little quickly to go to the shed for pails and cleaning cloths.

Nell washed the dishes, set up the ironing board. Not quite ten o'clock—six hours before she would meet Tony.

The telephone rang. It was Mrs. Peely. "Nell, will you come in,

31

this afternoon? I want you to go over the offertory we've been rehearsing."

"I can come early in the afternoon."

That, like the ironing, would help pass the time.

She had some food ready when Susan came back at noontime. They were alone; their father carried a sandwich to the plant and ate it at his desk with a cup of tea he brewed over a small kerosene stove.

"I'm going to Mrs. Peely's this afternoon to rehearse something," Nell informed Susan, when they finished eating. "She phoned me."

She knew instantly why Susan's face lighted—Susan was thinking she was not going to see Tony. She added, in a burst of honesty, *"Early in the afternoon—I've a date with Tony later."*

At that Susan lowered her eyes to her plate. She seemed to be at a loss to know just what to say. Perhaps she was not going to say anything. . . .

Then she spoke. "I don't like it, Nell—I mean, you seeing this boy every day the way I think you're seeing him. Why doesn't he stop for you here at the house—bring you back here?"

"You know the tiz Father'd go into!"

"Maybe if Father met him . . ."

This, from Susan! Nell stared at her sister's head. She could not know that Susan was struggling to tear up by the roots the conviction of a superiority to the people of the Flats to which she had been born. *"It's this tradition of separation I'd like to see scrapped."* Aloud, Nell said, "Huh," to Susan's suggestion, remembering the time Susan had brought in the young man from New Hartford, whom their father had damned before he turned the lights out after him.

Susan looked up from her plate. "I realize you're grown now, Nell— that I can't say what you should do and shouldn't, the way I have. Only—I hope you *think* of what you're doing—don't let yourself get carried away—do things you'd regret awfully afterwards. That—"

32

Susan paused, then finished a little lamely—"that would be talked about here in the village."

Nell tossed her bright head. "As if I care what the old women around here talk about! Why, Sue, if you did, you'd never do *any*thing! You might as well be dead!"

"I suppose so," said Susan, in a queer voice that held Nell's eyes on her again, wonderingly. Nell saw, too, the slight flush on Susan's cheeks. She got up from the table, threw one arm lightly around her sister's shoulders. "You're wonderful, darling—not to be reminding me that self-respect is the most precious and so forth ad nauseam! Now I've got to be off to sing praises to the Lord!"

She sang as she went up to her room to change. Wonder of wonders—Sue realized she was grown up, on her own!

Agnes Peely lived in an old house across from the Congregational Church. By virtue of two years' study at the New England Conservatory of Music in her youth, she was considered a musician of talent in Sweethome. During the week she gave a few piano lessons and on Sundays she played the organ in the Congregational Church and directed its choir of six mixed voices. The choir did not sing very well nor did Agnes Peely play the organ very well, but all were of Sweethome, gave their services free, so no one ever spoke critically of them.

The parlor had a faintly musty smell and Nell's nose crinkled in distaste as she followed Agnes Peely into it. Also, the old grand piano, covered with a fringed embroidered shawl and a great many framed photographs, was unpleasantly reminiscent to Nell of the hours she had sat on a stool in front of it, stumbling through scales and at the same time watching the hands on the grandfather's clock, back of the piano.

She glanced now at the clock. *In two hours . . .*

Mrs. Peely sat down at the piano. "I'll run through this, dear. It's a lovely oratorio. Mr. Wendell is *so* pleased that we are going to sing it! Now, listen . . . Tra-la-la, tra-di-da . . ." She trilled along with

33

the music, in a voice a little thin and uncertain from age. "The contraltos come in here—wish we had better contralto voices. Tradi-da . . . Oh, now—" she bent toward the music "—the sopranos! *'Praise ye the Lord. . . .'* It should be like angels' singing, *really,* it should!"

It was as much in Nell's nature to sing as in a bird's. She sang now: *" 'Praise ye the Lord!' "*

Mrs. Peely stopped playing, looked up at her, her small short-sighted eyes wide with surprise and delight. "Why, *dear*—I hadn't realized you had such a lovely voice!"

Nell laughed. "I didn't know it, either."

"It's so *warm,* and you don't hear many soprano voices that really are *warm!* It sounds so happy, too—as if—as if you *were* worshiping our Lord!"

"No; Tony," thought Nell.

Mrs. Peely settled herself more firmly on the stool. "We'll do something with this—let's begin again at the part where the sopranos come in—here." She put her finger on the page of music. "Can you see the words, dear? You won't mind really *working* on it? If *you* know it well you can lead the others—help *them* along."

Nell's eyes went again to the grandfather's clock. "I have to go at quarter to four."

"Well, until then . . ." Mrs. Peely began to play, eager and excited. "Oh, *lovely,*" she murmured as Nell's voice lifted above her accompaniment.

They went through it again, and then again. Neither heard the front door open nor saw John Wendell standing just inside the room—until Mrs. Peely dropped her hands from the piano keys. "That's *good,* Nell. With just a few rehearsals . . . *Why*—" she fluttered up from the piano stool— "Mr. Wendell! I didn't realize you were here!"

"I heard a new voice—I couldn't resist taking the liberty to walk in and listen."

"It's Nell Brent—you've met her, of course."

"How do you do, Miss Brent? No, I don't think I've met you."

"That's a jab at my not going to church," thought Nell. However, he was smiling, his eyes even had a twinkle in them.

He sat down at the piano, began to play. "There's one place, Mrs. Peely. Here . . . It should be pianissimo . . . *Who is like unto the Lord our God!* Then crescendo—to the last. Miss Nell, will you go through this part again?"

It was twenty minutes to four. "I'm sorry—well, just once!"

Annoyed by the delay, she sang it through indifferently, ignoring the suggestions he had made. He got up from the stool with some abruptness. "Thanks. I must be off myself. Next week, perhaps, Mrs. Peely, I'll help in the rehearsals."

"*Will* you? You will do it so much better than I can."

He was gone, then. Nell said, "I must go, Mrs. Peely."

"Yes, dear. Will you give me another afternoon—Friday afternoon? I've a lesson tomorrow. The Emory child . . ."

"I can come on Friday, early," said Nell, moving toward the door.

"It is just too bad Susan can't carry a tune, isn't it? She would love to be in the chorus—everyone in it feels that she's giving something of *herself*—you'll feel that way, too, dear. Though Susan . . ." They were at the front door, now, Mrs. Peely close to Nell's elbow. "I saw her go into the parsonage yesterday afternoon—she didn't come out until long after four. Almira Coggin met her outside and Susan told her she had been doing some typing for Mr. Wendell. That's very nice of her, but . . ."

But Nell was flying down the brick walk.

Her thoughts flew with her feet—not ahead to Tony, for a moment, at least, but to Sue. So Sue was at the parsonage yesterday—giving of herself! Keeping awfully mum about it, too. Perhaps . . . Could one fall in love with a preacher? Nell could not see how, but if he were the only man around . . . Then she remembered that his smile had been rather cute and that he was wearing gray slacks—old Winnie never had smiled and even on workdays wore black clothes.

35

Near the bridge she saw Tony driving across it. She stood still to get her breath. And he stopped his car with a grinding of its brake almost on her toes.

"Going my way, Carrot-top?"

"I beg your pardon—have I had the pleasure of meeting you before?" As she said it she climbed into the car.

They always met like that—Tony would say something silly and she would say something silly and then they'd laugh and laugh—or was it what they said that made them laugh?

"Where *are* we going, Tony?" He had said he had a swell place to go. Usually they just drove off into the country, stopped, went on, stopped and went on again, ending in Winsted for a Coke or a sundae. Tony had to get her back fairly early for he worked evenings at Sears, Roebuck's in Winsted, opening crates and cartons, setting merchandise on the shelves for the next day's sales.

"You'll see . . ." He turned the car around, drove on beyond the bridge. "Do you love me, my woman, as you did yesterday?"

"Did I—yesterday? Let me think . . ." But the moment for nonsense was over. Tony's eyes on her were darkening. She said, shakily, *"More . . ."*

He swung the car into a road that climbed up the hill, ground it to a stop. Then he pulled her into his arms.

"Tony . . ." Though it was not a protest, she just had to breathe his name. Now his eyes, close to her face, were all black; she saw the flash of his white teeth for the instant before his mouth came against hers, seeking.

"Kiss me, sweet!" he breathed against her mouth. "Like this— have I got to teach you how to love?" Now his hand moved across her shoulders.

But in almost the next moment he drew away from her, started the car. He often acted this way—just when you thought you were melting into nothing, he would stop making love. Perhaps he would not kiss her again this afternoon. There had been several afternoons when

36

he had not touched her. That made her want him to—want it terribly, and the sensation of wanting was almost like the sensation of melting.

He was continuing on the uphill road which turned, after a little distance, and ran along the side of the hill, up above the village. "Why this way?" wondered Nell but she did not ask. She was happy. She did not care where they went. It was enough at the moment to be with him, to look at him, his head, with the black hair springing thick up from his temples, the black line of eyebrow, his eyes, velvety brown when they were not close to you, with the thick short dark lashes that made them seem deeper-set than they were, the clear olive of his skin over the cheekbone, the faint shadow of blue-black where he had shaved.

Nell had met Tony in April of this year. The Y.W.C.A. in Winsted had opened a canteen for young people where, under chaperonage, they could dance or sit at the stools at a bar in one corner of the room and drink soft drinks; Nell and Ginny Wooley and Stella Butt had gone on the bus into the city to see what the new venture promised in the way of fun. Not much—until Tony sauntered into the big room, stood looking over it with a somewhat condescending air. One of the hostesses had gone up to him. He had told Nell later that he told the dame the only girl he wanted to meet was the little red-head. They had danced—he danced differently from the others, closer to you, more smoothly, more with the rhythm of the music. His arm across her back had a surer pressure, his eyes near hers, for he was only an inch or so taller than she, had had their dark look. . . .

"Want some of that poison over there?" He had nodded toward the bar. "Or what say we get out of this dump?"

"Let's . . ."

Then, outside, "Where do you live, Carrots?"

"In Sweethome. I came over on the bus with a couple of girls."

"You'll go home with me. I got a car parked somewhere around. I live across the river from Sweethome."

She had felt no shock in learning that he lived in the Flats. She was incapable of feeling anything more than his thigh against her own as they walked slowly through the half-dark of the street. At her suggestion he had let her out of the car a block away from her house. "You see the family expect me to come home on the bus," she had explained with some embarrassment. But he had said quickly, "Okay with me. Now when do I see you again?" But he had not kissed her. He had just made her want him to, awfully. . . .

She had not cared if Ginny and Stella told everyone in Sweethome that she had let this strange young man bring her home. What girl wouldn't let him? Nor did she care now who saw her meet him, afternoons, who saw her get into his car. It was more exciting to see him in this way; it made it something that belonged to just the two of them.

As well as working evenings, Tony worked until noon every day in a bar and grill on the Flats, cleaning up the place. He hated it, he told Nell, but he needed the money. When he had some ahead, he was going to New York, or Chicago—maybe South America. Going where there were bigger opportunities for a fellow than here in the sticks. It thrilled Nell when he talked of what he was going to do; the boys in Sweethome were content after graduating from high to take the first job that offered itself. With most of them it was in her father's plant.

Now that she knew Tony loved her she saw herself by his side, sharing his glittering achievements—a big banker who dealt with millions, perhaps, or a boss in politics. . . . "That's where you make the dough, baby!" Sometimes the daring of his ambitions, so far removed from the Flats, indeed, from Sweethome, took her breath but she never let Tony know.

Only once had he spoken of his family, and then, when she asked him if he had any brothers or sisters, he'd given a short laugh. "Have I? An even dozen. Maybe there'll be another by the time I get home." Something in his tone had told her not to ask him more. Well, she felt about family as he did.

The road came out of a stretch of woodland to open fields marked off by low stone walls. Dominating these stood an old house, its central part two-storied, one-storied wings running off on each side of it. Shutters hanging lop-sided, a tumbling chimney, the paint on the bricks which once had been white streaked now with a yellowish gray. The overgrown shrubbery around its wide door gave it an uncared-for appearance. The two posts which marked the entrance to the driveway had fallen over.

Tony swung the car into the driveway.

Nell sat up straight. "Tony—this is private!"

"Just curious—I've looked across at this old house up here on the hill a lot of times, wondered what it was like, close up."

"But it's trespassing! There's a sign—at least there used to be. . . ."

"What do we care? Anyway, who's going to see us?" But he took the precaution to drive to the rear of the house and park out of sight of the road. "Come on, sweet, we're getting out!"

Nell did not move. "There used to be a caretaker. . . ."

"Doesn't look as if he'd been around lately. If he comes, I'll tell him I'm considering buying the place!" Grinning, he caught Nell's hand, pulled her out of the car.

Was this the surprise he had for her? The swell place to go? Nell knew the house—her mother often had brought her and Susan when she called on Mrs. Hurrell. Mrs. Hurrell was an old woman, then, crippled so that she spent all her days in a wheel chair. She was childless but loved to have children come to her. Nell remembered, "Go wash your faces, Nell and Susan—I'm going up to call on Fanny Hurrell. She likes folks to come in and I guess not many do." Nell vaguely understood that that was because in her younger days she had written books, which, coupled with the fact she had come from some place in the Middle West, made her different. She had died twelve years ago. No one had lived in the old house since. It seemed to be dying, too.

39

She felt queer, remembering all this as she followed Tony up the path to the narrow back porch. Puzzled, too—it wasn't like Tony to be curious about a tumbling-down old house like this.

Tony went to a window and with a little upward push of the lower part of the frame, opened it. He turned, waved his arm. "Enter!"

She was staring at him. "Tony, how did you know?"

"Know what?"

"That that window would open . . ."

"Just guessed one of 'em might, in an old house like this. Let's have a look inside—can you climb through?"

He drew her to the window, helped her climb through it.

He was curious, she told herself, because he never had been in a rambling old house like this, with rooms and rooms; where he lived he had to crowd into two or three. Such interest *did* go with his big dreams! She was sorry she had acted so reluctant to come in with him. In the big, half-dark kitchen she held to his arm. "Wouldn't it be wonderful if it were haunted!"

They went from room to room. Nothing of the furnishings had been removed. It was all as Nell remembered it. Books still lined the walls of the smaller of the two front rooms where Mrs. Hurrell always sat in her wheel chair—the wheel chair was still there, close to the front window. Dust lay thick on everything, dimming the colors of old fabrics, the luster of old wood, to a uniform grayness. Dust hung in the air, graying the light that streaked in in a thin bar between the drawn hangings.

"Did they have dough—the birds who used to live here?"

"I don't know—some, I guess. They were the Hurrells—Mr. Hurrell farmed the place—cows, mostly. I remember his truck going along full of big shiny cans, the name 'Hill Farm' printed on it. Mrs. Hurrell was from away—Cincinnati, I think. She wrote books—maybe she had money."

Tony drew her to him. "That's the thing to do—marry a girl with a wad of money!" His eyes teased her but she saw them darkening.

"Some day, kid, I'm going to have a place bigger than this! Until then—we can play a little game. Make believe this dump is ours. . . ."

Nell pulled away from him—a thing she never had done before. "Tony, what do you mean?"

He laughed at her alarmed look. "Worrying about trespassing? No one'll know if we come here sometimes like we're doing today. Do a little dusting around so we can sit down somewhere. Say, it's a lot pleasanter than sitting in a drugstore or parked on a road where anyone's likely to come along! I want you alone with me. Like this . . ." He caught her up against him, kissed her long and hard, moved his mouth across her face, into her throat, back to her lips. "How about it, baby? Do we come here again?"

"I'd—love to," whispered Nell.

Tony dropped his arms, grinning, his teeth flashing. "Can't do any settling in today. You bring some cleaning rags with you, next time. Let's see what more we haven't seen." He drew her out into the wide central hall from which stairs curved upward to the second floor. "What's above—ever been up there?" He put his hand on the dust-gray newel post.

"No. Oh, yes, once . . . There's a bathroom and a lot of bedrooms —that's all." Tony's foot was on the bottom step. She said quickly, "Tony, let's not go up—not now, I mean. The house smells so—so shut-up! It's making me—making me a little sick, honestly!"

He turned from the stairs. "Okay, kid. We'll get out." He did not touch her as they went on through the kitchen to the back porch; he did not glance toward her.

Outside Nell drew in a long breath of the clean air. "That feels good," she said, a little shakily. She *had* felt funny, in the pit of her stomach, that moment standing there in the hall. But—it was gone, now.

She asked as they drove out of the yard, "Do you think anyone'd know if we opened some windows—I mean, when we come here next time?"

She saw him smile though he kept his eyes ahead. "Sure, we'll let in some air—make ourselves at home. The place is ours—nobody else wants it. Friday? I've got to drive one of the kids into Winsted to the dentist's, tomorrow."

Nell put her cheek against his sleeve.

"Friday's all right. Tony, we've forgotten something." She began to sing softly, "My love is yours through summer time . . ."

"And all time," finished Tony.

CHAPTER IV

JOHN WENDELL LOOKED over his study with a grin of pride. "Old Marcy couldn't have had it looking *much* tidier!" Magazines, pamphlets neatly stacked, books on the shelves which he had worked late into the night to finish and paint, the desk top clear, the table . . . It was nearing two-thirty on Friday afternoon.

The telephone rang.

"Mr. Wendell—this is Susan Brent. I can't come over this afternoon. I—I have to drive to Winsted. I'm—terribly sorry."

"Oh. I am sorry, too."

"I was thinking—couldn't you leave those notes at my house someday? I could copy them here."

"That's an idea—I may bring them around. But you're sure you have time?"

"Yes, I have time."

He was disappointed. He was puzzled, too. She had sounded offish over the phone, distant—not at all as she had seemed the other afternoon. Without doubt he had bored her by talking so much.

It left his afternoon free. There were innumerable things he might do but he felt a strong disinclination to do any of them. He decided he would go over to the Flats and have a visit with Father Duffy.

He had no car—when distance or time did not permit walking he went about on a noisy and evil-smelling motorcycle which he had had since college days. He went to the barn, got it out. He saw Mrs. Donnell in the kitchen window watching him straddle it. He roared off out of the driveway.

His acquaintance with the priest had begun one day soon after he had come to Sweethome when they had shared a seat on the bus, returning from Winsted, and had fallen into talk.

"The Congregational Church, eh? It has a beautiful steeple—I can see it from my window. I like to look at it."

"The old church is as beautiful—come over and see it." Instantly John Wendell had felt embarrassed—the older man might think his suggestion too forward.

But Father Duffy had smiled. When he smiled, one eye crinkled almost shut which gave it the effect of winking. "I will, someday."

He was a man close to sixty, John guessed, squat almost to deformity in build, with a big head and a thick-jowled face. But even on that first meeting John realized that he had a quality of friendliness that offset his unprepossessing appearance. John had needed, at that moment, to draw on friendliness. In the older people of his congregation, outwardly cordial though they were, he had sensed a wait-and-see attitude toward him. He had reminded himself that he should expect that; they knew no more about him than his record at the Seminary. He was here on trial and at any meeting of the church members or of the deacons they might vote to let him go. But even understanding their attitude, he had felt, and felt now, insecure and alone.

The priest had got off the bus first, that day. He had offered John his hand. "Drop in and see me sometime, my boy."

John had, very often, in the weeks that had followed. They never argued over theological differences in their work. "We labor in the same vineyard, don't we?" Father Duffy had said early in their acquaintance. And soon John had come to know that while the priest lived by the laws of his church, he had a wisdom, a faith, a love of his fellowmen that knew no such bounds.

They did argue over political situations, over books, over the complexities of human behavior, but whatever their talk, John always left his friend, stimulated and encouraged. He had felt no such pick-up after his encounters with Stephen Neal, pastor of the Sweethome

44

Methodist Church, a small, tired-looking, middle-aged man who, whenever they met, never quite concealed his envy of John's younger years.

Today, as he approached the rectory, a one-story stuccoed house, bare of any architectural pretensions, he saw Father Duffy out in his garden, a bulky figure, black against a wall of orange-red roses. He straightened at the sound of the motorcycle, threw up one arm in greeting. There was a little flash of sunlight against the steel of the clipping shears in his hand. "Come and see my flowers," he shouted.

John joined him in the garden.

"Ever see anything like 'em?" demanded Father Duffy.

His triumph was justified; they were beautiful, hanging in brilliant clusters against the glossy green of their leaves. And looking at them John remembered the yellow of Susan Brent's dress—the gay spot of color it had brought to the drab study. He knew now that his disappointment was not wholly because the work on the cards was held up.

There were other flowers in the garden at which he must look—delphinium already in bud, Shasta daisies, peonies. He followed the squat figure of the priest in and out among the beds. "I've an idea you say prayers over your seeds, when you plant them."

The priest cupped a shell-pink peony in his broad hand. "I thank God for the miracle of the seed—that men have it to see as a miracle. Shall we go into the house now? I've buttermilk on ice or—maybe you would prefer a cold bottle of beer?"

"The buttermilk. Mrs. Donnell refuses to get any—says it's fit only for slops."

They went into the house, to the kitchen. Father Duffy cooked his own meals—why put his parish to the expense of paying for someone to do it when he liked to do it for himself? As they sat down at the table in the spotlessly clean kitchen John wished he had no Mrs. Donnell—then he remembered his helplessness over the tea, remembered Susan Brent taking the pot out of his hands. . . .

"Well, what's weighing on your mind today, son?" asked the priest.

John Wendell laughed. A girl in a yellow dress who had not kept her date? "Nothing, at least heavy enough to be a burden."

"Still wishing you had slums to cope with?" Father Duffy's eye winked.

"Well, they'd give me more definite problems to go after. Though no one in Sweethome is rich, no one is in want, that I can find. At least, in a material way."

"But—spiritually?"

John turned his glass slowly around in his hand, frowning down at it. "I don't know. They come to services, go away—I can't know if anything I have said makes a bit of difference in their lives, one way or the other—whether I've given them anything. They're a good people—self-respecting, zealous in their work for the church, the women in the Church School, the Ladies' Aid, getting up suppers . . . the men in the committees. I call on them—they are cordial to me—but if any have a spiritual need, I don't know of it—as yet." He could be frank in admitting discouragement to the priest who had labored for so many years with spiritual needs.

He had told Father Duffy one day what had influenced him to go into the ministry. "My father. Though he'd blow his top if he heard me say that. He was a doctor—one of those who drove all over the countryside in all kinds of weather, night and day. He did not know a thing about psychiatry but he practised quite a bit of mental suggestion, guess you'd call it. I believe he had something in himself, some inner perception, without knowing it, perhaps. He'd tell me of some of these cases. We were close—there were just the two of us and I think he was lonely after my mother died. He died, my first year in college. All my life I had wanted to be like him and afterwards, when I had to give serious thought to what I would do when I was through college, that was uppermost in my mind. But I wanted to do what he hadn't—leave the physical ills to someone else, go after the spiritual ones.

46

"But . . ." John took a long swallow of his buttermilk. "There are times, Father, when I envy you your confessional—you get to the inner man!"

"No." Father Duffy shook his head. "We have to leave that to God." He smiled, then. "Discouragement is healthy, son, if you refuse to let it beat you. Wait and pray. You are just beginning—you'll soon find a lost sheep in your flock and even though it is only one . . ."

John broke in with a laugh. "Fact is, there is one! A girl who struck on going to church any more. She is the daughter of Will Brent who owns and runs that nail factory on the other side—one of our deacons. He spoke to me about her. But I can't haul her in by the hair—it happens to be red hair, at that."

"No. She has to do her own thinking. Speaking of nails—and you want some very rich in your flock, for contrast, say—why don't you go after this Rudolph Petersen? He told me he is planning to settle somewhere across the river. He's tired of living in big cities—too lonely, he said, which suggests an interesting side of him—wants to belong in a small community, likes the quiet living around here. He's a Protestant if he's anything . . . though he gave me a very generous check for my health service fund. He might build that community house you plan. . . ."

John had talked to the priest of those plans of his, as the priest had talked to him of the health service he wanted to see instituted on the Flats.

"I'll go after him—if I'm lucky enough to get the opportunity. Thanks for the tip." They both laughed, making it a small joke between them.

"You must take some of my roses back with you," said Father Duffy when John got up to go.

"I'd like to." See the expression on Mrs. Donnell's face when he told her they were from Father Duffy's garden!

There was little traffic as he went through the Flats, for neither

47

the mills nor the Petersen plant had closed as yet. But nearing the bridge he saw a car stalled at the side of the road, the hood of its engine uptilted, a woman bent over it. She straightened, turned, as he came up to her.

He brought the motorcycle to a stop. "Trouble?"

"It's in the gas flow, I think. The tank's full but it isn't feeding. Just bought the car out of a lot in Pittsfield so I am not well acquainted with it."

John was struck by the extraordinary pleasantness of her voice, a hearty quality in it, warm. He saw her a plain-faced, gray-haired woman, past middle age, evidently not one to give much concern to her personal appearance, for a streak of grease lay now across her cheek and her hands were covered with it and she did not seem to be aware of it. Or of John, himself. She was looking past him, down the road that led to the Flats. "I suppose there is a garage somewhere about."

"A few blocks over. But may I take a look at the engine? Perhaps I can get it going."

"I'd be delighted." She sat down on the runningboard. Now she looked at him and from him to the motorcycle. She began to laugh and her laugh had the same warm quality of her speaking voice. "I was just thinking—it would be *perfect* if I arrived back in Sweethome, riding piggyback on your motorcycle!"

John Wendell had not the slightest comprehension why it would be perfect but he laughed with her.

"You're going to Sweethome?"

"Yes. You know the village?"

"I'm getting to know it—I've been there for almost two months. I am the new minister of the Congregational Church—John Wendell."

"*You're*—the new minister! I heard that old Marcy had died." She looked him up and down, smiling. He knew she was thinking of his clothes, of the motorcycle, but in no disapproving way.

48

"I'm taking an afternoon off."

"Picking roses . . ."

"No, visiting a very good friend over here in the Flats. Father Duffy. The roses are from his garden."

"Oh . . ." She drew out the word, a lively interest in her eyes, but she made no comment on such a friendship.

He turned to the car, began examining the carburetor—usually with his motorcycle it was the carburetor at fault. The woman sat looking across at the village, a little smile on her lips.

"If I had a wire . . ."

"Look in the glove compartment. It's chuck-full of junk. Oh, if you find a rag or some waste—I could use it."

He did find a rag and a short length of wire. She began to wipe her hands with the rag. "I must look as presentable as I can when I meet my family." She read the question on his face and said, "I am Deborah Brent."

"A relative of—Susan's?" He reddened slightly under the quick look she gave him.

"I guess so—yes, I am. A half-aunt. Susan is one of Willie's girls, the older of the two, I think."

John went back to the carburetor, but he felt her smile on his back.

"The wire did it," he announced after a few moments. "The flow was choked a bit . . . I'll see if it picks up now." He got into the car. After a moment, with considerable sputtering, the engine began to turn.

"It should get you to Sweethome, at least."

He noticed, as he got out of the car, that the back of it was piled high with boxes and bags.

"Are they expecting you this afternoon?" he asked.

"I don't think so. I just wrote that I was coming soon. I flew as far as Albany, took a bus to Pittsfield, bought this old car there. . . ."

"May I go along with you on my motorcycle—help you unload this gear?"

"That'd be nice—a sort of escort. The roses for a finishing touch. Let's go. . . ."

"Before we start . . ." John drew a handkerchief from a pocket, offered it to her. "This is better than that rag—and there's grease on your face."

"Heavens! Thanks for telling me. You're a very nice young man, even though . . ."

"I am a minister," finished John for her, with a wide grin.

They drove off, across the bridge, the engine of the car still sputtering some, the motorcycle much more. They turned into Sweethome.

As he rode along beside the car, John realized that he was enjoying this encounter very much. Curiously it was as if he had met, for the first time, someone he had known for a long time.

She turned the car into the driveway of the old Brent house and he followed her on the motorcycle.

No one was about.

Deborah Brent got out of the car, stood still for a long moment, looking over the old house. "It hasn't changed a bit," she said, then.

John was lifting out the bags.

"Just put my stuff on the porch—I'll go over to the other house. Someone will be coming in soon—one of the girls or Willie. I suppose he's still at the plant. Or the boy. Thanks, immensely, Reverend. I hope you'll come in soon to see me?"

"I most certainly am going to, Miss Brent."

"It's Mrs. Brent. That's a story I'll tell you someday."

She put out her hand and he took it. He liked the quick, warm firmness of her handshake—somehow it confirmed his feeling of knowing her well.

At that moment Susan appeared, hurrying through the trellis between the adjoining yards. John saw the startled surprise on her face at sight of him with her aunt—confusion, too. She gave him one quick look and then looked away.

"I heard a car over here . . . Aunt Deborah, we didn't know you were coming today!" She did not move to kiss her aunt, or offer any other greeting.

But Deborah Brent took Susan's two hands, held them for a moment.

"You are Susan."

"Yes. Father isn't home yet—Nell isn't home—Bill's working at the store. But if you'll come over . . ."

"I'll go along now," said John Wendell.

Deborah Brent turned to him with a warm smile.

"Well, thanks again." To Susan, "My car stalled over the other side of the bridge—I'd still be there if this young man hadn't gotten it started for me."

"That was fortunate—I mean that he could help you." But Susan did not look at John as she said it.

He puzzled over that as he rode away. Somehow, it tied up with her telephoning to him that she could not come to help him. Had she, perhaps, taken an active dislike to him?

Then his glance fell to the slightly wilted roses in the wire basket on the handlebar and he thought of Deborah Brent. "Wish I'd left them with her. It'd have been something of a welcome. Didn't seem as if she got much!"

CHAPTER V

It was not a good day, this Friday, for Will Brent. His works-manager, Coley Coggin, had made a remark that had brought into the open a worry from another quarter than his half-sister's imminent return.

The Colton Construction Company was one of New England's biggest house-building concerns, with branches in every sizable city from Maine to the New York state border. One of the oldest, too; and it had bought its nails, each spring and each fall, from the Brent Manufacturing Company, even back in Will Brent's father's time. But no order had come as yet, this spring.

The Brent plant had no high-pressured sales force—the quality of its nails did the selling and even now, in a time of stiffer competition, Will Brent refused to see the need of one.

He had spoken to Coley this morning of the delay in the Colton order. "It usually comes in April."

Coley Coggin had studied his grimy fingernails for a moment before he answered. Then he had said, without looking up, "Maybe 'tisn't coming. Know what they're saying round the town, Will? That you haven't a chance to compete with the Petersen outfit, across."

"Nonsense!" He had said nothing more.

But after that the possibility that the Colton order had gone to Petersen loomed big in his mind. If so, it would be more than a serious loss to him, for it would indicate an alarming truth in the talk which Coley Coggin said was going on behind his back.

During the afternoon he dictated a letter to Kate Briggs, who typed his correspondence and kept his books. "Colton Construction Company, Worcester, Massachusetts. Sirs: We have been looking for your usual spring order so that we may fill it without delay to you . . ."

As he dictated, he thought, uncomfortably, "She'll tell her aunt. . . ." Coley Coggin's wife, Almira, was her aunt. It'd be over the village by nighttime that he was worried. He did not like to be the recipient of sympathy from his neighbors—he wanted their respect and felt that he merited it, but the kind of talk Coggin had implied was going on behind his back was distinctly distasteful to him. But the letter had to go—he had to know what was happening.

He was tired when he reached home, that evening. He went into the house through the kitchen door. Susan was sitting at the table, idle, a distraught look on her face.

"Father—she's here!" She whispered it.

"Who's here?"

"Aunt Deborah."

"Good God!" That he should speak so vehemently was a measure of his consternation. He groaned, "Today of all days!" But he did not explain to Susan why it was worse to have her arrive today. "Where is she?"

"Taking a bath. She flew from California—then she bought a used car in Pittsfield and it broke down or something over in the Flats— John Wendell fixed it for her—he came with her to the other house."

But her father was not interested in these facts. Nor did he notice the slight tremble in Susan's voice. He said, heavily, "Well, she's here. What about supper . . . ?"

"I'll—I'll get something. . . ."

"Where's Nell?"

"I don't know. Oh, yes, she was going to Mrs. Peely's this afternoon."

"I'll go upstairs and clean up—that is, when I can get into the bathroom!"

Susan said, after him, appealingly, "Father, she's quite nice—Aunt Debbie, I mean. She told me to call her that . . . that you always had."

He could hear the splash of water on the other side of the bathroom door. He went on to his room, closed that door.

She was here, Debbie. Here in this house. He took off his coat, loosened his tie. He had an uncomfortable sense of his mother's presence—that she stood at his elbow regarding him with the cold, tight-lipped severity which she always had shown when he was at some fault. Then from out of that past, flashed a memory of Debbie; Debbie taking the blame for something he had done. She often had shielded him—she always had laughed as if she liked doing it. He remembered the warmth of her laugh—a daring about her. And hadn't he leaned on it, back in those days?

He jerked off his shirt. Absurd to allow all that to come back to him now; more important was to know what Debbie was like after all these years.

He waited in his room until he heard Debbie go down the stairs.

Susan was getting supper ready but she was still distraught, taking things she did not want from the refrigerator, looking blindly over a cupboard shelf without knowing what she was looking for.

It had been a wholly wretched afternoon for her. She had had to make herself phone John Wendell and the instant after she hung up the receiver she had regretted terribly that she had told him she could not come. But how *could* she have gone there again, after begging Nell not to do things that would make talk? If she'd gone, Nell might have seen her from Mrs. Peely's parlor. . . .

But—what was it Nell had said? "If you never do *anything* you might as well be dead?" Going away from the telephone Susan had felt dead, indeed.

She had planned to drive to Winsted, shop a little, to give some truth to the lie she had told John Wendell, but she was too dead to bring herself to the exertion of changing her dress, backing out the car.

"I'll never see him again." Oh, in church and at church affairs, but not as she had on Tuesday. Even if he brought his notes here—and she doubted that he would—he'd just stop at the door. She would not have that wonderful, close feeling she had that afternoon, alone with him.

"I—I *love* him!" She had whispered it, though there were no ears anywhere near to hear.

For some time it had been a small and secret concern of hers that she never had felt a deep stir of heart over any man. She had tried to think she did, especially with Ethan Phelps, over in New Hartford, but after that evening she had had him here she had known she was forcing it—she had not cared enough about him to defend him before her father. There had been two other young men, Jack Albrecht here in Sweethome, and Peter Scott, the manager of the Food Mart in Winsted, with whom she had gone around some, to the movies, in Winsted, usually, but when first one and then the other went to jobs in other towns she had not felt the slightest loss or answered the few letters they wrote to her. She had wondered sometimes if she were not like other girls, lacking is some way. But now she knew she had fallen in love that first Sunday she saw John Wendell behind the pulpit. But knowing it only brought a deeper wretchedness to her. She had failed it.

She could not settle down even to any small task in the house. She was in the kitchen doing nothing when she heard a car and voices, next door. She gave it no heed until it drifted in to her unhappy consciousness that it might be Willet's truck from Canaan with the grass seed. She hurried across the yards.

Aunt Deborah—she saw the bags on the porch. But her only thought, after the shock of surprise at seeing John Wendell with

Aunt Deborah was that he would know she had not gone to Winsted, that she had told him a lie. He would think she did not want to help him. In her confusion she had not spoken a word of greeting to Aunt Deborah.

She realized that, and with contrition, as soon as John Wendell rode away. And Aunt Deborah was old—had come such a long distance. She had been very cordial to her, to make up for her first rudeness. Back home, she had insisted upon making her a cup of tea, then had urged her to take a little rest before supper. "You must have supper with us—Father will want to visit with you!"

Aunt Deborah had said she would be glad to. But that she wanted a bath more than a rest. Susan had taken her up to her own room, given her towels.

It was true, what she had said to her father—she *did* think Aunt Debbie was nice, even though . . .

Deborah Brent came out to the kitchen. "Let me do something, Susan."

"There's just the salad. I've washed the lettuce and there are the tomatoes and a cucumber. I was late getting started with supper." To let Aunt Debbie help would make her feel more one of the family, thought Susan. "Here's an apron, Aunt Debbie."

Deborah was at the sink peeling tomatoes and looking quite at home when Will Brent came into the kitchen.

"Good evening, Deborah."

She turned, dropped her knife, put both her hands out to him. "Why, Willie—Willie, how are you?"

He saw her gray hair, the wrinkles around her eyes and mouth, with a definite relief. Absurd of him, of course, to think she would not have changed with the years, sobered down. He had expected to see her dressed flashily, rouged up to look younger than she was, hung with doodads—instead he could see that under the apron she

56

was wearing a gray tweed suit, a plain blouse, and there was not an ornament of any kind in sight.

Bill came in just as Susan announced that everything was ready. He mumbled something that sounded like "H'lo" in answer to Deborah's greeting, then grinned a little shyly. "We heard at Higgins' that you'd come!"

Deborah laughed. "So soon? Now, where's Nell? When she comes I'll have met the three of you!"

"She'll be here any moment," said Susan. "She is in a chorus that is going to sing at the Commemoration Service at the church. The church will be two hundred years old in July, Aunt Debbie."

Aunt Debbie laughed. "Two hundred years—that's going to make the Methodists jealous—they're no more than a hundred."

Nell came, flushed from hurrying, her hair wind-blown, her eyes very bright. She made no apologies for her tardiness—she slid into her chair with an absent manner, as if she were not wholly aware where she was. She had met Deborah in this same way, casually, and with no surprise. Though she explained that. "I heard you'd come, Aunt Deborah! I met Abby up the block and she'd seen you drive in. . . ."

"Abby Boyd? I remember her—she had freckles all over her face and her nose was always running. . . ."

"It still is," said Nell with a giggle.

"I doubt you'll find many changes in Sweethome," said Will Brent. Susan kept some talk going—asking Deborah questions about California, the weather, the flowers, such things. Now and then Nell said something, but not in a particularly interested way. Bill just ate.

Those first apprehensions over Deborah's coming eased, and, momentarily, his concern over the Colton order forgotten, Will Brent found himself eating with good appetite. It was a creditable meal—Debbie'd see how capable Susan was. He saw her eyes resting warmly on first one and then another of the three children and he felt a sudden lift of pride in them. Satisfaction, too, in the pleasantness of

57

the room with its solid old furniture. Probably Debbie saw it very cozy after the roving life she had led.

His plate clean, Bill lifted his head. "Say, Aunt Debbie, there's a whopper of a big plant just been built over on the Flats. They make nails—bolts and screws and nails."

"Nails?" Deborah looked down the table at Will Brent. "A competitor?"

Will Brent answered a little stiffly, "Not yet—and I see no reason why it ever should be." He added, "A company from outside . . ." He stopped. Was he just imagining there was some concern in Debbie's regard of him?

But all she said was, "I noticed the Flats have built up. It would have been a good investment to have bought up land over there, when one could have gotten it for next to nothing."

"A real-estate firm over in Canaan bought most of it," said Bill. "Gee, I'll bet they made a wad of dough!"

"How are you going to make the dough when you're through school, Bill?" asked Deborah, smiling at the boy. "Nails?"

"He's going to start at the plant this summer vacation," said Will Brent. "As I did. . . ."

"*Gee,* Dad. Let a fellow have some fun!"

Will Brent caught Susan's eyes on him with some pleading in them —Nell's, too, but a little fire in hers. Before he could speak, Deborah asked, "What particular fun have you in mind, Bill?"

The boy turned to her quickly. "Soon's school over—three of us are goin' to see something of this United States—we're going to hitch-hike out West. . . ."

"Even so, it takes money," put in Will Brent, in a voice that said more.

"We'll work for our food—one of the guys read an article in a magazine about some fellows who did it. It's easy—you wash dishes, things like that. . . ." He looked at Deborah as he said it, not at his father.

Susan laughed. "If it's dishwashing you want, Bill . . ."

"Oh, *gee*," growled Bill, pushing his plate away from him.

Something of his first fears came crowding back on Will Brent. He had not missed the way the boy had looked to Deborah for a sympathetic understanding of this crazy plan of his. *Just as he had done at Bill's age.* "I'll speak to her—I am not going to permit her to encourage him in any wild ideas!" He remembered there were those other things he must speak about, too, when they were alone. Her financial situation—on a second look her clothes appeared a little shabby. This matter of calling herself Brent, again. And why she had come back to Sweethome.

Bill got up with a muttered, "Excuse me," and moved toward the door.

"Haven't you homework to do?" his father asked sharply.

"Did it study hour."

"Where are you going?"

"Oh—out. I told Jim Purdy I'd come over—maybe."

"I want you in by nine o'clock."

Bill slouched out through the door without answering. Nell got up, as she did so, picking up her plate and cup and saucer.

Susan said quickly, "Nell, Aunt Debbie, maybe, hasn't finished."

"I have, Susan. It was a good supper."

"Probably you'd like to go over to the other house—get settled for the night," suggested Will Brent.

"Father, maybe . . ."

Deborah seemed to anticipate what Susan was going to say. She gave her a little smile. "Thanks, no. I might as well begin right away, getting settled."

Will Brent said, "I'll go over with you, help you with your baggage."

"Well, breakfast, Aunt Debbie—come over for breakfast," persisted Susan.

Now Deborah's smile was warmer. "That's very kind of you, but

59

I bought some food while I was in Pittsfield. Goodnight, my dear. Goodnight, Nell."

While Will Brent carried in the baggage, Deborah went from one downstairs room to another of the old house. From the hall he saw her looking slowly, reflectively around each one. When he came down from upstairs, she was in the parlor.

"It's just the same," she said, in an oddly quiet voice.

"The furniture—yes. It's good old stuff. But I've had electricity put in and the plumbing modernized—oil heat, too. I had that done for Doctor Pryor. He paid good enough rent to warrant the improvements."

"Oh, yes, rent." Deborah went to a window, lifted the shade to the top to let in more of the lingering daylight. "How much rent did he pay you?" She spoke now with that odd quiet.

A little to his own surprise, Will Brent was sorry he had spoken of rent—he had a sudden realization of the great unfairness to Debbie of his father's will, leaving the old house and the plant to him. "He paid me seventy-five a month, but with you . . ."

She turned, came up to him, her eyes warm. "Willie, don't be embarrassed about it! Of course I expect to pay you rent—I'll pay you what you were getting." She put her hand affectionately on his arm. "There'll be ghosts pop up, probably, but don't let's let any of them come between us! I haven't held it against Father that he cut me off—I didn't, when I first knew he had. I understood how it happened he wrote such a will. So we'll not speak of it. Willie, it was *good* to see you and your children together—you've a very nice family. It is very sad that Mary had to die. I remember her as a young girl, a lovely girl. . . . Now help me carry my food to the kitchen."

She went ahead of him, bags in her own arms. In the kitchen, she switched on a ceiling light experimentally, exclaimed, "An electric stove! And a Frigidaire! You did fix up Doctor Pryor very well. Sit down, now, while I put stuff away."

He sat down at the table, a little stiffly, thinking this was not leading up to the talk he must have with her. His eyes followed her as she moved from cupboard to cupboard. Now she did not look her fifty-eight years. Her quick step, the straightness of her back . . . His own shoulders, of which he was rather proud, suddenly felt stooped. Her gray hair had an aliveness in the way it waved over her head to her neck, where it was cut short; his own was limp and thinning. He suspected that those wrinkles on her face which had contributed earlier to his surcease of worry, had come from quick changes of expression, rather than time. He was not so confident, now, that she had sobered down. That warmth in her voice which he remembered . . .

She was keeping up a little run of talk as she disposed of her things. "Where did Nell get that hair of hers? It is gorgeous! I imagine she has her own ideas about things, hasn't she?" She talked on without waiting for him to answer. "Susan is a lovely girl. Though there is something about her emotionally undeveloped. Young Bill—he's like you were at his age. It rolled back the years when I saw him." She looked down at the coffee in her hands as if the forty years were there in the red and white labeled can.

He did not like this talk of Nell having ideas of her own; Susan, emotionally undeveloped . . . absurd! As to Bill—it was the opportunity to tell her that she must not interfere between him and Bill. He said, stiffly, "I think I had more sense when I was the boy's age."

Deborah sat down across the table from him. "You followed the pattern made for you, didn't you, Willie? You never made one of your own. . . ."

He did not like the sorry tone in which she said this. "I've every reason to be satisfied with the way I've lived. At least . . ."

Deborah smiled. "It is better than the way I have, you were going to say? Maybe so, maybe not. Sometimes I think life doesn't owe me a thing. Oh, I would have liked to have had children but I didn't. I had a boy for a few weeks, and then he died. . . ."

Here was his approach and now he was in the mood to follow it through. But, first . . .

He said, coldly, "This matter of your calling yourself Brent again . . . Sweethome will think that is odd when you have a married name to use. More than one," he added.

Now Deborah laughed. "Of course they will! You can tell them it is mine by law and benefit of clergy. Mrs. Roger Brent. I met Roger at a party in San Francisco. We tried to track down some blood relationship but we couldn't, so, lacking it, we married."

Her light tone quickened all Will Brent's first apprehensions.

"Is he—still living?"

Deborah leaned across the table toward him, a faint scorn in her eyes. "Willie, is it worrying you so—my coming back, dragging what you think a dubious past along with me? Yes, Roger is still living. We agreed to a divorce and it's a nice clean divorce for incompatibility. Not a co-respondent mentioned. The others—died in respectable fashion. Paul of tuberculosis. Dale Curtis of a ruptured appendix." She paused and Will saw one hand close on the edge of the table. "Does that relieve your mind?"

"You married again very soon after Curtis died."

"Three years. A much longer time when measured by loneliness. You had your children after Mary died."

Her manner changed. The scorn left her face; she looked only tired. She said, "I was hoping you would be glad to see me! That you'd kept something from our growing up together, here in this old house. But I don't suppose you had a chance. Willie, do you know one reason I came back?"

"I've wondered . . ."

"I wanted to go back to the beginning—see myself as I was, when I was a child. To understand how much hate had to do with what I became. Your mother hated me, you know. No—don't deny it. You wouldn't have known, perhaps, at your age then, but she did. I understand why—she hated my mother, was jealous of her—she'd

62

wanted to marry Father when he married my mother—and there I was to keep it alive in her. And I hated her. I want to know, if I can, what it did to me. You see, I am planning my memoirs."

"Memoirs!" Will Brent almost shouted it in his fresh alarm. "What . . ."

"I know—I've done nothing to make me a celebrity. But—couldn't the story of just an ordinary woman—a woman who has experienced almost everything life has to hand out—make interesting reading?"

One marriage after another . . . Chill prickled up the back of Will Brent's neck. "I am not a judge of such reading. But—I didn't know you wrote!"

Deborah laughed. "I don't. I am not planning to do the writing. I've a friend coming here soon to visit me, who writes. It was he who suggested the story. Rom Barcek. He is Polish."

Will Brent pushed back his chair. He could not listen to more. A Pole—she was bringing a Pole here to stay with her. Probably a Jew. Maybe a Communist. "I must go over home. I put your bags in the upper hall—I did not know which room you'd use."

"My old room. Thanks."

She went to the door with him. At the door she put her hand on his arm as she had in the parlor. It asked for some sign of affection he knew, but he stiffened under it, and she drew it away.

"Goodnight. I'll write out a check for the rent tomorrow—I'll leave it with Susan."

As he crossed the yards, he carried with him, along with his heavy apprehensions, an echo of disappointment in her voice.

CHAPTER VI

GHOSTS DID GO with Deborah Brent, the next morning, as she moved about the old house, settling her belongings in convenient places. Perhaps they had stayed here all this time, like the old furniture in the rooms, solid, dull stuff that no antique dealer would drool over, too much in each room, too ponderous. The kitchen, in spite of the electric stove and the Frigidaire and the occupancy of those tenants of Will's, was as she remembered it—the same cupboards where, day after day, she had put dishes away after wiping them. *"Deborah, are you sure that is clean?* And don't dally so!" The walled-in fireplace with the doors behind which the wood to feed the stove had been kept. *"Get me some firewood, Deborah."* The deal table . . . how many times had she set it? The small wooden clock on the shelf which had ticked off the minutes so slowly.

Rom Barcek had said of her coming back here, "You'll remember— you will see yourself as you were."

She did. A lonely child, hungry for affection, for a closeness to someone and hiding it down deep in her. Pitting young hate against the older hate—never in words, but in a deliberate defiance, in small triumphs of wilfulness, of daring . . .

She saw her father, shut up in himself, driven into himself by Sarah Brent's stronger, harder will, which he had not the courage to defy. "He must have loved me," reflected Deborah, a little sadly. "But he never dared show it or stand up for me!"

Had that hungry childhood made her more ready in later years to give of her affections? Rom with his more analytical mind would know the answer to that. But she recognized now, without his help, that all through those years she had kept, deep down in her, that long-ago yearning to belong to someone.

That was why, without encouragement, she had written to Willie from time to time—it was a thread of family to which she wistfully clung. A thin thread—she remembered the coldness with which he had bade her goodnight, last night. Yet in the old days he had been fond of her, in a boy's way.

Lately she had taken to talking aloud to herself—it made for company when she seemed too much alone. The lonely feeling was beginning to creep into her now and she said aloud, "Perhaps you were crazy to come, Debbie. Live here with ghosts!"

Then her glance went to the window, crossed the yards to the other house, and suddenly her heart warmed as it had last night to Will's children. "Maybe they'll let me love them! Become fond of me . . . Especially that nice Susan. Nell—I don't think she is interested just now in anyone but herself! And Bill's a boy. . . ."

At that moment, as though summoned by her wishful thinking, Susan appeared through the trellis between the yards. She was carrying a basket. Deborah hurried to the door, threw it open. "Good morning, my dear!" she called out gladly.

"Good morning, Aunt Debbie. Did you sleep well?"

"Like a top—though just how tops sleep I wouldn't know. Come in—there's still coffee on the stove. Let's have a cup. Sit down—it's nice to have you come over."

Susan put her basket on the table. "It's—I brought over some jam and jelly. . . ."

"That you put up?"

"Yes. We have much more than we can use. I thought you'd like some."

"I shall. Thanks a lot!" Deborah took out one of the jars. "Strawberry—and what a beautiful color!"

65

Susan was looking around the kitchen. "You look settled—I thought perhaps I could help you—show you where things went."

Deborah turned to the stove, picked up the coffee pot. "You forget— I lived here for almost nineteen years."

Susan flushed. "I had forgotten! You don't mind being alone in the house?"

Deborah said, "Not a bit. Not with all of you next door. I'll probably have company often. John Wendell promised to come in soon. I like him!"

She saw a flush again on Susan's cheeks but this time it came quickly, warmly. Susan became very busy with stirring her coffee.

"How does Sweethome take to his motorcycle?" asked Deborah.

"I—don't know. Father thinks it's undignified. But he probably *hasn't* a car—probably can't afford one with what we pay him! They gave Doctor Marcy one and when he died they sold it. Used the money to paint the vestibule!" Susan did not hold her indignation back from her voice.

"Perhaps they are waiting to see if John Wendell is cut to their pattern. Where's Nell today?"

Did she imagine that Susan's face looked a little troubled as she answered?

"She's gone to Winsted to buy a new dress."

Deborah remembered the young Debbie going into Winsted to buy a new dress but after so much unpleasantness with her step-mother over it that there was no excitement left in the expedition— except that of getting her own way. She wondered if Will were stingy with his children or, perhaps, did not have the money to hand out to them.

"You've carried considerable responsibility since your mother died, haven't you, Susan?"

"It never seemed much—the meals weren't anything—I knew just how Mother had done everything. And Nell and Bill were kids. But now that Nell's older, sometimes—" Susan *was* troubled, Deborah

66

knew—"sometimes I don't know just what to do or say to her." She finished warmly, "I'm glad you're here, Aunt Debbie! Someone older —and in the family!"

In the family? She loved hearing that from Susan. She would forget Will's attitude toward her the evening before.

"I don't know how good my help would be, but you come to me if anything gets too much for you to handle."

"I will," said Susan simply. She added, a little hesitantly, "Sometimes I think Father isn't very understanding."

Deborah made no comment on that. She did not want to risk offending Susan.

At that moment there was a knock on the door. Susan sprang up to answer it. John Wendell stood outside.

"Oh!" said Susan.

"Good morning, Miss Brent. I stopped . . ."

Deborah came to the door. "Come in, come in. We're having some coffee. Will you join us? Pull a chair up to the table while I heat up the pot. Of course it isn't Post to entertain the preacher in the kitchen."

"It happens that this particular preacher prefers kitchens." John Wendell gave Susan a little smile. "I really stopped, though, to ask you if you'd like to have me take your car over to a garage and have someone check it over."

"Why, you're wonderful to think of that! I'd be ever so grateful. I will not need it, maybe for days."

"But I am going to enjoy this coffee first."

"And a doughnut." Deborah produced some doughnuts. "Store-bought. Probably an insult to offer them! They're a weakness of mine—I couldn't resist getting some when I was shopping for food."

"I'll make you some, Aunt Debbie," said Susan in a voice that rang differently on Deborah's ears.

On John Wendell's, too? He said, "Let me know when and I'll be coming in to eat some. By any chance did Doctor Winfield Marcy have stomach ulcers? Mrs. Donnell feeds me as if I were on a diet."

Deborah took one of the jars of jelly from the basket that was still on the table. "Susan brought this over to me. She made it herself. May I give John one, Susan, to take home with him?"

Susan's "Of course" had the different lilt in it.

John Wendell took the jar. "Will I flaunt that in Mrs. Donnell's face! Thanks, Susan." He used her name without any self-consciousness.

"I thought it was the custom to invite the minister to supper with some regularity—feed him up that way. It used to be, I remember."

"It may have fallen off as Doctor Marcy grew older. I understand—from Mrs. Donnell—that he liked a light supper every night and went to bed at nine o'clock. She highly disapproves of the late hours I keep. Runs up the electric light bills, she reminds me frequently."

Deborah's eyes had a little gleam in them. "Is that all she disapproves of?"

John Wendell laughed. "As far as I know—to date." He got up from his chair. "I'll get your car out if you'll give me the key. And I'll be remembering that promise of a doughnut." He looked at Susan.

"Mr. Wendell, those notes—you will bring them to me?"

"Oh, yes, those notes. Yes, I'll bring them."

Deborah gave him the key to the car and he went out to the barn. Susan gathered up the coffee cups. Deborah left them to her to wash and went into the parlor. She came back with a check in her hand.

"Will you give this to your father, Susan? I told him I would leave it with you. It's for three months' rent."

"*No,* Aunt Debbie!" Susan drew back, startled, ashamed. "You mean Father's letting you—it isn't right—this was your home!"

Deborah tucked the slip of paper into the pocket of Susan's dress. "Don't hold it against your father, Susan. It isn't his fault—there is a great deal to it you don't know, and I doubt it's in you to understand, if you did know. Don't worry about it—I'd really rather have it this way."

"I hate it," said Susan, low.

Deborah Brent put her arm over the girl's shoulder. "To have you right next door—to get to know you, my dear—is going to be worth a lot more to me than that check. So forget it."

"Forget the whole darn past," said Deborah aloud, to herself, after Susan had gone. The present always offered so much more to dwell upon. Little unexpected things happening, like this hour, just over. John Wendell coming in, Susan . . . Soon Rom would be here.

She spent the rest of the morning pressing out her clothes. She ate a little lunch, cleared her dishes away. "Now I suppose I must go and see Clare."

As she had for Will, she had kept a fondness for Clare Hersey through the years. Another thread . . . She was looking forward now to seeing her, yet dreaded it a little, too, for she might find that there was nothing left between them on which to renew the old relationship. Almost forty years, and only an exchange of letters in that time, one or two a year . . .

She put on the tweed suit, and started out, bareheaded. Clare lived the other end of the village but she did not hesitate to walk the distance. She drew in a long breath of air. "I'd forgotten a New England spring was like this!" Rom must come while there was still this tangy freshness in the air.

She walked along Central Road and everything around her was pleasantly familiar—the old trees, older, of course, their branches reaching further, the old houses, older. Probably some one of the same family still lived in each one. She checked the families off to test her memory. "The Purdys, here, Cochrans across the street. The Jamisons . . . I wonder what happened to Alida Jamison. Clare never wrote anything about her. . . ."

She saw the houses, there on the dry stonewalls of their foundations, somehow impregnable against the changing tides of living.

The houses on River Road, though not quite so old, built, perhaps, only a hundred and fifty years ago, were like that, too. All Sweethome. Homes . . .

And suddenly she was conscious of a feeling of belonging to its solidity, its impregnability. She would not feel that way, she reflected, if she went back to any of the other places where she had lived— Etna, the milltown, in Pennsylvania; that lumbering settlement in northern California—most certainly not in the Russian Hill area of gilded and ungilded apartment houses in San Francisco. "There's something in roots, I guess."

Nearing the Hersey house she thought of Clare as she remembered her. A pretty girl with blond hair and big blue eyes, a giggly girl. Timid. Deborah Brent remembered her frequent, *"Deb,* would you *dare? I* wouldn't!" And always that had spurred her on to greater daring.

Clare never had married. She had written, sometime after Deborah left Sweethome, that she was engaged to a Winsted man, Bert Jones. But he had been killed in the first world war. Then Clare had written, "I'll never love anyone else."

She kept house for her younger brother, Fred, whose wife had died a number of years ago. Deborah remembered him—a spiritless boy with a long neck and skinny wrists. Clare always had referred to him in her letters as "Poor Fred." Yet apparently she was devoted to him.

Out of a long-ago habit Deborah walked around the house to the side door. A porch had been built on, and on a swing on the porch sat Clare.

Clare stared at her and Deborah stared back, faintly repelled. For the woman she saw was immensely fat, all shape of a human figure lost under billows and rolls of soft flesh. But her eyes were still blue, her hair still flaxen.

Then Clare stirred, though she did not get to her feet. "Debbie! *Deb!* When did you come? No one told me! Though no one's been in this morning. Oh, I can't believe my eyes!" Deborah saw tears in her eyes. "I can't get up unless you give me a hand. You haven't changed a bit! Oh, of course, *some* . . . I guess it was surprise I didn't know you right off. I was sort of asleep. There, darling, just a hoist—when I'm once on my feet I'm all right. Isn't it dreadful I've got like this? It's some gland thing. Let's go in the house. I want to hear *every*thing about you, Deborah Brent!"

She waddled ahead of Deborah into the house, on into the parlor. There she sank down onto a sofa, pulled Deborah down beside her.

Deborah heard the old warm affection in Clare's voice, something of the old giggle, and forgot her shock at her physical appearance. The parlor was almost exactly as it was, those years ago, except that a framed photograph of a young man in an outdated uniform stood on the round marble-topped table where the waxed flowers under a glass dome had been.

"Your letters never told *enough,* darling," Clare went on, her hand over Deborah's. "I always had to read between the lines! And I'd think, 'That's just like Deb Brent!' And married twice, too!"

It came, startlingly, to Deborah that Clare might have read a gay, careless off-with-one-man-on-with-another life between the lines of those letters. Her own fault, for she had avoided the truth. She was not disturbed—all her life she had been indifferent to what others thought of her. More important, in her creed of living, was what one thought of one's self. If Clare had enjoyed a vicarious excitement from thinking it, she would not disillusion her. She said, smiling, "Three times."

"Deb, *no!* Really? How *do* you do it!"

"I'm divorced, now."

Clare gave a little shriek. *"Deb,* at your age . . ."

"What has age to do with it?"

"Well, I suppose nothing, only you'd think . . . I believe you are the only woman in Sweethome who is divorced! Who was he, Deb? *Where* is he?"

Deborah told her of meeting Roger Brent, of their short acquaintance, their marriage. "He's in San Francisco. He put me on the plane to come East."

"You mean—you *see* him!" Clare's eyes on Deborah, as wide as they could stretch between the puffs of flesh, were agleam with excitement.

"Yes, I see him quite frequently. He may come East—if he does he's coming to visit me." Before Clare could exclaim at that she said, "Now that's enough about me—tell me of yourself, Clare."

"Darling, there's nothing to tell! I live like a vegetable!" Clare's eyes went to the photograph. "There's never been any man to take Bert's place . . . I've never wanted there to be. Everyone here was wonderful to me, after I got the word—I guess everyone's understood why I never married. I had Mamma and Papa and now I have my brother, Fred—poor Fred, he does most of the work here in the house. I don't get out much but everyone comes to me and they tell me everything that's going on, so I don't feel left out of things. I *do* miss getting to Sunday service, though—Fred likes to sleep late, Sunday mornings, and, poor man, it's his only chance—he's off with his truck every morning soon after seven. There's a new minister here—that's why I want to go. Deb, you should hear the *talk* about him—well, he invites it—the things he says in his sermons. One Sunday he said that physical ills were really ills of the soul come out in the body or something like that, and he looked straight at Julia White when he said it and you know, though, of course, you don't though you must remember Julia—she's always complaining about something that's the matter with her and when he singled her out, and others told me he really did look straight at her—she almost had a stroke, she was so mad!"

"He might have just happened to be looking in her direction. Or it was a case of the shoe fitting . . ."

Clare giggled. "It was that, all right!"

"What did he suggest as a cure?"

"Prayer. And he says very few know how to pray!"

"Do we?"

Deborah saw some surprise come into Clare's face—that *she* should put such a question.

"Well, saying that to the regulars who ought to know how to pray by this time! There's a lot more to the talk than what he says at service—the clothes he wears and that awful motorcycle he goes around on. He goes over to the Flats and visits with the Catholic priest there. Mrs. Donnell—she comes in often, evenings, to see me—said that he brought in some roses yesterday—stuck them under her nose and told her they'd come from that Father Somebody's garden. . . ."

"A rose is a rose. . . ."

"But there's more, Deb. Mrs. Donnell took the afternoon off the other day and when she came home she knew he'd had someone there—there were two cups and plates on the sink and they'd eaten some of a cake she had made and she knows it was a girl because she got the smell of perfume when she went into the kitchen. . . ."

"Well, what's wrong about it's being a girl?" Now Deborah had difficulty in keeping the light level in her voice.

"To pick out an afternoon when Mrs. Donnell wasn't there—that's what's suspicious about it." Then, her bits about John Wendell exhausted, Clare asked, "Deb, was Willie glad to see you? And his girls?"

Deborah said, "Yes, he seemed glad." He had, at suppertime, and she was not going to tell Clare of the rest of the evening, the matter of the rent, of Will's growing coldness to her. She added, "The girls are darling."

"Susan is a nice girl. Most everyone here thinks it's a shame that she's so tied down—seems as though Will Brent could pay a housekeeper though I don't know—some are saying his business isn't good. Did he say anything about it to you?"

"He hasn't yet."

"And there's that new plant over on the Flats. Everyone here thinks

73

that that Rudolph Petersen had *nerve* to built it—right across from Will's! You should see him driving around in his big car, right here in the village. You'd think he owned Sweethome! Everyone is just waiting for him to go to church some Sunday . . . he'll see, then. But just the same, I should think Will'd be worried. And, Deb, there's some talk of that younger girl of Will's. . . ."

Deborah got to her feet. What had been amusement at Clare's avid prattle, then some impatience, now was a sort of shock. She could not listen to any more. "I must go back to the house—finish getting settled."

Clare caught her arm. "Oh, *Deborah!* We've just begun to talk! I haven't asked you half the things I want to know! One—were you sorry afterwards that you—you ran away with Paul Bouvais? I always wondered. . . . I remember everyone said you'd be. . . ."

"Sorry? No. I'm afraid everyone has to be disappointed."

"Mamma always said it was *her* fault—you know, your stepmother's. That if she'd given you more loving you wouldn't have done it. Mamma stood up for you!"

Deborah's coldness yielded swiftly to a warm memory of the kindly, motherly woman who had made this house seem more like home to the young Debbie than her father's house. She said, "I wish I could thank her!"

"I wish I could give a party for you, Debbie. Though there aren't so many of our old crowd here—Julia White and Win Corbett, they'll want to see you—but I just can't get about to do more than feed poor Fred and myself."

"I don't want any parties, so don't feel badly about it. Don't get up—I should know my way to the door!" She pressed Clare's hand. "I'll be seeing you soon."

Clare's eyes filled with tears. "You said that the way you used to! Your voice . . . Oh, Deb, I'm so *happy* you're back! I didn't think you'd ever *dare* come!"

Deborah laughed. "Well, I did."

She thought, a little sadly, as she went back along Central Road, that there *was* nothing on which to renew the old friendship between her and Clare, except loyalty and some pity. She said aloud, "Poor Clare."

She remembered something Rom had said once, "To have life you must live." Clare had been too timid to really live. "She hid behind me when we were girls, then it was her father and mother—the tragedy of Bert Jones—now it's her flesh. She nourishes herself on the crumbs of gossip that are brought to her."

Suddenly she laughed aloud. "She'll have a whole loaf to hand out herself, now!"

"Yes, I know Deborah Brent's back. She came in today. And what do you think? She's divorced!"

She felt as she walked along that the windows of the houses were eyes, taking her in, that the few whom she met, though strangers to her, recognized her and turned to have another look at her.

But reaching the old house she stopped on the walk outside to consider it. "It needs painting. I'll tell Will I'll have it done. White, of course. Those bushes should be trimmed. . . . It *is* a sweet old place!"

And though she did not think of it as so, by these decisions she was claiming her right to be here, in spite of the wording of her father's will, in spite of Will's restrained welcome, in spite of what Sweethome thought of her. In Clare's word she had "dared" to come back! Without knowing it, she held her head higher as she walked into the house.

CHAPTER VII

THE EMPLOYEES of the Brent Nail Works lived in Sweethome or in the country near by. It had always been that way, sons following their fathers in the plant. There were no foreigners among them. There were no unions. There was no talk of unions.

Will Brent believed this contentment came from his men sharing his pride in the quality of his product; each one felt he had a part in keeping that quality up to its high standard. He lost no opportunity to tell them that that was so. His attitude toward his men was more that of a fellow worker than an executive. A neighbor, too. Petersen hired foreigners—a lot of Negroes, just lately. On that bit of information, Will Brent's satisfaction in his own industry had been greater than ever.

But lately it threatened to crack. Disturbing anxieties were piling up—doubts that had no place in his thoughts.

What Deborah had said the other night at supper. "Are you still using the machines that were there in Father's time?"

"Yes. They do the work."

"But there must be newer ones that would speed up production."

"Probably, but they'd be an unnecessary expenditure."

It was over a week since Deborah had come and Susan had had her in for supper three evenings in that time. He had made no protest to Susan—it was just as well to show the village that he and Deborah were on good terms. And, seeing Deborah now and then, he could have some idea of what she was up to.

At the moment it was a notion to have the house painted. He'd told her he could not afford it and she had said she'd pay for it. But he did not know if *she* could afford it. He knew nothing yet about her financial situation more than that her check for the rent, drawn on a San Francisco bank, had been honored. However, he was not going to take any opinions from her on how he should run his plant. So he had answered her in a tone of finality. But the thought stayed in his mind that the money spent on new machinery might mean more money coming in.

For years Fred Hersey had trucked the spools of wire to the plant. "Too bad the railroad wasn't run on this side of the river," Coley had said, once. "You could have had a sidetrack laid."

"We get along—and it gives Fred a living."

No letter had come from the Colton Construction Company in answer to his.

He was turning over his mail in the hope of finding one when Coley Coggin came in.

"Joe Briggs and Denny Smith are quitting, Will."

Will Brent looked up, astonished. "Quitting—*why?*"

The two men had been with the plant for eight years; their fathers had worked here before them. They lived on a back road but close enough to be considered natives of Sweethome. They were both very good workers.

"They're going over to Petersen's."

A vein bulged out on Will Brent's forehead. This was close to treason. "They'll be working along with niggers? I'll talk to them!"

"They've gone. I saw there wasn't any use trying to argue them into staying—they'd have got some of the others to thinking things. I paid 'em off and they went."

Had they already got some of the others to thinking things? Will Brent started to put the question, when Coley spoke.

"We don't need to get any men in their places—we're just about caught up on orders."

"We are," thought Will Brent, grimly. Higher wages! He'd have to cut them, lay off men, unless the Colton order came in. He looked at Kate Briggs' back—could he get along without her? He could keep his own books. If Nell knew how to type . . .

Nell. That concern belonged to out-of-office hours, yet it cut in now to the exclusion, for a moment, of every other. Nell had not come home for supper last night. When she did come she had met his questions evasively. "I went on a picnic. Oh, with some of my friends . . ." Then, defiantly, "I don't have to tell every place I go—who I go with! I'm not going to!" She had walked out of the room, her head high, gone up to her own room, slammed the door.

He had seen the startled, almost frightened look on Susan's face.

"I'll have it out with that young lady tonight! If Debbie isn't around . . ."

He reflected, wearily, that if Deborah were a different kind of woman he could turn this problem of Nell over to her. The matter of Nell's refusing to go to church. But Deborah, herself, had not gone, either of these Sundays she had been here. She would be of no help to him.

Kate Briggs got up from her desk. "It's almost noon—shall I put some water over for your tea, Mr. Brent? I brought a sandwich today." Sometimes she did this instead of walking home for her lunch.

"Thanks—yes." Though he felt a little uncomfortable accepting even this small service when it was in his mind to lay her off.

Kate sat at her own desk to eat her sandwich and drink her tea. She was a plain-faced woman, who seldom had anything to say. These qualities had had much to do with Will Brent's hiring her— she would not get any ideas of marrying him and he had not been unaware, after Mary died, that several women were looking upon him as a possible mate. But at this noon hour, to his dismay, she showed some talkativeness.

"That Petersen—you know he's staying over in Lenox but they say, maybe, he's thinking of buying a place in Sweethome. *Living* here! Someone told my aunt that she saw him and that real-estate man from Canaan stop at the Wheelers' house, the other day. The Doctor over in Winsted told Jeannie Wheeler she has to live in Arizona on account of her asthma so Jim Wheeler has to sell the house. They must have gone through it for they were inside quite a long time. He'd have his nerve to settle right there in the middle of the village!"

Will Brent put his half-eaten sandwich down on the paper plate, drew a sheet of figures in front of him, hoping it would stop Kate's talk.

But she went on, after a swallow of tea, "You'll like to hear, Mr. Brent, that Agnes Peely says Nell has a perfectly beautiful voice! She thinks she should take singing lessons. If she did she might be a great concert singer or even get into the Metropolitan Opera."

"Lessons cost money," said Will Brent curtly, running his eyes down the sheet of paper. "Now, Kate, I have to total these figures."

"Oh. I'm sorry. But, Mr. Brent, you ought to take *some* time off! You haven't finished your sandwich!"

Was there some instinct of compassion in this concern of hers? She had overheard his and Coley's talk. She'd go home and tell her aunt he was too worried to eat. He picked up his half-finished sandwich. "That's so—I haven't eaten it."

The afternoon went on. On his ears fell the hum of the machines, not as loud as usual, but agreeable to hear. His life, he thought, leaning back in his chair to listen to it. His father's, his grandfather's. Before that it had been the sound of iron against anvil. And before that men digging ore out of these hills roundabout, smelting it—his people among them. An honorable heritage of enterprise.

A car passed the window, a gray-and-chrome-bodied car, its top down. Kate Briggs saw it.

"Why—that's that *Swede!* Coming *here!*" she cried out indignantly.

Will Brent sprang to his feet, stiffening in every muscle.

79

So tall and broad of shoulder was Rudolph Petersen that he seemed to fill the doorway as he paused on its threshold. "Brent?"

"Yes."

The man came on into the room, a little hesitantly. If Will Brent had not been so affronted by his presence here he would have recognized some shyness in his manner. He had put out his hand, then drew it back. "I'm Petersen—your neighbor across the river. I stopped in—thought it was time the two of us met."

"Take a chair," said Will Brent, coldly; with a motion of his hand he directed Kate to leave the room.

"I've known of your product for some time—Brent's nails. It's rather exceptional to have quality keep to such a high standard for so many years!"

"Three generations," informed Will Brent.

He disliked the man more on closer sight. Older than himself by a few years, he'd heard, yet he appeared to have the vigor of a man in his thirties—the clear blue of his eyes, the healthy red of his skin, the length and breadth of him.

"Three generations," repeated Rudolph Petersen. "And I can claim only fifteen years!"

Will made no comment on that, nor any effort to break the little silence that followed. Let the man know they had nothing to say to each other.

Rudolph Petersen finally spoke, squaring his shoulders so that he bulked bigger in his chair. "One reason I wanted to meet you, Brent, is to sound you out on a proposition that's been shaping up in my mind. Speak of it so that you can be thinking it over. It's that we merge, in a way. It'd go on being Brent's nails—a superior quality for which we could ask a higher price. I'd give you shares proportionate to the value of this plant here. . . ."

Will Brent was on his feet, his face white with outrage.

"I am not interested in any such proposition, Mr. Petersen."

Rudolph Petersen rose to his feet. "I'm sorry, Brent. But I'll leave it open—maybe you'll change your mind."

"I am not likely to. Good day."

As his caller went out, Will Brent dropped down into his desk chair, shaking with anger. *"Sorry!" What did the fellow mean?*

Kate came back into the room. "Mr. Brent—you look dreadful! Can I get you something?"

"I am all right." He spoke loudly to reassure himself as well as Kate.

He made a show of going back to what he had been doing when Petersen came into the room, though he was still shaking. He'd tell no one of this insulting proposition—lucky that Kate was out of the room. He told himself that he had met it very effectively—left no doubt in the fellow's mind of what he thought of it.

He'd settle with Miss Nell in the same way.

One of the many things he admired in Susan's housekeeping was the regularity of the meals. Until that evening of Deborah's coming, and he had been too taken aback that night to give it any thought, supper was always ready when he got home. But tonight there was no sign of supper in preparation; he heard the clack of the old typewriter Susan kept in her room.

He called to her, a little sharply.

She came running down the stairs. "Father! I didn't know it was so late!"

"What were you doing?" He never had spoken to Susan in that tone.

"I—it's that typing I said I'd do—for John Wendell." Susan went on to the kitchen as she spoke.

He followed her to the door. "Where's Bill? Where's Nell?"

"They'll be coming, any minute. It won't take me long to get something ready—I've some dried beef I can cream."

He turned away, went up to his room, his step heavy. His heart heavier. Now it seemed to be Susan to whom he must speak—working for Wendell when she should be getting supper. Why had Mary had to die, he thought with weary irritation.

He remembered the quiet, smooth running of the household, when she was here—her gentleness with the children when she had to discipline them. How they were always running to her with scratches and bruises to be healed, or to tell her something. Then came the startling thought: "They've never come to me!"

He frowned at the thin, tired face in the mirror over the washbowl and the face frowned back, somehow reassuring him. Mary had not had to meet any situations like this with Nell!

Nell came in as they were sitting down at the table. She greeted them gaily, "Hello, folks!"

"Apparently she is indifferent to giving me cause for displeasure," thought Will Brent.

He ate little supper; he said little and that to Bill about his final grade in algebra which had not been creditable. "What kind of a man will you be if you are satisfied in just skinning through subjects, as you put it?"

"A lot of fellows didn't do that," Bill answered with pride.

The meal over, Nell started to clear the table.

"Let that wait, Nell. Come into the parlor—I want to have a talk with you." He tried to say it gently, as Mary would.

Nell followed him to the parlor.

"Hope it isn't too long—we're rehearsing tonight."

Will Brent closed the door. "It will depend entirely upon you, how long it is. I want to speak about last night—your attitude when with every right I questioned you as to where you had been. Your impudence in speaking to me as you did I will overlook—it is more important to have you tell me it will not happen again."

He saw her face change, the vividness go out of it, a hard stubbornness come in. Her eyes met his squarely.

82

"I am not going to say it won't happen every time you ask me a lot of questions. I *don't* have to tell you everything I do and I am not going to!"

She did not fling this defiance at him as she had last evening, but the quiet with which she said it was worse, the cool look in her eyes. Will Brent's control broke. He said harshly, "We'll see about that, young lady! If necessary . . ."

"You'll lock me in my room?" With that she turned and walked out of the parlor.

When he went to the dining room, through the window he saw her crossing the yards to the other house. *"Going to Deborah . . ."*

Susan was finishing clearing the table. She looked as she had the evening before, frightened. She said, a little uncertainly, "Don't be too angry with Nell—she's—she's just beginning to feel grown-up and wants to show her independence. . . ."

Will Brent only made a sound in his throat in answer to that. He frowned through the window. "Are you two girls running over to the other house all times of the day?"

His back was to Susan—he did not see the quick way she put down the dishes she held, stood straighter.

"I don't know what you mean by all times of the day. Nell doesn't—but I go over quite often. Aunt Debbie's there alone, at least most of the time. And I like her." When her father did not speak she added, "Is there any reason why we shouldn't?"

Was that defiance in Susan's voice? Will Brent felt a helplessness crawling over him. "I don't want her putting any of her ideas in your heads." He thought suddenly of the man Deborah was bringing here. "Or take up with her friends."

There was silence behind him for a moment, then Susan said, "She had a little party this afternoon. Coffee and doughnuts. John Wendell was there and he brought Father Duffy from the Flats. I was so glad she asked me to come—it was a grand afternoon!"

Will Brent swung around from the window. The vein stood out on

83

his temple again. Deborah, taking up with the priest from the Flats! But he kept that back. He said witheringly, "Such a grand afternoon that you came home and typed for Wendell and forgot supper . . ."

Susan's dark eyes met his as squarely as Nell's had, a little time earlier. "Yes," she said, as quietly as Nell had spoken. Then she picked up her dishes and went to the kitchen.

CHAPTER VIII

IN THE OLD HOUSE Deborah Brent sat alone at the kitchen table eating a light dinner and enjoying a great contentment. Her little party had been particularly pleasant. John Wendell's idea—he had said he wanted her to meet Father Duffy. If he could use her car he'd bring Father Duffy to her. This afternoon was free for him—was it for her? "You'll like him!" He was boyish in his eagerness to have her share with him his liking of the priest. He often had seemed boyish when he was here, which had been frequently, running in informally, for a few minutes, every day or so.

It was John who suggested that Susan might come over, too. That had delighted her—and to see Susan blossoming out in her pleasure of the occasion.

She liked Father Duffy—she had liked the talk between him and John, the genuine friendliness in it even when they disagreed. The humor, too. She reflected, now, on how, all her years, she had enjoyed men's talk more than women's. She would have other afternoons like this. Rom would be here. Father Duffy would be good for Rom, who was inclined to be too cynical. Susan'd come over. . . .

She did not plan further than that, nor did she have any desire to do so. Julia White and Win Corbett had called a few afternoons ago, as Clare had predicted they would, but she had sensed almost at once that it was curiosity that brought them rather than friendliness. Their eyes, boring over her from the top of her graying hair to the toes of the old shoes she was wearing, had betrayed that. In their

85

talk, mostly of their husbands who had been Sweethome boys, and their girls, Julia's Libby and Win's Paula, "They're both of them stay-at-home girls," there had been a smugness intended, Deborah suspected, to show up their virtuous lives in contrast to what they believed hers to have been. It had made her certain that Clare had fed them well on what she had read between the lines of those letters. She had listened and smiled and said that, yes, it was nice to be back in Sweethome, and get acquainted with Will's family, and, no, she did not know how long she would stay, through the summer, surely, and had wished they would go. When they did go she had said aloud, "What *dull* women! I can do without them!" Happily—here in the old house which, with each day, surprisingly seemed more home than any place in which she had lived.

She was thinking of that and of the peace of it—"It's like slipping your mind into a pair of comfortable old shoes"—when, without a knock, Nell opened the door. She got up from her chair, surprised and pleased. Nell had been over only once, commissioned by Susan to bring her some asparagus from the garden.

"Nell, how nice! Have you had dinner?"

"Yes."

She saw that Nell was wrought up over something but she said lightly, "Well, sit down with me while I finish mine!"

Nell sat down, rested her chin against her clenched hands, her eyes blazing over them. "I had to get out! Go somewhere, away from Father! I hate him!"

The word sent a slight chill over Deborah Brent. But she told herself that, with that hair of Nell's, it would take only a small issue between her and her father to throw her into a temper. Probably this was over something in the way of clothes the girl wanted which Will considered an extravagance. She said, placatingly, "It's hard for a man to understand all the things a girl likes to have, especially at your age."

"He doesn't understand *anything* except his old nails!" said Nell,

86

scornfully. "He won't realize that I'm old enough now to do what I want to do!"

Some instinct warned Deborah to listen to no more of this. She opened her lips to tell Nell that, when she saw the anger suddenly leave the girl's face, tears in her eyes. Touched, she said, gently, "What is it you want to do, Nell?"

"I'm in love, terribly in love with a boy, Tony DiVito. He's from the Flats. You know what Father'll say, how he'll act! But I'm going to marry Tony! Only—sometimes I'm scared, thinking of the fuss there'll be. You know—you must remember. . . ."

So that was why the girl had come to her! Deborah Brent did not speak for a moment, then said in a strangely unwilling voice, "Yes, I remember."

"You ran away and that's what I'll do when I marry Tony!"

Deborah got up from the table, her face strained, her hands tight on her chair. She spoke sharply. "Don't do such a thing because I did it! We're two different individuals—the circumstances of your situation are not what they were in mine. And you must think whether you are strong enough to pay the price of your rebellion."

"What price?" demanded Nell.

"Estrangement, for one thing. The loneliness it brings." Abruptly, Deborah controlled herself. She said more quietly, "I suppose you meet this boy away from the house—does he like it that way?"

"No one dates at one's home any more!"

"Do you go with him to the parties here?"

"There aren't any here—oh, things at the Grange and the church suppers but they're an old crowd. Anyway, he works evenings."

Deborah fell silent, her eyes on her hands where they held to the chair. Yet she must say something, say the right thing. . . .

"It isn't important on which side of the river your Tony lives—what is important is whether you love each other enough to wait a while—you both are young—wait and give yourselves a better chance to make a good life together. . . ."

Nell sprang to her feet. "You *can't* wait—you've forgotten how it is, Aunt Debbie. I've got to run, now—there's a rehearsal of that chorus this evening and I'll be late." But halfway to the door she paused. "Aunt Debbie, you won't tell Susan what I told you? She knows about Tony but not that I might run away with him. I just had to say it to someone—or choke."

She looked so young, so uncertain in spite of her show of independence that Deborah went to her, put an arm around her. "No, I will not tell Susan. Now go and sing, darling—sing your heart out! Come see me again!"

After Nell had gone she went back to the table, sat down in her chair. "I was her age—then" she said, aloud. "Paul only a year older . . . We wouldn't have listened if anyone had told *us* to wait!" She put one hand over her eyes. She did not want to remember the price she and Paul had paid—if she had to think back to those two years they were together she wanted only to remember Paul's sweetness, not the other things.

Yet they came back to her—those endless nights at the Corner Inn where Paul played his violin for what went as dancing, and she waited on table—the smoke in the room, the noise around the bar—men's hands on her arms, sometimes on her hips when she put the thick cornbeef sandwiches and beer mugs down in front of them. All she had got for her work were the tips, and Paul was paid only a little more than that and yet they were afraid to quit! Fear—the awful fear that was always with them, along with the loneliness. Their young dreams of gypsying over the world had ended, oh, too quickly, in fear.

The room they lived in, back of a delicatessen shop. Cheap because the only heat it got was through the walls from a kitchen. One meal a day, excepting those days when Mrs. Lesser needed her help in the shop and paid her with provisions. Paul growing thinner, thinner, coughing . . . No money for a doctor—*afraid* to go to a doctor. No money to move away from the mill town where the air was laden

88

with noxious gases. *"My mother'd know what to do for my cough."* Oh, how many times afterwards she had remembered that!

"Oh, Paul, we were too young to face it all—I was too young to know how to help you. . . ." Both too young to fight fear and homesickness.

Yet there was some good to hold in memory—Mrs. Lesser's kindness, after Paul began to have hemorrhages. Mrs. Lesser knew a doctor who wouldn't charge anything. Doctor Levi's kindness to Paul and to herself. Mike Daley, the bartender at the Corner Inn—he'd taken up a purse for Paul's burial. The priest, a friend of Mike's, who had said prayers over Paul . . .

Deborah felt her cheeks wet, dashed her hands over them, sprang up from her chair. "Well, you let it all back—and what was the use? You don't think Nell would listen if you tried to tell her! She'd say it couldn't happen to her and Tony. Maybe it couldn't. . . ."

She went into the parlor, switched on the lights, looked over the room to summon a satisfaction in the changes she had made in it that would bring back the contentment she was enjoying when Nell came in. New creamy-white ruffled curtains hung at the windows, half of the old furniture had been taken out. She had found a cobbler's bench in an antique shop and put it in front of the old sofa—she had served coffee from it this afternoon.

Tomorrow she would finish the curtains for the front bedroom which Rom would use.

But though she sent her thoughts resolutely this way and that, the burden of Nell's confidence still weighed on them—the feeling of responsibility, the urge to do something. Yet what? Warn Will? Never! He'd only drive the girl faster into a runaway marriage.

Perhaps she had not the right to try to do anything—it was part of life for young people to learn through their own experience. What another had learned over years of living was of no use to anyone but himself.

CHAPTER IX

John Wendell decided while he was shaving that the time had come to settle with Mrs. Donnell, once and for all, the matter of his having two eggs for breakfast. He had spoken of it, half-jokingly, but she had gone on giving him only one.

It was the morning after Deborah Brent's little party and he was feeling in high spirits. It had been a very pleasurable occasion—and there'd be others like it, he hoped. They were real folks, Mrs. Brent and Father Duffy. And Susan . . . In this mood he could smile as he planned his attack on his housekeeper.

She had told him when he came that she always had done the buying. He had been glad to let her do it; he knew nothing about it. "A woman knows more how to save," she had said. Well, if she looked upon two eggs at breakfast as extravagance she could cut out those puddings she put before him at every noon and evening meal. Evidently his predecessor had had a liking for them. He must get it across to her that he was a different person from that esteemed gentleman.

He whistled as he went down the stairs, into the kitchen. "Good morning, Mrs. Donnell."

She was opening the refrigerator door. "Good morning," she said without turning. John saw her take one egg from the box—a pullet's egg, at that.

"Two eggs, Mrs. Donnell, if you please." He put authority into his voice.

She went to the stove, put the egg in water. "There won't be enough to go the week."

"Get some more . . ."

Now she turned, leveled a coldly disapproving look on him. "I've got to save somewhere to pay the electric bills with you burning the lights to all hours."

"Those puddings you make—may I suggest that you cut them out? They take eggs, don't they?"

"They fill you up cheaper than meat, now that meat's so high."

Plainly he was not getting anywhere. Suddenly he found her implacability irritating, where before it had amused him. Fire her? He'd like to on the instant, but he couldn't, old as she was. He drank his fruit juice, to get the impulse out of his mind.

She put the boiled egg down in front of him, some toast and a cup of coffee, all without a word.

"I brought some doughnuts in yesterday—I'll eat them with my coffee."

She opened a cupboard, took out a paper bag, holding it between a thumb and forefinger, away from her. "I wondered how this got here. . . ." Disapproval of it was in her voice.

Was she thinking that perhaps it had come from Father Duffy's, like the roses?

"Susan Brent made them—we had them at a little party at her aunt's house, yesterday afternoon." Admiration for Susan's accomplishments led him into explaining the doughnuts. He added, "They are very good. Sit down and eat one."

Mrs. Donnell put the bag on the table in front of him, sat down across from him. But she did not move to eat a doughnut. She folded her hands. "It isn't my business to speak, maybe, Mr. Wendell, but you're young and you're new here and a word of warning might be only Christian."

"Warning?" John put down the cup he had lifted.

"Your running over to Deborah Brent's. Maybe you don't know, a stranger as you are, but she's never been what she ought to be. And Susan's too nice a girl to get *her* talked about!"

Red ran up to John Wendell's temples but he kept his rising anger out of his voice.

"In what way have I made Susan Brent a topic of gossip?"

"You had her here alone with you a whole afternoon—picked out an afternoon when I was out. I found your dishes and Mrs. Coggin saw her come out."

He still spoke quietly. "She was typing some notes for me! Surely there was nothing in that to cause talk."

"You are our minister—we expect seemly behavior from you." Mrs. Donnell added, "In other things too."

"Such as? Please go on."

"Well, your hobnobbing with that Roman priest over in the Flats. No one sees you going to the Reverend Neal's house. Riding around on your motorcycle—it isn't fitting for your position. Some of the things you say in your sermons—no one knows where you get them in the Scriptures! I see it only kindness to tell you what they're saying —before it's too late."

"Kindness." He repeated the word under his breath, at the same instant praying for control of his tongue. It was given to him. He said, quietly, "Thanks. But at the risk of criticism I shall remain friendly with Father Duffy—continue, too, to ride my motorcycle. As to my sermons—I am certain that, with an intelligent study of their Bibles, the members of the church will find a substantial backing for every word I say from the pulpit. . . ." He stopped. Mrs. Donnell was not listening. A satisfied smile was pulling in the corners of her mouth. She'd done her duty, it said.

He got up from the table, went out of the kitchen. He shut his study door, stood against it a moment.

Susan. That was why she had not come the second time, why she had been embarrassed before him, that day! She had heard some word of the talk. A part of his shock and anger was that it was his thoughtlessness that had exposed her to it. Fool, not to know that he should not have let her come here when he found that the housekeeper was going out. But the pure *rightness* of their being together, alone, that afternoon . . . He remembered the warm interest in her eyes when he told her something of what he hoped to do in his work. Of how much it meant to him. He thought of her as she sat, yesterday, not saying much, in Deborah Brent's parlor. She'd had on the yellow dress he liked. He remembered the flush that had touched her face when he told her that her doughnuts were out of this world.

And Deborah Brent wasn't what she ought to be!

He felt a strong need to get away from the house, from the sounds of Mrs. Donnell in the kitchen, to go to Deborah Brent—she wasn't like these other women.

He found her making a pie. "Lemon," she told him, motioning to him to sit down, "A little treat for Will. I remembered that he used to be very fond of lemon pie and Susan says he doesn't like the kind she makes."

She was enveloped in a huge butcher-type apron. A streak of flour lay across her cheek. John Wendell thought of his first meeting with her, the grease on her face to which she was so indifferent. Of the way he had felt, a little later, that he had known her all his life. What quality was this in her that gave one such a feeling?

She went on mixing, measuring, stirring—flour now on her arms which were bare to the elbow. He asked, "You like to cook?"

She laughed. "Yes—perhaps because it is the only accomplishment I can claim."

"I don't think that that is so."

"Well, it's the one that has supported me most of my life." She put her mixing spoon down on the table. "Have you ever heard of Excelsior Bean Soup? Probably not, here in the East."

"Can't say I have. What is it?" Though, at the moment, he was not much interested in knowing.

Deborah Brent hesitated and when she did speak, she had the

93

manner of bringing her words out from undercover.

"It used to be called 'Debbie's Special' by about a hundred lumberjacks around Twitchel in California. We lived on it for a month when we were snowed in and all that was left of provisions were beans and onions, salt pork, a few potatoes. I boiled them all up together—it'd go further that way—then added some of my herbs I'd grown and there it was. Its fame spread, for months jacks would come from camps fifty or so miles away for some of it."

Now he gave her his full attention and there was frank amazement in it. "You've lived in a lumber camp?"

"Seven years. Dale Curtis, my second husband, was boss of it." She went to a cupboard, took a can from a shelf. "Here it is—take it home."

He read the bright label on it. "Why isn't it still 'Debbie's Special'? 'Excelsior'—that doesn't mean anything!"

Deborah laughed. "It means a lot to me, my boy! A good security in my advancing years. I sold the recipe to a big soup-canning company in San Francisco—and drove a hard deal with them. A down payment that was not small, and a share of the profits from it. It is selling more now than at first, out in the West. Frozen Foods are after it, so you can see why I don't care what it is called."

John stared at her as if he were seeing her in a new light. A tougher fiber in her, living in lumber camps as she had, driving hard bargains. From a slight grimness in her voice as she spoke, he suspected that she had had to fight against odds, through these years. Valiant—the word slipped into his thought, stayed.

Then he remembered what Mrs. Donnell had said of Deborah Brent and anger swept over him again.

Deborah Brent pushed her mixing bowl aside. "What is it, John? If you feel like telling me . . ."

It was that about her, her quick understanding of one's feelings. She'd known his, all the while she was talking of her soup.

He did not speak for a moment, but it was because he did not

94

know how much to tell her. Then he said, "I've wanted to find some problem in my congregation to work on—up to date about all I've done is to lead the services, the group meetings, call around on the community. No one has died, no one has married, no one has been seriously ill. No one has sought *me* out, for spiritual help. And now I've found one and it appears to me so serious that I don't know how to deal with it. It's—gossip."

He saw amusement in Deborah Brent's eyes. "You didn't know—and you told me you grew up in that small New Hampshire town—that that is the popular pastime?"

His guards broke down. *"Pastime!* Then call any wickedness that!"

Deborah put her hand across the table toward him. "John, may I make a guess? That it has hit you personally—and I don't have to be too bright to suspect that it came through your Mrs. Donnell. And that it concerned me, Deborah Brent, legendary fast woman of Sweethome, who dared to come back here! Am I right?" She was smiling.

John flushed with embarrassment. It was far from his wish to tell her what Mrs. Donnell had said.

"She spoke of my coming here. Also of my friendship with Father Duffy. And a few other things I am not doing in a 'seemly' way. She saw it a kindness to tip me off!" He let his anger into his voice.

She put her hand out further, patted his where it lay in a fist on the table. "John, think it through. It *can* be evil, gossip, but not for the most part. These people here do not mean to hurt—talk of everything and everyone is a habit with them. They just don't *think.* . . ."

"You'd defend them?" demanded John.

"Well, where I'm concerned, it's partly my own fault. I've kept in touch through the years with Clare Hersey. She was my closest friend when I was a girl. But I never wrote the real facts of the way I was living. You may not know, at least not yet, that I ran away from here with a boy from the Flats. My family disowned me. I've married twice since then. I'm divorced, now. So, don't you see, some think of me as a bad character? And Clare knew nothing to spoil their idea of me. But, John, if I'd written in those letters of mine even half of the truth—only mostly it was what you don't put down in black and white—their attitude toward me might be very different. They might—" her eyes twinkled "—think it was pretty wonderful I'd come through it all. I believe they would. There's one thing I've learned, through these years—there's some goodness in every human being, believe it or not. I've found it in one and another, in the queerest ways, too. I guess it's been to me what your religious teaching was to you. It's been—God." She stopped, pushed her hair back with a floury hand. "Whew, that was a long speech for me! I'm exhausted. There's still some coffee in the pot, put it over the fire, John, and we'll have some."

He got up, switched on a burner, moved the coffee pot over it. On his way back to the table he put his hand on Deborah's head. "You're good for me, Mrs. Brent!"

"You might, when we're together, call me Aunt Debbie."

"Aunt Debbie. Thanks."

"The cups are in that cupboard over there. There are more doughnuts, too, in the breadbox. Can you explain, Reverend, why food always is a comfort?"

John remembered his breakfast. "Not always." But he did not explain his comment. He brought the cups and saucers.

They drank their coffee, ate the doughnuts. John thought of Susan, with a deep relief that her name had not come into their talk. When they finished, Deborah said, "Your job, my boy, is to think impersonally about this, isn't it?"

"Preach a sermon on it?"

"Well, you can give them something that'll start them thinking." She laughed. "*I* should be telling *you!* But, one thing, John, be yourself!"

"I'm afraid I am not likely to be anything but myself."

96

She rubbed a finger up and down over her cheek, in a moment's deep thought. Then she asked, "Isn't there a church supper coming along soon?"

He thought she was teasing him. "Next Wednesday. Chicken. Mrs. Coley Coggin is in charge. Tickets one dollar. The money to be used to meet the expenses of the Commemoration Service. Speaking of that—do you realize that your niece Nell has a voice out of the ordinary? I heard her sing at a rehearsal of that chorus Mrs. Peely's gotten together. Mrs. Peely says she never has studied—it's a pity she doesn't. She could do something with it."

"Is that so? I haven't heard her sing."

He got up from the table, the can of soup in his hand. "Perhaps Commemoration Sunday, two Sundays from next, would be good timing for that sermon you suggest. Could I hope that you'd be there?"

"I might."

Deborah Brent finished her pie. As she worked she dwelt on what John had said of Nell's voice. "If Nell got interested in taking singing lessons, she might be content to wait a year or so to marry her Tony. . . . It would give her something else to think about . . . she hasn't anything now. . . . I doubt she has had enough here in Sweethome of the good times a young girl should have. . . . And with Willie . . ."

She put the pie in the oven, shut the door, addressed the stove. "I'll pay for them. Willie wouldn't. . . ." She remembered what he had said at supper a few evenings ago. "We've fortunately been spared any influx of these crackpot artists and writers who have been buying up places roundabout." At the time she had thought he was merely giving her a dig at Rom's coming but now she thought that most likely he really was scornful of all the men and women who found a profession in any one of the arts.

Then her resolution came up against the question that had been in the back of her mind since last evening. Did she have any right to interfere in Nell's life?

"I'll ask Father Duffy!" He'd looked so wise, yesterday. He would listen to it all impersonally.

Directly she had finished her lunch she got out her car and headed for the Flats. She drove slowly after she crossed the bridge to observe the changes the years had brought: the rows and rows of cheap small houses, some trimly kept, others not; the stores, small, too, yet with a look of up-and-doing about them; gas stations. A bar-and-lunch place at a corner. A one-story frame school. She thought of it as she remembered it—narrow, meandering mud roads, the "shanties," separated by stretches of vegetable gardens, marked off with dilapidated fences. She could not locate now where the Bouvais farm had been— over toward the further line of hillside, she remembered, but lost now in the development of the community.

She had gone there once with Paul. Paul had wanted her to meet his mother. She tried now to bring that visit back with some vividness but it was confused. A hot sun on everything—chickens on the steps of the house—and small children, gaping. Paul had shooed them all away, disgustedly. Paul's mother—dark of skin, broad-breasted . . . Paul had said something in the patois most spoken on the Flats, and his mother had not answered. Deborah could remember vividly enough the cold rejection of her look.

"She didn't like me." Hadn't she said that to Paul as they walked away?

"That's because you're not of our faith." She did remember Paul saying that. And that he had kicked angrily at a stone in the road as he said it, and then yowled because it hurt his toe and then they both had laughed. Gone on along the road, holding hands, laughing . . .

But *"Mother'd know what to do."* It struck into her heart, with something of the old pain.

It was easy to locate the church by the cross above the low stuccoed structure. She thought as she stopped the car in front of the rectory gate that the simplicity of the place was like Father Duffy himself. Then she saw the flowers abloom in his garden. "He has a green thumb!"

He opened the door at her ring, his eye winking in his warm greeting. If he felt any surprise at seeing her here, the day after they had met for the first time, he did not betray it. "Come in, come in!"

He took her into his study—a room as bare of any comforts as a cell, yet with books on shelves to the ceiling, used-looking books. He waved her to one of the two caned chairs. "Sit down."

"I've come for—advice, Father."

He nodded. "I'll be glad to give it to you, if I can."

For just a moment Debbie hesitated. She wished she were in a confessional box—it would be easier, she imagined. "It's about my niece—she has told me that she is planning to run away, marry a boy who isn't much older, I think, than she is, and that is only a little more than eighteen. And I am wondering—have I, knowing it is in her mind, any right to interfere?"

He smiled, though it did not reach his eyes. "To what extent? 'Thou shalt not' seems to have no weight these days. Interference of the kind to which I think you refer, more often than not is a wasted effort. But what is wrong—why should not two young people who love each other marry, even at eighteen?"

Deborah felt some embarrassment but she went on frankly. "The boy lives on the Flats here. My brother, Nell's father, clings to the old tradition of a superiority to the people our side of the river—Nell knows the unpleasantness he would make over it. She never takes the boy to her home. It would mean—estrangement from her family, perhaps from his. And could it be happiness for them, if that were so?"

Father Duffy was fingering a small crucifix he wore. "Not if their sources of happiness depended upon material things . . ."

A sudden impatience fired Deborah Brent. After all, what could this man know of it? She drew forward in her chair, spoke a little tensely. "I didn't intend to tell you, take your time to listen—but years ago I ran away from my home in Sweethome with a boy from here—I was Nell's age—he was as young. My family took it as her father will. And we—we paid for it. In loneliness—in fear. We were too young to face it."

He let the crucifix fall back against his shabby cassock, looked up at her, his eyes very gentle.

"I know all about that. From Jean Bouvais."

Deborah Brent drew back in her chair. *"Paul's brother?* Did—did Paul ever write home to them?"

"Yes. Just once—I think just before he died. Jean found the letter among his mother's things after she died."

"And she never answered it!"

"No." The priest said it with a great sadness and he touched the little crucifix again.

"Oh, if she had . . ." cried Deborah Brent, then stopped. It was too long ago, too—past. It did not matter now.

"Yes, if she only had," repeated Father Duffy. Then he gave her a grave, considering look. "But tell me, Mrs. Brent, didn't that experience of yours, unhappy as it may have been, leave with you some strength, some knowledge that helped you?"

"It must have," answered Deborah, with some grimness.

"Well, then . . ." Father Duffy smiled. "Perhaps it is not right to deny experience to others—as long as it is not sinning against God. Does that help you any?"

"Yes. I asked myself that. But I needed someone else to answer it. Thanks." She got up from her chair.

"You say this boy is from the Flats—perhaps I know him. I might be able to reassure you about him."

"His name is DiVito. Tony DiVito. I suppose it's really Anthony."

"DiVito. Tony . . ." Deborah saw the expression on his face alter, a frown come between his heavy brows for just an instant. "I knew

100

him when he was younger." But he did not say any more to reassure her.

He pressed a cup of tea on her but she refused. She did let him pick some flowers for her, his first delphiniums, some Shasta daisies. They shook hands and she drove away.

But she was more troubled than she had been before. Father Duffy's frown had betrayed that he knew something about Tony that was not good. "Oh, Nell, Nell," she sighed.

And then aloud to the road ahead, "I'll write right away to some schools of music for catalogues. Boston, New York. It isn't interfering to be *ready* to do something!"

CHAPTER X

THE COMMITTEE on arrangements for the Commemoration Service had been meeting since early spring. Nothing in their preparations must be overlooked, for this service would be the most impressive, most solemn event in the annals of the parish. Dr. Slade, the State Superintendent, and ministers and deacons of other Congregational churches were to be invited. It would be, too, a sort of Old Home Week, for quite a few members who had moved away from Sweethome were coming back to attend it.

This week it met at Clare Hersey's instead of at the church. Almira Coggin had proposed that. "Poor Clare, her heart is in all that we are doing and she can't get out to help us! We can each take something for lunch and make the coffee there." The others instantly declared that it was a wonderful idea. "And *kind* of you, Almira, to think of it!"

"We can cut out the robes," said Mrs. Higgins. "The cloth will surely be here by then."

The women assembled at the Hersey house at eleven o'clock, with food, scissors, pins, thimbles, thread. They approved heartily the purple sateen Ham Higgins had got at wholesale for the robes of the members of the chorus. "It's sort of solemn!" cried Mrs. Peely, clasping her hands over it.

They fell to work at once, cutting off lengths, pinning them together, basting and stitching. Clare could baste and pin, if someone brought the cloth to her. But now and then she let it rest in her lap to feast her eyes on the crowded parlor. It had been years since so many women had been in her house at one time. Why, now, some had to sit in the dining room. She was so happy she wanted to cry.

The pattern for the robes was too simple to require concentration on the work of cutting them out and basting them together. Talk ran around the room freely. Of their children's grades in the spring examinations, of gardens, of recipes—who was coming to the Commemoration from outside, who was not coming. Of the Commemoration itself.

"Two hundred years," exclaimed Mrs. Higgins. "Our church has stood just where it is now for two hundred years! I don't believe there's another one that old in this part of the state."

"It isn't the same church," someone reminded her. "The first one burned, you know."

"Of course I know. Years and years ago. My grandfather used to tell us about it. It was struck by lightning. But it's the same corner-stone, the same foundation—and that's really the church, to my thinking."

Others approved this by nods of heads bent over the work.

Mrs. Coggin waved her scissors at them. "Why, I almost forgot to tell you—a reporter from the Hartford *Courant* called Coley about the Commemoration. He's going to write it up for his paper. He wants a story about the church, its history, its beginning. *I* think Coley should write it, because it was him the reporter phoned to but he says he can't—that he couldn't put two words together that'd make sense—you know the way he talks. *He* thinks Will Brent is the one to do it—his family was one of the first to settle here and I guess a Brent has been one of the deacons of the church ever since. Only, Coley says poor Will has an awful lot on his mind, just now. Things aren't going well at the works. . . ." She stopped with a manner of closing her lips on what was not going well at the Brent Nail Works.

"It'd be nice if there were some confessions of faith made before that Sunday, so as to have some new members to welcome," said Agnes Peely.

"Who's to make them? Everyone in Sweethome belongs to our church or the Methodist."

"And just among us, if there *was* anyone, I can't see this John Wendell influencing him to join—not with *his* sermons," said a voice from the dining room.

At the name almost every head came up. Mrs. Coggin abandoned her scissors. "What do you think is his latest idea? He spoke of it to Coley. He wants Stephen Neal and all the Methodists invited to attend the service. He said if it were the other way round, the Methodists would invite us and we'd all want to celebrate it with them. Coley agreed it'd be a nice neighborly gesture—you know Coley, he always agrees and then thinks a thing over, but he said it'd depend on what Will Brent and Lem Sims thought about it. Though Coley *did* speak up about another idea of John Wendell's— just the other day. A community house here in Sweethome with a gymnasium and a playground—a place where there could be dances, things like that! And it'd be for *everyone,* not just us. Coley said there wasn't the money here for anything like that. And *I* say, what's the need of such a place when *we* have our Sunday School rooms to get together in."

Martha Purdy spoke, her voice clear above the murmurs of agreement.

"I think it is a wonderful idea! It'd keep our young people, *all* the young people here, from eternally running to town to the movies or to hang around drugstores or goodness knows where."

She was one of the few in the room who had not been born and raised in Sweethome. Walt Purdy had met her and married her in Hartford and they had lived there until a few years ago when he opened an insurance agency in Winsted and they settled in the old Purdy house on Central Road. She had joined the church by letter, Walt having joined in his youth, and she had come into the Ladies'

Aid because she considered that was what the wife of a man who sold insurance should do. For the same reason, when she was with them, she never had lifted her voice in disagreement with anything any one of them said. Until this moment . . .

So they looked at her in surprise. Then Mrs. Coggin said, with some tartness, "Well, if the parents can't control that, I don't see how a gymnasium is going to do it!"

"Don't you?" said Martha Purdy, smiling a little and looking down at the hem she was basting.

Mrs. Higgins asked, "Has anyone any idea what his sermon is going to be on that Sunday? I really think one of the deacons should find out!"

"Well, if it's any of that healing talk I'm going to get up and walk out of the church!" said Julia White, bridling. "I'd like to have him have my arthritis for a while!"

"Maybe there *is* something in what he said—that we don't think right!" It was Martha Purdy again. She added, in the same level voice, "We don't think of God enough, maybe."

An affronted silence met this. To bring up God's name so casually at an occasion like this was sacrilege.

"That's a personal affair," said Mrs. Coggin.

In her chair in a corner, Clare was sensing undercurrents that threatened to spoil her enjoyment in the occasion. She asked Mrs. Peely, a little quickly, to change the talk, "How is the chorus going?"

"Oh, *beautifully!* Really the way everyone in it is just loving it! No one misses a rehearsal! Except—" her face clouded a little, "—Nell Brent. She's missed the last two—I had them at five o'clock so that the men could come and she said, both times, she was busy. And we *do* need her voice in that lovely oratorio."

"Well, we all know what Nell Brent's doing," said one of the women.

"Of course—running around with an Italian boy from the Flats. Guess everyone in Sweethome knows about it, except her father and

Susan, maybe, and I'm not so sure Susan doesn't know."

"I feel sorry for Will—it's enough for him to worry about his plant and that Swede, right across the river, and then to have Nell start something is just *too* much!"

"Funny, how often a strain like that shows up in a family," observed Mrs. Higgins, shaking her head over the fact.

"Like what?" asked Martha Purdy, a little bluntly. "You mean—Deborah Brent?"

"Yes, I mean Deborah Brent. You haven't been here long enough to know about her."

"Oh, I've heard all about her! Abby cleans for me once a week. But—that was awfully long ago. And it was rather romantic!"

"Romantic! Well, if you want to call it that. But it showed what she was like. Married three times and now comes back here divorced, at her age. Ask Clare about her!"

Hands still, they turned to Clare, expectantly.

Clare felt her breath shorten as she struggled between the temptation to feed out bits of information and a sudden quickening of loyalty toward Deborah Brent. "I've—told all I know. I guess Deborah's been the kind who just can't help getting married—and her husbands *have* died—except the last one. And she says he and she are very good friends. He saw her off when she came East."

"I saw her go into the store—she wanted to ask Ham the name of a painter she might get—and I thought she looked dowdy! Those husbands couldn't have left her with any money or else she went through all they had."

Julia White bit off an end of thread.

"Win and I called on her the other afternoon—we thought we should, at least once, for we were in school with her—and she was wearing an old suit I wouldn't be seen in!"

"I saw her pass the house, the other day," said Martha Purdy. "I thought she looked interesting—I liked the way she walked!"

106

The others ignored that. Almira Coggin said, "Will Brent's probably sorry she came back. She had John Wendell at her house the other afternoon, a sort of party, and that priest from the Flats was there. *And Susan*. How's Will going to like her getting Susan into her goings-on? John Wendell told Mrs. Donnell about it—he brought some doughnuts back with him that Susan had made. And then that afternoon she went to the parsonage . . ."

Martha Purdy dropped her work down on a table. "Anyone mind if I put the coffee over?"

She left the room but the prospect of coffee did not silence Mrs. Coggin. "I watched Susan Brent in church last Sunday and I didn't see her eyes lift *once* to the pulpit. And she had the funniest look on her face, as if she were ashamed of something!"

"Libby noticed that, too," said Julia White.

Clare had again the uneasy feeling that this occasion was not so pleasant as she had thought at first. Again she was moved to say something to get them to talk of something else, and the only thing she could think of to say was, "Deborah's going to drive me over to the church supper."

This had the effect she wanted.

One of the women cried, "You mean *she's* going to it *herself?*"

"She said she would."

There was instant and lively interest. They'd see Deborah Brent up close. . . .

There came soon from the kitchen the smell of coffee percolating. Work was put aside. Different women hurried out to unpack hampers of food, spread it out. There was some laughter, exclamations. "Good, you brought some of your grand potato salad!" "Look at that cake! And I'm trying to diet!"

One of the women helped Clare out of her chair. Clare was happy again.

They ate. They washed the dishes, put them away. They went

back to the parlor, gathered up their work, some volunteering to take the unfinished robes home and put the last stitches in them. "Then they'll be done!"

The women went away in groups of twos and threes, except Martha Purdy who waved her hand to them all and set off briskly by herself.

She knew they would begin at once to talk about her but . . . "I could have said more than I did! That I'm *sick* of their yappity-yap!"

Until now she had accepted it as the sort of sociability that prevailed when women who knew one another well got together. It was not unlike the "yappity-yap" that went on in the restroom of the big insurance office where she had worked before she married Walt. But today, suddenly, she had not been able to listen in silence while they pulled John Wendell to pieces.

Both she and Walt found John Wendell a stimulating change from old Doctor Marcy. They expected that others would think that, too. But apparently they did not—not behind his back! They had their knives out, too, for this Deborah Brent, who had come back.

Absurdly, because she never had met the woman, Martha Purdy wanted to champion this Deborah Brent, just as she was moved to stand up for John Wendell.

She knew Susan and Nell slightly, living so near, and Bill, the boy, came often to the house to play with her boys, but she had only a bowing acquaintance with Will Brent. Walt definitely disliked him, perhaps because he would not let Walt even begin to talk policies to him. "Big stiff" was Walt's opinion of him. "Thinks he's the Lord God Almighty!"

But Walt's feeling toward Will Brent need not stop her from being nice to Deborah. Martha had come to her own walk. She paused, looked across the road to the old Brent house. "I believe I'll go over and call on her tomorrow afternoon. I'd like to sort of make friends with her before the supper."

Mrs. Peely and Mrs. Coggin walked home together. They talked of Deborah Brent. Mrs. Coggin said, "You could have knocked me over when Clare told us she was coming to the supper next week! I would have said a church affair would be too dull doings for *her* liking."

"Perhaps we have her all wrong," suggested Mrs. Peely, mildly. She hesitated a moment. "I'm wondering—do you suppose Clare really knew as much about her as she claimed to, all this while? I don't mean Clare'd make up lies but sometimes I've suspected she lets herself *imagine* a lot, so as to have something she's telling us more exciting."

Mrs. Coggin had thought that of Clare quite often, but she was not going to admit it now, or that there was a possibility that Deborah Brent was a respectable woman. She said, crisply, "Well, we'll see!"

They had reached the Peely house. Agnes Peely said, a little breathlessly, as if it took courage to bring it out, "I can't help but think—if it were *me* in her place, coming back. . . . *I'm* going to be nice to her at the supper! Goodbye, Almira, I'll see you at our next committee meeting, if not before."

She turned then and hurried up the walk to her house.

CHAPTER XI

DEBORAH BRENT WAS as startled as the women of the committee by her decision to go to the church supper.

It had sprung from a stir of pity at Clare's shut-in-ness. "I wish I could get there," Clare had mourned. "But Fred simply will not go—he's too tired evenings, he says, to wash up and change!"

"I might go. I could drive you over."

"Oh, Deb, *will* you?" The ready tears had sprung to Clare's eyes.

Deborah had regretted her impulse almost at once but then had realized that it was, after all, what she should do whether she wanted to or not; for Susan's and Nell's sakes these women here must be given an opportunity to know her as a respectable woman.

It would in a way be a campaign, she reflected, over her coffee on the Monday morning of the week of the supper. "I have to sell myself. . . ."

She laughed at that. "If Roger could hear you, Debbie."

It was Roger Brent's campaigns, one after another, that had brought about their separation. He was a salesman, gifted in that specialty beyond most. He had begun in youth with vacuum cleaners, gone on into automobiles, then to electrical equipment, then into bigger deals. At fifty he had accumulated enough to retire from business, but had gone on selling—community causes, charity drives, candidates for political offices. . . . Very quickly he found himself with the reputation of the only man in San Francisco who could put a big thing over.

Deborah had known all this when she married him. She had known that he had his own way of going about it. "Groundwork," he called it. "Get the right ones together, a few at a time, and sell them the idea. Let the other fellows go on from there." He did this mostly through small dinners or cocktail parties—good food and good drinks usually softened the toughest shell. The right places to eat, too, were important—the high-ups would be insulted by anything that was not ultra-exclusive, and the lesser high-ups were flattered to be entertained where dinners were six dollars and more a plate.

They had met when she was beginning to negotiate to sell her soup recipe; he had taken the matter over with a lively interest, advised her what to demand, how to stand against less than that. But she had not known when he suggested that they marry that he would expect her to take an active part in these campaigns that were the breath of life to him. She had thought he found her a good companion.

Her coffee was cold. She emptied her cup, filled it, sat down again at the table, sent her thoughts back to those ceaseless dinner parties, cocktail parties, sometimes luncheons, that had been her life after their marriage. If they had been friends, gathering together . . . But they were not. Sometimes, seeing Roger's selected victim yield to his gifts of persuasion, she had thought it all a little dishonest.

"And the *clothes!*" She said it aloud, with a half-groan, a half-laugh. Always from Celeste's, the most expensive and exclusive dress shop in the city! Evening wraps, jewelry.

"You look very elegant, Mrs. Brent!"

She had played her part—for over three years, then, suddenly, could not go on with it. She had told Roger that she couldn't.

"One thing about Roger—you never had to talk all around a thing to him!"

He had looked stricken. "I can't drop out of things—I've too many irons in the fire."

"You mustn't think of that for a moment. I'll go to Reno—keep it as quiet as possible. Everyone will say—if anyone says anything—

that it was just a mistake you made. That we both made. Maybe it was—you should have met a younger woman at that Rotary party."

"I don't like young women—they bore me. The only thing they think about is themselves. You're sure about this, Debbie?"

"Yes, I'm sure. I'd let you down some time terribly—and I don't like to do that to anyone."

"No, you wouldn't."

Could these women here, could Willie, ever bring themselves to believe that, at her age, she had walked out on a life which must look to anyone as the softest of cushions? That she had refused to take with her those clothes of Celeste's that filled clothespresses in their apartment? She had begged Roger to sell them or give them away.

She had gone to Reno, lived there the required number of weeks, then gone back to San Francisco, rented a small furnished apartment in an unfashionable section of the city, remote from Russian Hill. A week after she settled in it Roger had come in. After that he dropped in often, afternoons, and they talked of whatever iron it was he had in the fire at the time. She had liked his visits—she was really very fond of him—and then to have him go, and go herself to eat her dinner in some near-by inconspicuous restaurant.

She gathered up her breakfast dishes, smiling, carried them to the sink. "I must write to Roger that I have a campaign of my own now! That it opens with a church supper!" He knew nothing more of Sweethome than that it was a New England village where she had been born; his opinion of it was that it should have changed its name a long time ago. If she wrote about her situation here he would laugh at her, write back, *"You,* worrying your head over what anyone thinks of you! I don't believe it!"

It was difficult for Deborah to believe it!

She held a plate up in her hand, spoke to it. "I suppose I should get a new dress for the supper. I can't appear in that tattered old suit. They'd think I'd come back, impoverished, to live on Willie."

"Go buy some new duds for that evening, Debbie." Roger always

had said that, when he was about to plunge some very important iron into the fire.

Later in the day, she asked Susan to go with her to Hartford the next day.

"I loathe picking out clothes—I'm likely to buy the first thing I see and you can keep me from making a dreadful mistake. We'll start early, have lunch there and get home in time for supper."

"I'd love to go," Susan said.

She did not ask Nell. She had seen Nell only once since that evening she had burst in on her, and then the girl had avoided looking at her or speaking directly to her. "She's sorry she confided in me what she did! She doesn't trust me," Deborah had told herself.

Susan took her part in the shopping expedition seriously. She shook her head at the first dress the salesclerk brought out, after examining the fabric and the price tag. "I'm sure you'll find something you like better, Aunt Debbie."

She whispered it, but the salesclerk heard it. "We've some that have just come in I'll show you." She disappeared, returned with a print with every primary, secondary and tertiary color in its pattern. She held it up. "Older women are wearing these bright things—it gives them a dash."

Deborah laughed. "A dash is just what I must not have!"

The clerk drew herself up haughtily. "I'm sorry—I've a navy I could show you but it is one of our expensive models." She let her eyes go coldly over Deborah's tweed suit.

"Bring it out, please."

Oh, shades of Celeste!

It was of fine sheer material, its dash in its plainness and its price. "Eminently suitable," said Deborah of it, a twinkle still in her eyes. She tried it on, bought it. "I suppose I ought to get a hat!"

Now the salesclerk was gracious. "Millinery's on this floor, madam. I'll go over with you and introduce you to the buyer. I'll take the dress with me. You'll want to see it with the hat. And shoes, madam?

Blue gabardine, perhaps? Shoes are on this floor, too."

With the salesclerk and the buyer hovering over her, Deborah bought a small blue hat with two sober wings its only adornment and blue pumps of gabardine with moderate heels.

Susan had approved her selections, each in turn, but with a troubled look growing on her face. "Perhaps I'm not going to appear the respectable woman I think I will," thought Deborah.

"There that's done. Now let's find a place to eat."

But on the main floor she stopped at the jewelry counter. "I'm going to buy something for you, Susan, and for Nell."

"Oh, *no*, Aunt Debbie!"

"Earrings? I never wear them—can't draw attention to my ears— but I like to see them on young people. Look at this pair, Susan." They were leaf-shaped, of pearls. "They will look lovely against your skin. And a necklace to match?" She was addressing a clerk, now.

Susan's face flushed. "Really, Aunt Debbie, you mustn't! They're lovely—I do like earrings but—Father wouldn't like it."

"Your father has nothing to do with this," said Deborah.

The clerk was taking a necklace out of the showcase.

"Try them on, Susan," ordered Deborah, pulling a standing mirror toward Susan.

Susan fastened the earrings to her ears, the choker around her neck.

"You must look your best at the church supper, Susan!"

Now the flush was deeper on Susan's cheeks. She unfastened the necklace, her fingers fumbling over it.

"I'll take these," said Deborah to the clerk. "And please show me something in green." To Susan, "Don't you think green would look well on Nell, with her hair and eyes?"

"I guess so." Susan's voice had a helpless note.

She was quiet through lunch and on the ride home. The packages lay on the seat between them and Deborah Brent saw her eyes go to them every now and then. Then suddenly she burst out, "Aunt Debbie, I *wish* you hadn't spent all that money on Nell and me!"

"Is that your New England conscience? Twenty-four dollars for that sort of thing. Or—" she stopped speaking while she passed a truck—"are you worrying that I can't afford to spend twenty-four dollars when I want to?"

"I—guess so. It does seem a lot of money for costume jewelry. And—" Susan paused a moment, embarrassed, then finished, "we don't really know much about you, Aunt Debbie! Father's never told us much."

"No, I suppose he hasn't." Deborah realized she had allowed a regret in her voice that would have no meaning to Susan. And she ought to be feeling only glad that Willie had not prejudiced his girls against her. "Your father didn't know much to say—I've been away so long and neither of us were strong on writing letters. But I'll tell you, to relieve your mind, that I *can* afford to buy those things for you and Nell. There, are you happier about it?"

"Oh, yes! I do love my pearls! I've never had any really good costume jewelry."

Now it was Deborah who was quiet. She thought, "Is it that Will won't give the girls the money to spend—*or can't?*"

They reached Sweethome about five o'clock. "Have supper with us, Aunt Debbie. Then you can give Nell her present!"

"If you'll let me help you get it, I'd like to."

"Oh, I'll let you help—I like your company, Aunt Debbie."

Deborah put up the car, took her packages into the house, came back through the yards. Susan had changed into a cotton dress and was in the kitchen, filling the tea kettle with fresh water.

Her face was radiant.

"John Wendell called this afternoon, Aunt Debbie. I found his card under the door. He wrote on it he was sorry I was not home."

"I found a slip of paper under my door. Mrs. Purdy's name. And some flowers. We picked out the wrong day to shop, I'm afraid."

"Maybe John Wendell wanted something special. . . ."

"I've no doubt he did," put in Deborah, smiling.

"I mean, some more typing."

"Well, typing, too, perhaps." Deborah saw Susan struggling to hide her confusion, went to her, put her hands on her shoulders. "Susan, my girl, if you like this young man—if you love him—*don't* be afraid of it! Let yourself go!" She could say that to Susan. . . .

Susan drew away from her, turned to the stove. "It's—oh, they *talk* so much here, about everything you do."

"And you *care?* When it is something that is so *right?* That is wholly your own affair?"

"Father does. He's drilled it into us from the time we were little that we must never do anything that would *start* talk. He's—very particular about it. And they *do* look up to him, in the village!"

"I am sure they do," said Deborah, dryly. "Salad tonight? Let me make the dressing." She went to the refrigerator, got out the ingredients. "I've a notion to start an herb garden!" Safer to talk of herbs than of Willie.

Susan apparently was glad to talk of something else. She said quickly, "What kind of herbs? I buy some, sometimes."

"Oh, marjoram, basil, bergamot—a lot of others. I had a good place to grow them, once, the right soil, enough shade for some, enough sun for others." No need to tell Susan that her herbs had contributed to her being able to buy expensive geegaws now. "I like to see things grow. Anything—flowers, vegetables, young people. By the way where are Nell and Bill?"

"Bill's probably playing ball—Nell may be at a rehearsal." Deborah heard the small troubled note in Susan's voice that came now when she spoke of Nell. She longed to tell her that she knew what she was worrying over, perhaps, by some word, lighten a little the responsibility Susan shouldered, but she could not—she had given Nell that promise.

"John Wendell says Nell has a very good voice."

"Did he? I've always thought so—it's so true. She sang in the Glee Club at school. A solo, one time. She wanted to take voice lessons, after she graduated from high but Father thought she should study something more—well, practical."

"And she hasn't done anything," said Deborah, giving the bottle in which she was mixing the salad dressing an unnecessarily vigorous shake.

Susan's preparations for supper went ahead, but every now and then she paused in them to look out of a window. "I *wish* they'd come," she said, finally. "It makes Father so cross when they're late. And this last week he's looked so tired when he comes home!"

"Has it occurred to you, Susan, that he may be worrying about business rather than the children?"

Susan gave her a startled look. "He's never worried about business, Aunt Debbie! Why do you think of that?"

"Well, these are rather tough times—competition, cost of materials, labor—all that."

Susan's eyes were on her, still startled. "He's never . . . Is that why you said what you did about the machines being old?"

Now Deborah regretted turning the talk to Willie's business affairs which she had done to take Susan's mind off Nell. Yet she was impelled to say more by a sudden anger at Willie for his blind satisfaction in himself.

She answered, a little crisply. "Yes. I would have thought he would have put in new machinery years ago—or expanded in some way. . . ."

His step outside the door brought their talk to an abrupt end.

"Good evening, Deborah. Good evening, Susan." He put his hand on Susan's shoulder as he spoke to her. Susan turned, impulsively, and kissed his cheek.

"Supper ready? I'll go and wash."

There was weariness in his voice, a little sag to his shoulders. Deborah prayed that Nell and Bill would come.

Nell did come in before her father came downstairs. "Sorry . . ." She tossed that to Susan, for not helping with supper, and made little

117

more than a sound of the word. "Hello, Aunt Debbie." That over her shoulder as she turned and went out of the kitchen.

"Where's Bill?" asked Will Brent, frowning, as they sat down at the table.

"He'll be here any minute, Father," said Susan.

"We will say grace."

He repeated the words. They began to eat.

"I don't like this—Bill knows at what time we have supper. It'll do that young man good to start working at the plant. Next week—his school's over then, isn't it, Susan?"

"Yes. At least there's just Commencement, next week. Aunt Debbie, may I bring down your presents—show Nell hers?"

Deborah smiled her agreement. Nell lifted her head. "Presents?" Susan came back to the table with the small boxes.

"Couldn't this wait?" asked Will Brent. But Nell was giving a little squeal of delight and his question went unnoticed. "Who from? Why?"

"Aunt Debbie. We went to Hartford today, shopping, and she insisted on getting these for you and me. See mine?" Susan held out the boxes, open. "Look, Father!"

It was nervousness, not pleasure in her pearls, that gave Susan's voice its unaccustomed loudness, Deborah knew.

"I see them," said Will Brent. "I suggest that you eat your dinner."

Susan put the covers back on her boxes, but Nell fastened her choker around her throat. Deborah saw the defiant look she flashed at her father as she did so.

"Thanks, heaps," she said across the table but without looking directly at Deborah.

Will Brent's silence, as he went on with dinner, was reminiscent to Deborah of nights when his mother had sat at table in the chair in which Will sat now, not saying a word, but exuding disapproval like a fume over them. She'd speak of it later but she always had taken time to let it gather to storm force. "And the storm usually broke on

118

my head!" Well, let Willie's now. . . .

Nell was asking Susan if she had seen anything luscious in the store windows, where they had eaten lunch . . . But there was no envy in her voice to make Deborah sorry she had not taken the younger girl along. On the contrary she spoke as if she really were far above this interest she was showing. "She's just left her Tony," thought Deborah.

Bill came. "Gee, I didn't know it was so late."

"Your supper's on a plate in the oven, Bill," said Susan, quickly.

"It's your business to know what time it is," said Will Brent when the boy came back with his plate. "If I hadn't learned that a long time ago . . ."

Bill did not let him finish. "Well, if you'd give me a wrist watch, like I asked . . ."

"I didn't own a watch until I was twenty-one."

"And I suppose you got it then because you hadn't smoked," said Nell, in a level voice.

Susan got up from the table a little hastily. "Nell, will you bring out the plates? I'll fix the dessert—it's a jelly mold."

Bill was wolfing his food. Suddenly he stopped. "I forgot—I've a letter for you, Aunt Debbie. Mr. Higgins saw you drive past without stopping for the mail and gave it to me." He produced it from his pocket, slightly crumpled.

Deborah took it, glanced at it, said delightedly, "At last!" To Will, "It's from Rom Barcek. You may remember I spoke of him that first evening I was here. Now I'll know when he is coming!"

She looked down again at the letter but not so quickly that she did not see Will's face whiten about the lips—just as his mother's used to.

"Why—he wrote this from New York City! He'll be here day after tomorrow!"

Susan and Nell came in with the dessert. "Who'll be here?" asked Nell.

Deborah folded the letter, smiling. "A very good friend of mine,

Rom Barcek. He's very interesting—he writes books."

Nell's interest, now, was genuine. "I've never met a real author."

"You knew Mrs. Hurrell," reminded Bill.

Red rushed up Nell's cheeks. "She was *old*," she retorted.

"His name's funny," said Bill. "Rom. I never heard *that* one before."

"He's Polish. It's not an unusual name with them. Rather nice sounding, I think."

"And Barcek," Bill turned that on his tongue, then put a big spoonful of jelly in his mouth.

Susan was saying nothing. Deborah noticed how she kept her eyes on her plate. Was it her awareness of her father's disapproval—or was she thinking what her father was thinking? "Oh, child, don't be *that* much inhibited!"

She got up from the table. The tension was becoming intolerable. "May I eat and run, Susan? And Will, I wish you'd walk over to the other house—there's an upright on the back porch which perhaps should be bolstered some before the painter gets to it. If you'd look at it . . ."

She was inviting the storm, she knew. But—"Let Willie get it out of his system."

He went with her, examined the support she indicated. "That should be good for several years," he pronounced.

"If you think so," agreed Deborah and sat down on the step.

Will Brent drew out a handkerchief, wiped his forehead. "Deborah, I'll take this opportunity to say what's on my mind . . ."

"Please do, Willie."

He drew himself up straighter. "I don't want you to be filling the girls' heads with extravagant ideas. I don't know whether you can afford it or not, but—I cannot. Another thing . . ." He stopped.

"Rom?" prompted Deborah.

"Yes. It isn't any of my affair how many men you keep trailing after you—as long as you are a long way from Sweethome. But to bring your practices here, flaunt them in the faces of the respectable people here, is too flagrant."

Deborah got to her feet, faced him. He was taller than she. "Sit down," she said, and pushed him so forcibly that he had no choice but to drop down into the chair that was behind him. "Now listen to me!" She went on, her voice low, with more scorn in it than anger. "What do you know of my practices? Nothing! You've held all these years to what your mother impressed upon you—that I was bad. That I'd always be bad. I can hear her saying it! And can't it occur to you that she might have been wrong? But we'll skip all that. It's only important if you are that stupid about everything else! As to Rom Barcek—he's only twenty-eight years old, only a little older than my boy would be, if he had lived. He has no one—his father, mother, sister were murdered by the Nazis—he was here studying at Columbia. He went back after the war and they were all gone. . . . If anything I do to help a boy so alone, any kindness I show him, is *flagrant* to these people here in Sweethome—well, they're not worth thinking twice about."

She dropped down again on the step, exhausted, shaken.

Will Brent got up from the chair. He did not speak for a moment, then he said stiffly, yet not with his usual decisiveness, "If there was someone else living here with you . . ."

Deborah laughed. "A chaperone? Perhaps Nell—you couldn't spare Susan!"

He ignored the implication in that. He went down the steps. "I am only trying to tell you that there will be talk. It's on your head, but I intend to keep my girls out of it."

"Of course," said Deborah.

He stalked off across the yards without another word.

"Poor Willie," murmured Deborah, watching him go.

She sat on, then, where she was. "If Willie knew I picked Rom up in a restaurant!" A small eating place in a basement under some stores, and usually crowded because the food was exceptionally good.

"Will you mind sharing a table?" the waitress had asked her, with Rom right behind her, a shabby-looking, too-thin young man. He had ordered only a bowl of soup—ten cents. Her plate was heaped with hearty food. She had seen his eyes drawn to it more than once. He was hungry—she knew the look. They had talked. "Though I did most of it, I remember."

She had suspected that he hungered for more than food. The next time she saw him at the little eating place, at a table with his bowl of soup, she had gone directly to him. "May I join you?" He had nodded an assent but with some warmth coming into his dark eyes. She had invited him to go back to her apartment with her. "It's just around the corner. I live alone and it'd be nice to have someone to talk to for a little while."

It was a chill, foggy night, that night, and some heat had been turned on in the apartment house. She had seen Rom thaw under it, under the home-like atmosphere she had achieved with little things here and there in the rooms. She had brought out cheese and crackers and milk. He had talked, a little, of himself, of his book which had just been published—*Dark at Noonday*. The reviews had been very good but it was not selling too well, he had admitted. He was writing another. . . .

But who could write, do *any* job, on soup? Even her soup . . . So she had contrived excuses to feed him something, evenings when he came in. And always in her mind was the thought that her boy— Waite, she and Dale had named him——might have been, through circumstances, up against just this need for food and affection and understanding.

That was two years ago. And in that time she had come to feel very fond of Rom and he to trust that affection.

"I want to put you into a book, Aunt Deborah."

At one time and another she had told him sketchily of her life—a little about Paul, of those years she had worked as a servant in the Mulford family, of her experiences in Twitchel, afterwards . . .

"A story of a woman's integrity."

That had pleased her but she had laughed. "Guts is the American word!"

She could not by any stretch of her imagination or of vanity see herself material for a heroine of a story, but to encourage him she had expressed enthusiasm over the idea and out of that had grown her suggestion that they both come to Sweethome where he could get an understanding of the community in which she had grown up, and she could relive that unhappy time.

She got up from the step. "And now you'll have to tell Rom that you've been too busy with the present to think of the past!"

CHAPTER XII

DEBORAH, DOWN in the kitchen, could hear Rom's step as he moved about in the room upstairs. Unpacking, perhaps—though he had brought only a small bag with him.

She had sensed almost at once after meeting him at the station that he was very low in his mind over something—she had seen a new hard look on his mouth, in his eyes. He had appeared glad to see her, for his greeting had been warm, but then he had fallen quiet, too quiet. To cover it she had talked, explained the Flats and, after they crossed the bridge, a little of Sweethome. She had thought he must see the village as a unique community but he had shown no sign of interest. She had not been certain he was listening.

He might have had some discouraging interview with his publishers when he was in New York. Or some bad news from Poland. Whatever it was she must wait until he spoke of it. "And feed him!"

So she was cooking chicken in a special way she knew. The dough for rolls which she had set to rise in the morning was in the oven, baking. Potatoes and peas were over the fire. She hoped the savory smell of it all would reach him upstairs and sharpen his appetite.

When the supper was ready she called to him to come down. "We'll eat in the kitchen—it's a custom that rather goes with old houses."

He looked over the kitchen. "A pleasant room," he observed, but with no feeling in his voice. He drew a chair out for her and as she sat down, he said behind her back, "But I should not have come."

Deborah was startled. "Rom, why not? You can work here just as well as anywhere else—better, I believe. We agreed that you would find a change of surroundings stimulating, didn't we? If it's a matter of pride, my boy, you'll find any number of ways to pay for what we call here your 'keep.' I'm always needing a man to do something around the house."

"It isn't pride," he said harshly. He sat down, stared down at his plate, which Deborah had heaped with food. Then he looked up at her, his eyes pleading, "Will you forgive me, Aunt Debbie—if I don't talk about it?"

"Of course. Just eat your dinner."

He began to eat, but as if he did not know what he was doing. She had little appetite herself; she was still startled, troubled. Her good dinner was wasted.

When he moved to help her with the dishes she waved him away. "Go outside—these June evenings are something special in this little corner of the world. There're cigarettes over there on the shelf, if you haven't any on you."

"I must leave him to himself," she said as she ran water into the dishpan.

She had seen him in a low mood often, but until now she had been able to guess the reason for it pretty accurately from some word he dropped. Usually it was because his writing was not going ahead as fast as he wanted it to. Her answer to that always was that he was trying to do two jobs, for daytimes he worked in one of the telephone exchanges. Or he would be brooding over the meager royalty returns of the book he had written.

"I suppose to the people over here it is just another war story," he had said once, with bitterness.

He had talked often about his father. Evidently they had been very close, yet it was his father who had insisted that he must finish his education in America. He talked of his father's school. "It was his world. He was dedicated to his teaching. . . ."

One time he had cried out, "He was the gentlest of men! Incapable of being an enemy to anyone, anything! He believed too much in man's ability to think for himself, to speak what he thought. He taught his pupils English, French, Italian, Russian, because he believed one had a better understanding of these people if one knew the language each spoke. He taught me. . . . He's gone—*but his school can be rebuilt for others to go on with his work.*"

She had been very certain, then, that he was half-starving himself, going about in his threadbare clothes, shunning the cheapest of the pleasures a young person normally would seek, to send every dollar he could scrape together back to his home town to rebuild his father's school. She had thought, more than once, that he was too young to give himself so wholly to this single purpose. It was not good for him.

In his present depression she sensed a fresh, terrible hurt. It had been naked in the appealing look he had given her at the table.

She hung up her dish towel. Through the window next to the drying bars she could see him sitting in one of the two folding chairs she had bought in Winsted and placed under the cherry tree. She had told herself that she must leave him alone, but he presented such a desolate figure, hunched forward, elbows on his knees, staring down at the burning cigarette in his fingers that she was impelled to join him.

As she crossed the porch Nell came through the arch of the trellis.

"Hi," she sang out with a lift of her hand.

Rom's head jerked up. He got to his feet but the hard set to his face did not alter. Deborah said, "Hello, Nell. I'd like to have you meet Rom Barcek. My niece, Rom."

He gave a slight bow in acknowledgement of the introduction, but he did not speak. Nell's eyes flicked coolly over him, then she turned to Deborah. "I had to come over to tell you, Aunt Debbie—I'm going to sing a solo at the Commemoration Service! Part of the oratorio.

Mrs. Peely asked me this afternoon if I would. She as much as said it was John Wendell's idea and I suppose *his* idea is that it'll get me going to church again!" A light laugh disposed of that possibility. "But it's going to be a lot more fun than singing with those older people—some of them are off key most of the time. I'm on my way to rehearse it now. 'Bye." She included Rom in the word, with the briefest of glances, and that airily scornful; then with a light step and a swing of skirts went on out to the road.

Deborah saw a dark blaze in Rom's eyes as they followed her. Then he dropped his cigarette to the ground, dug it to shreds under his heel.

"Rom, she's *young!*" She was annoyed at Nell for coming over—she knew it was curiosity over Rom that had brought her, rather than any need to share her distinction in singing solo, but at the same time she was moved to defend the girl. "She's only eighteen and sometimes she seems younger than that. . . ."

"I hate them all," said Rom with a violence that startled her. Even in his bitterest moods, she never had heard it in his voice. Then he pushed one hand through his hair, looked about him, as a man might look who has lost his bearings. He took a step or two away from her, turned and came back. "I told you I should not have come—but I'm here. God knows you are the only one I can call friend but it isn't very considerate to inflict myself on you just now."

Deborah said, in the brisk voice and manner she often had used on the jacks in the lumber camp—more often on Dale, those years when he was sunk in discouragement, "That's what friends are for, boy. Now I've quite a few things to do. Why don't you take a walk? You were cramped up on that slow train for a long time. You can't get lost—there's the steeple of the church to show you the way back. I'll leave the back door unlocked. You can have breakfast any time you feel like it—even midafternoon. Now be off with you!"

"Thanks," he muttered and turned and strode off toward the road.

Deborah watched him, until he disappeared from sight. "It's a girl that has him upset," she said aloud. But the conviction left her a little puzzled. By his own word she knew he had no young women friends in this country—he had said he had neither the time nor money nor desire to seek them out.

"These young people—everything is so terribly *permanent* to them! They don't know what time can do!"

She knew. . . . She dropped down in one of the chairs, a little wearily. Heartbreaks, hardships, privations—time pushed them back by rushing new experiences in their places, dimmed them into a balanced pattern. Happiness, too. You had a few hours or days or months of a special kind of happiness which you told yourself you would hold to forever—but, no, time dimmed that into the pattern. When you thought of it, the specialness of it was gone.

The happiness, the sadness of those years with Dale. First, his high hopes of his venture in lumbering. He had bought up a vast tract of redwood timberland. People were just waking up to the superiority of redwood over the Douglas fir, that they were disease resistant, had less shrinkage in weathering and processing. . . . He had talked constantly about it. He was staking everything he had in it, of himself as well as money. "We'll either be millionaires, Debbie, or flat broke. Will you take a gamble on it with me?" That had been his way of proposing marriage. She was in Portland, then, working in the Welcome Center. She was lonely. She had needed to meet someone like Dale, big-built, hearty of spirit, daring.

Oh, it was good to think of him as he was then!

She had loved the life in Twitchel—the hum of saws by day, the men's voices, and at night the vast stillness. A roughness in their living, and a camaraderie. Remoteness, too. A world far removed from Etna, St. Louis, Portland—from Sweethome. From those struggles to exist . . .

She and Dale spent hours of evenings over plans for the house they would build. They chose a site for it, a mile or so from the camp. "The place has got to be big enough for a pack of kids," Dale had said.

128

Their boy was born. "You'll own all the timber in this part of the state, sonny, some day!" was Dale's promise to him.

When did his high hopes begin to fail him? She never had known —perhaps it had been before he let her know. He grew quiet, untalkative. She thought it was losing the baby. Then he became irritable when he did speak, given to dark moods, darker than Rom's tonight. A different man—and yet she loved him no less.

"I'm not going to make good," he burst out on her one evening. "Do you want to quit me?"

"Do you want me to say yes?"

"No!"

"Well, I'm not going to. We'll get through this!"

They hadn't—Dale lost everything he had put into the venture. They had gone to San Francisco, where she had taken a job as cook in the Blue Bonnet Tearoom. For weeks Dale had looked for work but his confidence in himself was gone, his grip on himself. He had begun to drink. . . .

As with Paul she had had to see the man she loved dying before her eyes, slowly, slowly, over the months. But she was older—she was not afraid. She had learned in Twitchel not to be afraid. She had her soup recipe, too. The Blue Bonnet featured it Thursdays; each Thursday more patrons came. She was made assistant manager of the tearoom, with a larger salary. Though she saw to it that no one but herself prepared the soup.

Yes, time had blurred the sadness of those months.

On this same evening John Wendell was pacing the length of his study, trying to summon ideas for his Commemoration Day sermon. It must, of course, express a rededication of the church to God's service, a rededication of the spirit of those who worshiped in the church. But he wanted to say something which would awaken in these people's hearts a sense of oneness, one with the other, out of which would spring a truer neighborliness. He turned phrases from

129

the Bible in his mind. "Love thy neighbor . . ." "Do unto others
. . ." "Judge not . . ." and though no better ones could be found,
he discarded them. They, these steady churchgoing men and women,
would say they did all of that—they really believed they did. He
tried to phrase something of his own—to reject it as quickly.

He was still terribly disturbed by what Mrs. Donnell had revealed
of the gossip in the community, mainly because, through his own
stupidity, it involved Susan—*Susan*.

That first Sunday he had preached here—his glance had happened
to rest on her for a moment and the rapt look on her face had given
him some reassurance that he might be saying something worth
listening to. Every Sunday after that, irresistibly, his eyes had sought
her out, and the attentiveness of her listening had heartened him as
much as though she had stood on her feet and said, "You're good!"
He had not seen her often outside church—not nearly as often as some
of the other younger women, and, when he had, she had appeared a
little distant. Until the day she had come here to help him . . .

He realized that she had been in his thoughts almost constantly
since that day. In his heart? He dared not ask himself that. He was
in no position to fall in love—he had to make good in his job here,
first.

Last Sunday he had noticed a difference in her manner; she had
sat through the service with her eyes lowered to her hands clasped
on her hymnal, a curious constraint in her face.

Now he saw Mrs. Donnell a purveyor to the other women in the
village of everything in his private life. *"He went to Deborah Brent's
the other afternoon." "Susan Brent made doughnuts for him." "He
wants two eggs for breakfast."* He hated this, and the certainty that
these tongues, so ready to wag, would misconstrue even the simplest
of friendships between him and Susan. She knew this, where he had
not, until the knowledge was forced on him.

He had found himself pausing before his telephone, moved to call
Susan on some pretext. But, no, Mrs. Donnell was within hearing.

The other afternoon, passing the Brent house, he had stopped, re-membering that Susan still had the last of the cards she had been typing and at the same time thinking that Mrs. Donnell was not anywhere near. Then, instantly, that others might see him at the door.

"A pastime," Deborah Brent had said of the gossip. If he could see it with her tolerance! *"They just don't think!"*

He brought his step to a halt. "The sin of unthinking . . ."

He sat down at the desk, drew a pad to him, began to write on it. The words ran crazily uphill on the pad but he wrote on.

He was aware of the sound of singing coming through the open window but for a while it was only an accompaniment to his swiftly moving thoughts. Then, suddenly, he put down his pencil, listened. Nell Brent, at the house across the road.

Evidently Mrs. Peely had gone through with his suggestion that the girl sing alone in that particular part of the oratorio. He had offered it when Mrs. Peely had told him that Nell had not come to the last few rehearsals. "And we do need her voice!" Mrs. Peely had said sadly.

He appreciated how hard Mrs. Peely was working over her part of the Commemoration Service, but he had dropped in on the rehearsals often enough, and knew enough about music, to realize that Nell Brent, with her true ear, well might find the uncertain pitching of the other voices a little trying. "If she sang that soprano part solo— one voice would be more effective anyway." Then he had spoken of a hymn he thought would be very fitting in the service. "Spirit divine, attend our prayers, and make this house Thy home."

"You mean—Nell Brent sing *that* alone, too?"

"Yes."

Mrs. Peely had looked a little troubled, he remembered. But then she had nodded her head. "It'd be lovely! And it might get her to going to church again."

He had not thought of that possibility and he doubted it now. To be "starred," as it were, in Mrs. Peely's program of music probably

131

appealed to the girl's sense of importance, but it was not likely to stir in her any desire to go to church. He had thought more than once, since that day at Father Duffy's, of his one "stray lamb," but each time he had come up against the fact that he did not know how to bring this particular lamb back into the fold. He had sensed some defiance in the girl, the brief time he had been with her at Mrs. Peely's, that afternoon. She saw him a representative of authority, perhaps, and she might be going through a phase of rebellion against authority in any shape, from God down. He remembered that one of his impressions of her father was that he was a man who would hold to a stand he had taken through hell and high water; it was easy to imagine frequent differences between him and this girl. But as long as she was rebellious, any words he might speak would fall on deaf ears. "There must be a deep need, first. . . ."

Nell was singing the hymn now, dragging it a little, perhaps because of unfamiliarity with it. Mrs. Peely was dragging the accompaniment, too. After a moment he sprang to his feet. "That won't do!" He hurried out through the door to go over to the other house.

He saw a girl standing in the deep shadow of the big maple in front of the Peely house but, such was his rush, he did not recognize her as Susan Brent until he was fairly upon her.

"Susan!" His deep pleasure in the unexpected encounter shook his voice.

She wheeled around. "Oh!" She brought it out on a quick-drawn breath. She caught her hands together. "I—I heard Nell practicing— I was walking past—I'd gone to Higgins' and I came around this way—I stopped just a minute to listen. . . ." She moved to go on. "But I must get home!"

"Don't," he begged. "I haven't seen you since that afternoon at your Aunt Debbie's."

She stood still but he saw her look over her shoulder down the street before she spoke. "I'm sorry I wasn't home when you stopped. The cards are all done. . . ."

"I didn't stop for the cards. I wanted to see you. And I'm going to try it again and hope for better luck."

The shadow of the tree was not so deep but that he could see the soft line of her mouth, the curve of her cheek. A desire to take her face between his two hands, lift it to his, swept through him.

"If you'll phone, first . . ." Susan brought it out a little breathlessly. She looked again over her shoulder.

"I'll do that." Now he did reach out and take her two hands in his, felt them trembling and held them more closely. "Susan . . ." He stopped—too much was coming to his lips to say to her.

> *"Descend with all Thy gracious powers,*
> *Oh, come, great Spirit, come,"*

sang Nell.

Susan drew her hands free. "I'm so glad Nell has this chance. She loves to sing more than anything—and just now, she's awfully restless."

"Let's go in. I was on my way to go in."

"No. Nell would hate that—I mean, if *I* did. And I really *must* get home!"

"Then—goodnight."

"Goodnight." She turned and walked swiftly away from him.

John crossed the road back to the parsonage. He did not care at the moment whether Nell dragged the hymn or didn't.

In his study he began to walk the floor again, but he did not try to bring his mind back to his sermon. He thought only of Susan. He knew now all that she meant to him and the knowledge went deep, warmly to the core of him. He could still feel her hands in his, quieting under his hold.

133

"And why was she afraid?" he said aloud in a burst of indignation. "Why can't we meet and talk in the dark like any girl and man! What if someone did see us?"

"I saw them—him and Susan Brent—standing under a tree— holding hands. He didn't even have a coat on . . ."

That was his answer. He gave a groan, walked to his desk. His eyes fell on the notes he had abandoned. A more definite answer was there! He must discipline himself where Susan was concerned— he could not let it be gossiped about that he was angling for security here in the church by going after the daughter of one of the deacons.

CHAPTER XIII

FOR THE FIRST time since she had been meeting Tony at the appointed place near the bridge, Nell was a few minutes late in arriving there, the afternoon of the next day. She was out of breath, too, and warm, from hurrying.

It was Susan's fault—Susan had come into the kitchen just as she was wrapping sandwiches and had said a few things which she had had to answer and it all had delayed her.

"What are those for?" Susan had asked.

"To eat, darling."

"I mean—where? Who?"

"By Tony and me. Maybe sitting in his car—maybe not."

"Do you do this every afternoon, Nell?" The troubled tone in Susan's voice.

"Can't she leave me alone?"

"Yes, and why not? I suppose you've missed the peanut butter and cookies and such—I'll tell you now that today I took some of the cold chicken. You won't have to go snooping in the icebox!"

She herself had heard it as a nasty crack and she had had to take time to tell Sue she hadn't meant it, that she didn't know why she had said it, that she knew Sue did not snoop—all that. Talk until the hurt look left Sue's face.

She had the sandwiches in a shoebox by that time, a piece of string in her hand with which to tie it. And then Sue began again, and of all things, with the church supper, this evening.

"I wish you'd go, Nell. You might enjoy it—some of the younger crowd may be there."

"No, thank you." She had the box tied.

"What I really was thinking—it would please Father!"

She should have walked out without answering, but she could not resist a retort. "*I* do something to please Father? Let him be decent to me for a change."

"Oh, Nell!" Then Sue had said, "I think he's like he is at home, Nell, because I'm afraid things are not going well at the plant."

"What things?" She had been suspicious that Susan was making this up to get her to go to the church supper.

"Everything. He told me last evening that he has to lay off a lot of the men. And he's going to discharge Kate Briggs. He asked me if I didn't think you could manage here at the house so that I could do Kate's work in the office."

"*Me!*" She had let her tone effectively reject the idea.

"It isn't settled yet—he's only thinking it over."

"He'd better think of something else, then. I'm off, darling. Have a good time at the supper!"

Their talk had done more than delay her—it had left her with a queer apprehension of change which she could not shake off. She had taken it for granted that her father would go on manufacturing nails as long as he lived, Bill after him—that he might not do so was as difficult for her to believe as though she saw the hill across the valley suddenly flatten before her eyes.

Then she remembered. "It won't make any difference to me—I'll be married to Tony!" But, somehow, that did not banish her uneasiness.

She felt the sun was too warm and moved into the shade of a tree. She wanted to look fresh and cool when Tony drove up. She wanted, oh, just to be thinking now of Tony—nothing but Tony! And their hours ahead . . .

They had been going up to the old Hurrell house almost every afternoon. They had opened windows, dusted the furniture, even rearranged some of it, cleared the kitchen a little, daring more each time they were there. Oh, it was *fun*. Sometimes Tony was simply clownish, making her laugh until it hurt. He had a talent for mimicry—he would pretend he was old Mr. Hurrell with his cows, or a gangster—one afternoon he had taken off Red Skelton, so well that she could believe he really was Red. Today she could tell him that *she* had a talent—that she was going to sing a solo at the Commemoration Service.

She began to feel some impatience—it was quite a bit past four and Tony had not come. They would have that much less time up at the old house. He had been late in meeting her on two afternoons but both times he had had trouble starting his car—*and he had not been as late as this!*

Suddenly, her impatience was a terrible fear, clutching at her throat. Maybe he was not going to come! Her knees went limp; she dropped down on a hummock of grass.

Maybe . . . "Say, we're just a couple of crazy kids," he had said one day. And it might be that he had tired of their game, saw it as too juvenile, the daring to trespass and all their nonsense. But there were the moments when he made love to her . . . "We're not kids *then!*" she whispered into the sun-warmed peace about her.

Or maybe—if she had let him, the other day . . . But she had said, "No, Tony—no." She could not explain to herself her instinctive withdrawal. "Why *didn't* I? For I will, sometime!

"I'll tell him, maybe today, that I'll run away with him!" Her intention to do so was as fixed as it had been the evening she declared it to Aunt Debbie. She dwelt on it constantly, but she had not told Tony of it. She wanted him to speak of it first. But now she would not wait for that. She would tell him today—if he came. . . .

And just as the fear caught at her again, his car appeared on the bridge. She sprang to her feet.

"Why, see who's here!" he called out as he stopped his car. "By

137

any chance are you waiting for someone?"

She got in the car before she answered. "Just a poor gal thumbing her way!" She began to laugh, a little hysterically, put her face against his sleeve to smother it. "Oh, *Tony!*"

"You didn't think I wasn't coming, did you? A row at home—and it held me up. I've got some wine—we'll make this a real party, sweet. Say, you're not crying, are you?"

"No, just laughing." "At myself," she might have added. She cuddled up to him with a happy sigh. "I've some chicken sandwiches." Then she was sorry she had said it, for it sounded juvenile.

But Tony said, "We'll set it all out in style, my girl." He had turned into the hill road. He stopped the car where he usually did to kiss her. He kissed her. Everything—oh, everything was all right.

"What was the row about, Tony?" she asked as they went on.

He grinned down at her. "Me running around with a girl!"

Nell sat straight in utter astonishment. "What's wrong about me?"

Tony's grin vanished. "She's got a girl all picked out for me, nice French-Canuck girl, lives a few doors from us. She'd like to see me get a job at the mills, and settle down where she could keep her thumb on me!" Irritation roughened his voice.

"Parents are simply *pests!*" cried Nell with spirit. "My father'd put me in a strait jacket if he knew where to find one!"

"Of course what my mother's afraid of is that I'll light out any day—which is just what I'm going to do!"

It was the opportunity to tell him she would go with him. But they were turning into the driveway of the old house and, too, at that moment a motorcycle roared up behind them, went on along the road.

"Who was that?" asked Tony with some sharpness.

Nell laughed. Long ago she had lost her first nervousness at trespassing. "That new minister in Sweethome—he rides all around on that awful old motorcycle."

"Do you think he recognized you?"

"He's only seen me once, that I know of. Anyway, what if he did?"

"We'll be going away from here very soon," she thought.

His irritation seemed to stay with him even after they were in the house. He did not pull her at once into his arms as he usually did. He moved around the room restlessly. He looked different—older. And she felt younger. She did not know what to say, what to do.

Then he said, "Come on out to the kitchen—open the bottle."

"Yes, let's."

In the kitchen he found two small glasses in a cupboard and filled them. She sipped at hers, not liking the sourish taste but Tony emptied his in a gulp, filled it again. He had forgotten the style he had planned.

"Tony, this girl—is she awfully pretty?"

"Which girl? Oh . . ." He laughed, though it did not have a pleasant sound. "Got a shape like this." He moved his hands in a gesture that suggested a barrel. "A cast in one eye. Crooked teeth. But she never misses Mass or going to confession!"

He had said, "Which girl . . ." Nell asked, a sudden small chill in her heart, "Are there other girls, Tony, who—you like a lot?"

He gave her a quick sharp glance over his uplifted glass. "Who's been telling you things?" Then he grinned. "Sure, dozens of them. I fall for them, soon as I lay my eyes on them. But none of them are *you,* baby. Just remember that!"

She would—oh, she would.

"Tony, I'm going to sing a solo in church a week from Sunday— will you come to hear me?"

Tony laughed again. *"That*'d top the whole works! Me, sitting in your Protestant church! I thought you told me you were finished with all that pap? Same as I am."

The word shocked her a little. She had only told him that she was through with sitting in a hard pew for an hour, listening to old Doctor Marcy's singsong voice. And, having made that declaration to her father, she had had to stand by it. But, the rare times she thought of religion, she had not thought of it as "pap."

She answered with some spirit. "It's a special service and they needed me. My voice, I mean. I really can sing! You might sit there long enough to listen to me. *I'm* not cross-eyed or fat or . . ."

"You're . . ." Tony put down his glass, took her roughly into his arms, kissed her over her face and throat. She felt his hard breathing against her breasts and it became part of her own.

After a moment he muttered against her lips, "Let's go upstairs, baby."

"Tony, not—now!" The words spoke themselves.

He stepped back from her, his face dark, flushed, angry.

"Stingy!"

"Tony, it's . . ." Then, to her horror and shame, she burst into tears.

"Why, kid!" Tony spoke gently, pulled her head against his shoulder, roughed her hair. "Don't cry about it! A lot of girls hold back that way, I guess. I like you more for it."

"Everything's different today—it started all wrong," she whispered through a little sob. "Tony, you *do* love *me?*"

"My love is yours through summer time," he sang low in her ear, "and all . . ."

She lifted her head, her eyes wet but shining back of the tears. His, on her and close, had the dark look she knew.

"Atta girl! Now let's have a drink on it!"

The wine warmed her as had Tony's avowal in her ear. "Tony, let's—just light out, like you said!"

He stared at her, pretending an exaggerated shock. "Miss Brent, this from you!"

"Neither of us can stand our families—we'll just go away—then they can't bother us any more—we'll be married!"

Her breath gone, she put her hand to her throat. "Oh, say something, Tony!" her heart pleaded. For Tony had put down his glass and was standing looking down into it.

Then he spoke, but, before he spoke, he laughed. "You *are* a kid, Nell! Sounds real good—but what'd we live on?"

Never in her dreaming had she anticipated this answer from him. She was terribly confused, her heart sank. "Why, you'd get a job— I'd get one. . . . We wouldn't need much, we'd have each other." It was frightening to have to seem to plead with him. "And you'll do all those things you've talked about. . . ."

"Yes, that I've talked about!" He said it with a sneer. He walked across the room to a window, stood there, his back to her, his hands dug down in his pockets, his shoulders hunched. Then he swung around, a look on his face she had never seen before, hard, bitter, somehow naked. "Look, what chance has a guy like me to get anywhere? Haven't even got a high school diploma. Had to get to earning some money before I could finish because there was always another baby coming and not enough money to feed what there were. Even when I was a kid I couldn't play with the other boys—no, I had to deliver for the A and P, pick up coal where it dropped to the tracks from the cars, earn a nickel here, a nickel there—lie to keep some of it for myself. It's the same now—I don't let my mother know how much money I'm getting—I've a right to some of it. She's dumb —she thinks Sears Roebuck's gave me the flivver to use. Oh, I've talked big—maybe I had to, and I'll get away someday and soon but—what can I do anywhere else better than a job in a mill or unpacking a lot of rotten crates and it'll be like it is here."

Nell was shrinking back against the drainboard. This was not Tony—this was a stranger, frightening. . . . Then another emotion swept up over her alarm, too new in her experience for her to know as compassion—she knew only that she must comfort Tony, make him believe in the future he had talked about, in himself.

She went to him swiftly. "That isn't so! It's just that fuss with your mother that's made you discouraged! Why, *anyone,* knowing you, knows you're going to get ahead fast, once you've started!"

She put her hands on his shoulders, her eyes very blue and bright with earnestness. "Tony, you can do *any*thing! I *know* you can!"

The bitterness went out of his face, the hard look. He took her hands, held them. "You're my girl, all right! You're a sweet kid!"

She did not want him to think of her as a kid—what she had said might have sounded young, but inside of her she was feeling very mature and wise with this new knowledge that there was more to loving than love-making.

She twined her fingers into his tightly.

"Tony, we'll wait until you get a start in something somewhere." She was too moved to hear this as an echo of Aunt Debbie's advice. "Even if it's—months. Or even a year. Then I'll go to you wherever you are!"

Tony dropped her hands. His eyes fell from hers. "What if you find out I'm not worth waiting for?"

"As if I'd ever think that! As if I don't know by this time what you are. . . . Tony, don't say a thing like that ever again! Now—" she gave a gay, if shaky, little laugh—"it's all settled—let's have our party!"

"Party?"

"The sandwiches—they're super. Let's take them outside—it's such a perfectly heavenly day. If we stay in the back no one can see us from the road." She went to the table, opened the shoebox, tore off the wax paper around the sandwiches. "I'm famished!"

They chose a shady spot under an apple tree near the back door. They did not say much as they ate. Nell's quiet was from a curious hush in her heart. *"I'll come to you wherever you are!"* It was like the words of a song. "I will set it to music and have it to sing. . . ."

She felt closer now to Tony than she did when she was in his hold. His quiet, she was certain, was because he was feeling as she did. She told herself she would remember this moment all her life. She looked up into the tree, off over the old barns to the hillside to film in her memory the setting of the moment. She would remember the sunshine, the smell of the fields. . . .

"Tony, I shall always love this place! I didn't want to go into the house, that first time—I felt just like a burglar, but now it seems ours."

"Just the same, I guess maybe we'd better stop coming here."

"Tony! *Why?* Not because that Wendell man rode along. He was going pretty fast—maybe he didn't notice us. Or he thought we had a right to be coming in. Anyway, he wouldn't be likely, a minister, to tell it around. . . ."

"I don't care about him," put in Tony. "It's . . ." He took on a masterful air. "I might sometime make you do what you don't want to do!"

A warm color swept up to Nell's temples. "Oh," was all she could manage in answer and that in a small sound. But she was moved now by a thrilling sense of being taken care of—not the wanting she always had felt when he gave her an ardent look.

Tony got to his feet, drew her up to hers. "I'd better not be late, getting in to supper tonight." He said it with a significant laugh. "And we've some clearing up to do."

She slipped her hand into his as they went back to the kitchen. Through the door, for, some time ago, Tony had found an old key that unlocked it. They wiped the glasses with a piece of cloth Nell had brought one day, put them back in a cupboard.

"Everything okay?" Tony looked around the room. Then he drew her into his arms, kissed her lightly on the cheek. "You're a sweet kid, know it?"

"Tony, if we don't come here . . ."

"Sure I'll be seeing you—can't tomorrow, but next day, same time. We'll cruise around, like we did."

"Until you go away . . ." added Nell.

Out on the road, a little way from the house, she said, "Stop, Tony. I think I'd like to walk, from here. It's early. The family's going to a church supper, so I don't have to hurry."

"Okay. Just as you say . . ."

He stopped the car. She wished he would kiss her again but he made no move to. "See you day after tomorrow, same time."

Her impulse to walk all the way home sprang from a strong reluctance to arrive there before the family left for the church supper. She did not want to see anyone until she had adjusted herself to the changes the past hour had brought.

She dropped down on the grass at the side of the road to think it all out, beginning, not with what Sue had hinted at, which now had gone entirely out of her mind, but with that moment when Tony turned around from the window and startled her so. Oh, poor Tony! She hugged her knees up to her, put her face against them, wanting to cry over Tony's lot.

He must get away and he was right about getting a start at something before they married. But, instead of shedding tears, she breathed a little sigh against her knees. It had been so wonderfully thrilling, planning to run away with Tony, thinking of it almost every minute of every day, sometimes dreaming of it when she slept. Part of the thrill was that it would be the final, telling, declaration to her father of her right to do what she pleased. And now, to wait—that meant living on at home, weeks and weeks and weeks, one day like the other perhaps, with her father and Sue watching her, checking up on her, with nothing to do. "But, Tony, *Tony,* darling, I will wait!" She started to repeat aloud, "I'll come to you . . ." lifted her head to give it the proper drama and broke off, abruptly. A man was walking along the road, almost in front of her.

She sat straight, startled and furious, seeing him a trespasser, not only on her thoughts but on this private domain of hers and Tony's. Then she recognized him as the writer who had come to Aunt Debbie's. "Hello," she said, though not pleasantly.

His step halted abruptly and his head jerked around as if he had not seen her there. "Good afternoon," he muttered, and went on.

"Well, of all the *drips!*" Nell threw after him. "What Aunt Debbie sees in *you!* You look like something that's been left out in the rain for *weeks!*"

He had spoiled the moment—even after he walked out of sight around a curve in the road she could not slip back into the exalted feeling he had rudely interrupted.

Anyone might come along—old Si Carr lived on a farm a mile further along, the Hodgsons beyond that. The minister had ridden past, earlier. It had been only pretense—their adolescent game—that the old house and the fields around it were a seventh heaven that belonged exclusively to them.

She got to her feet.

"I might as well go home."

Before she reached the bend in the road she stopped to turn and give a last long loving glance at the old house. It looked lonely, and as she walked on, she felt something of its loneliness creeping into her.

CHAPTER XIV

Deborah had just finished dressing for the church supper when Susan came in.

"I'm not going, Aunt Debbie." Even though she was wearing her pearls.

"Why not, Susan? What's happened?" By Susan's tone and the look on her face Deborah knew that something had.

"Father telephoned that he was staying at the office to do some work."

"But that need not keep *you* home, child!"

"I'm going to take him some supper. He said to leave something for him on the kitchen table but—he might not eat it. Aunt Debbie, I don't remember his *ever* staying at the office long after closing time. And he has never missed any of the church suppers. He thinks it is his duty as one of the deacons to go to them!"

"When Willie misses a duty, something pretty serious is afoot." Though Deborah did not say that to Susan; she did not want to affirm Susan's worry, which she herself really had started.

"Can't Nell take something to him? You said the other day she was not going to the church thing."

Susan shook her head. "Nell—might annoy him. Anyway, she isn't home."

"And you look so pretty, Susan," said Deborah, regretfully, as Susan turned to the door.

It was business at the plant, no doubt, that had Willie down—and what could anyone do when he refused to see it an antiquated set-up, probably worth no more now than the ground on which it stood.

She put an apron on over the new dress to lay out some supper for Rom. She had not seen him since the middle of the morning when she had persuaded him to drink some coffee. But she told herself that walking in this clean sweet air, even to the point of exhaustion, was the best thing he could do, just now.

She was putting his food on the table, cold ham, a green salad, a pitcher of milk, when he came in. She had to look quickly away from the haggardness of his face.

"I'm going to a church dinner, Rom—I didn't think you'd be interested in it so I've fixed a little something for you. . . ."

He frowned down at the food.

"You should not have gone to the trouble."

"No trouble at all, if you eat it! Now sit down." She untied her apron.

He sat down but he dropped his head into his hands.

She doubted that he was aware of her in the room, hanging her apron away, putting on the new hat, taking a last quick survey of herself in the square of mirror that hung over a chest. She went out of the door quietly, without a goodbye.

Clare greeted her excitedly. "Deb, what a stunning dress! And look at me in this old thing. But what's the use of *my* caring what I wear? Will you do the zipper for me, darling? Poor Fred always has an awful time with it."

Deborah fastened the zipper. Fred came out to help Clare up into the seat of the car. He shook hands with Deborah: "Glad to see you." Though well past forty he still had in his manner something of the shyness, the awkwardness Deborah remembered—the long thin wrists, too.

In the car Clare gave a little giggle. "It's just like old times, Deb, the two of us going to something together!"

"Not much like," thought Deborah. But she was touched by Clare's loyalty to their old friendship—a little ashamed that she could summon back so little of its warmth.

"*Look* at the cars!" cried Clare as they neared the church. "Park here, Deb—I can walk from here. Oh, hello, Agnes!"

Agnes Peely was pausing in the walk beside the car. "Can I help you, Clare?"

"I'm managing—I sort of edge myself off. There! You know Deborah Brent—you must remember her. . . ."

"I—sort of do," Agnes Peely's hand fluttered out in Deborah's direction. "Welcome to Sweethome!"

"Thanks. I remember you—you recited pieces in school and you had long curls and always wore a big bow of ribbon on top of your head."

"Imagine your remembering my silly hairribbons! I think that is *sweet* of you, Mrs. Brent. It makes me feel as if—" Agnes Peely took a little breath and some pink came into her cheeks—"as if we were good friends! Is that an awful thing to say?"

It was so much more than Deborah had dared to hope for that she said warmly, "Not awful at all! Thanks," and she tried to forget that she and Clare had made fun of those hairribbons. They went on, the three of them, toward the church, Deborah between Clare and Agnes Peely. "Forward into battle," she thought, smothering a zany impulse to sing the words.

In a recent renovation of the church the basement had been divided into rooms for the Sunday School classes and various meetings, but in such a way that the partitions could be folded back, leaving one long open space. This was as Deborah remembered it—the long tables spread with borrowed cloths, the borrowed knives and forks and spoons, the smell of stewing chicken from an adjoining room, the babble of women's voices, the small children milling around, the huddle of older children waiting outside of the door for the call to dinner. For an instant it seemed no forty years had passed since she had come to a church supper, but the next she knew they had, for,

148

on her appearance, a sudden silence fell on the room, eyes came to her, sharpening with lively curiosity.

Clare was panting a little from the effort of walking her bulk up the path to the church so it was Agnes Peely who said, brightly, a little loudly, "You *all* remember Deborah Brent! Isn't it *nice* to have her back here with us?"

There were murmurs of greeting from the women nearest to them, others smiled. But there was no warmth. . . .

Then a younger woman came up to Deborah, her hand outstretched. "I'm Walt Purdy's wife—your neighbor. I was sorry you were not at home the other afternoon when I called."

Deborah was quite certain that the distinctness with which she said this was to tell the women within hearing that she *had* called. Deborah said, "Thanks for the flowers you left."

Julia White came up to her. "Hello, Deborah! Like old times, isn't it?" Though her eyes belied the friendliness her words suggested.

Clare had got her breath. "That's just what *I* said to Deborah, coming over! That it *was* like old times!"

"Though I guess anything like this must seem awfully dull to you, after . . ."

Mrs. Higgins interrupted Julia. "I'm Hattie Higgins—I was Hattie Ballin before I married Ham. Maybe you don't remember my folks—they lived in the house on River Road that burned down. Someone said Will isn't coming. Or Susan. I don't know of a supper we've had when they haven't been here!"

"He was delayed at the office," said Deborah.

"But Susan . . ."

"Something came up which she had to do."

Hattie Higgins plainly was not satisfied with this explanation. She was opening her lips to ask more when Almira Coggin came through the door from the kitchen. "Hasn't Reverend Wendell come *yet?* Everything's ready—we might as well sit down and eat while the dinner's hot."

Ham Higgins stepped out from the huddle of men in the corner. "I know what's delayed him! Si Carr was took worse, dying, mebbe—wanted prayers spoke over him."

"But he's a Methodist!" protested Almira Coggin.

"That girl who's been working up there come into the store—she'd been sent to get Reverend Neal and he'd gone to Hartford, wouldn't be back till tomorrow and she come in to ask me what she'd do. Reverend Wendell was in the store and he said he'd go up."

"Maybe old Silas won't like that—he was pretty regular at his church when he was well."

"A man who's dying can't be too particular," said one of the men with a chuckle. "And mebbe Reverend Wendell knows some Methodist prayers."

Ham Higgins said, "Let's eat—have the grace said later."

But at that moment John Wendell came in. He looked tired, grave. "Sorry I am late—I was hoping you were not waiting."

"Sit there at the head of that table, Reverend Wendell," directed Almira Coggin. "Everything's ready."

He went to his appointed chair, stood behind it. The others pulled out chairs. Deborah found Martha Purdy next to her, Clare at her other side. Agnes Peely sat across the table from her. The young people came in, gathered around a table at the end of the room. Bill was one of them. Deborah smiled as she watched him sidle away from two giggling girls, slide awkwardly into a chair, almost knocking it over as he did so. Willie had been like that at that age, clumsy hands and feet, hair that would not stay smoothed down. . . . And Deborah sighed, thinking of Willie as he was now.

"Those are my two boys with Bill," informed Martha Purdy. "They get along very well, the three of them. They were planning to go camping for two weeks up the river—Walt was going to rent a tent and a boat for them. But now Bill's working at the plant it's all off, I'm afraid. Unless . . ." She gave Deborah a quick, inquiring look.

"I could persuade his father. . . ." Deborah shook her head. "Not a chance! My brother started to work in the plant when he was sixteen, so he thinks Bill should do the same."

Martha Purdy gave a little sound of impatience. "That's like everyone else in this town! They wouldn't ever *think* of doing things differently, for a change! I told Walt that maybe it would be a good thing for something to happen here that would shake them up good and hard, just once! But nothing will!"

"Is Silas bad?" Ham Higgins asked John Wendell.

"He's—gone. He died before the doctor got there. I—stayed with him."

"Well, he was close to eighty, wasn't he?"

"He's had that bad heart for years."

Debbie could see that these men and women here were not shaken by the news of Si Carr's death. A few spoke appropriate words of regret but most fell into lively speculation about his wife's future.

"What'll Minnie Carr do? She won't want to stay there. . . ."

"Maybe go to that niece's in West Hartford."

"Would she have room? She's got four children. . . ."

"And a boarder. She wouldn't have room for Minnie."

"And that girl who's been working up there—she isn't as bright as she should be. What'll become of *her?*"

"There're institutions. . . ."

"Who'll be responsible for the Hurrell house now? Though guess it's been more'n a year since Si could do anything round the place."

"I've got the keys," said Ham Higgins. "Si brought them to me early spring. But it don't follow I'm responsible for how it looks. Let that bank in Watertown worry about that!"

"You wouldn't mind selling it if someone came along?" said Coley Coggin with a laugh. "Get a good commission."

"Who'd buy it—run down as it is!"

Now everyone was served. Almira Coggin, as chairman of the supper committee, took the chair next to John Wendell. "If you'll say grace, Reverend."

John Wendell repeated words of thanks in a grave, clear voice, then sat down.

A few moments later Deborah saw his glance move swiftly along the table. Was he looking for Susan? Then his eyes reached her, a surprised, pleased smile broke the gravity of his face and he lifted his hand high in a salute. It was his answer to his housekeeper's warning, perhaps indiscreet on his part, but she loved him for it and waved her hand back to him.

Hattie Higgins looked from her to John Wendell and then down at her plate.

Clare, next to her, began telling, between mouthfuls of food, who this one and that one was, prefacing each bit of information with, "You remember . . ." And though faces and figures had changed with the years, Deborah did remember. Some of them had been ahead of her in school, others in lower grades. Some had not been born, but she had known their parents. By every right she should be welcome among them, as one of them, and instead she felt very much alone.

With some abruptness Hattie Higgins spoke her name from across the table.

"Mrs. Brent! Bill says you have a young man staying with you. A foreigner. A writer. Is he any relation?"

A committee of one, appointed in the kitchen, perhaps, to "find out." Deborah remembered what Will had said. She was aware that the women within hearing had stopped eating to hear her answer.

She felt herself stiffening but met Mrs. Higgins' challenging eyes squarely. "Yes. Rom Barcek. He's Polish and he is young and he had a book published two years ago. No, he is no relation—just a very good friend."

A little too quickly and breathlessly, as if she were throwing herself bodily into a breach, Agnes Peely cried, "We've never *had* an author right in Sweethome, have we? If we got up a silver tea or something perhaps he'd read from his works! Anyway, you *must* bring him to the Commemoration Service, Mrs. Brent! There's going to be special music, you know."

Deborah thought of Rom as she had left him; then that she must reward Agnes Peely. She said, "I've been told that you are arranging a very lovely program of music."

"Well, I'm doing my little best!"

At that Hattie Higgins turned a punishing look on Mrs. Peely. "You think so, Agnes, but I'm going to say right here and now that I think it was a mistake your letting—leaving the sopranos out of that part of the oratorio. After they've worked so hard on it. *They* don't like it and I don't blame them. Of course we all know why you did it!"

For a moment Agnes Peely's face quivered like a slapped child's. Then some defiance came into it. "It's really *much* more effective— one voice singing that part. That was the reason I made the change. I explained that to the others. And we *all* want it to be just as lovely as we can have it."

"Huh," breathed Mrs. Higgins, her jaw outthrust.

But Agnes Peely was leaning forward toward Deborah. "Your niece has a perfectly *beautiful* voice, Mrs. Brent! It's a pity she doesn't have it trained!"

"Perhaps she will, someday," said Deborah.

Clare said, *"You* used to sing, Debbie. Remember? In the entertainments at school. I believe Nell's just like you!"

Deborah was saved any reaction to that, even from Hattie Higgins, for the supper committee, of which Hattie was one, was getting to its feet to remove the plates and bring in the dessert.

The dessert was pie, and the talk, among the women, turned to the making of pie crust. Some used ice water, others put the crust in the icebox to chill, some used prepared flour, others scorned it.

"Are *you* a good piemaker, Mrs. Brent?"

Deborah thought of the pies and pies and pies she had made over the years. What if she told them? "Yes, I was paid for making pies."

153

But she answered, pleasantly, "Well, what I've made seem to have gotten eaten."

At last the supper was over, the women were clearing the tables, the young people were disappearing into the out-of-doors, the men following them. All but John Wendell who came straight to Deborah.

He held his hand out to her, said in a low tone, grinning, "I think I know why you are here, Mrs. Brent."

She laughed, said in a voice as low as his, "I didn't get anywhere, I'm afraid. Oh, two on my side," she added, remembering Agnes Peely and Martha Purdy.

"That's a start. Where's Susan tonight?"

"She drove out to the plant—her father had work to do there and she thought she could help him."

"Will you tell her . . ." He stopped, reddened a little. "Never mind."

"Any reason you can't tell her yourself that you missed her?"

"Reverend Wendell . . ." Almira Coggin spoke behind them. "I'm sure you'll excuse me, Mrs. Brent, for interrupting your little private talk but I have to ask Reverend Wendell just one question. Has it been decided where Doctor Slade is going to stay?"

"At the parsonage. I did not know there was any question about it."

"Of course the Superintendent always *has,* when he's come to our parish. But we didn't know how you felt about it. I'd be glad to have him. . . ."

"I've already written to him and he has answered my letter. He'll get here Saturday afternoon. That will give him time to go over the reports of the different committees."

"I'll tell Coley. You don't want to give us just a *tiny* idea of your sermon on that day?"

"No, I'd rather not."

"We're sure it will be inspiring! Now go back to your tête-à-tête—it was nice in you to honor us tonight, Mrs. Brent!"

Deborah saw John frowning at Mrs. Coggin's departing back. She put a finger on his arm.

"Go along, John. But for goodness' sake, take that look off your face!"

Martha Purdy helped Clare back into the car. But she declined Deborah's invitation to ride home with them. "I have to pick out my forks and knives and shoo my boys home. But I'm coming over soon."

"I hope you will," said Deborah, heartily.

As Deborah started the car, Clare leaned back against the seat with a happy sigh. "I wouldn't have missed tonight for anything! Debbie, did you see the way the women looked at you? I'm so glad you wore that lovely dress. They'll be talking about it for weeks. We don't go in much for smart clothes, here in Sweethome, you see. Almost anything's good enough. They'll know you're getting good alimony!"

"I'm not getting any."

"You're *not?* I thought in divorces the wives always got some alimony."

"Not always. With Roger and me . . . Oh, let's skip it, Clare." For suddenly she was too tired, too indifferent to say any more; to get it all straight in Clare's head she must work through layers and layers of fat and it was not important enough to go to that effort.

Clare said, in a slightly hurt tone, "Well, tell me sometime—I mean what you're living on!" She straightened, then, in the seat. "Oh, that reminds me—Fred says there's a rumor that most of the men at the Brent plant are going to be laid off. Fred hasn't been trucking for them for two weeks. Has Will said anything to you, Deb?"

"No. But it may only be the usual slack time of the year."

"It'd be awful. Most of Sweethome works there. Even in the depression and through the war Will somehow kept things going! It's probably that Swede's fault! I wish somebody'd tell him what we think of him!"

They had reached the Hersey house. At the sound of the car in the drive Fred came out. Clare called to him, "It was a wonderful supper, Fred! There—just give me your hand. Thanks, Deb. You'll come over soon? Though, I forgot, you have company—that young man. . . ." Clare giggled. "You *do* do the most unconventional things, Deborah."

Deborah had to put down a desire to answer Clare as she had Will. But this wasn't the time. She said evenly, "My young man takes care of himself. I'll be over soon. Goodnight—goodnight, Fred."

She gave a long sigh as she turned the car homeward. No, she had not got very far in her campaign. Now they would have Rom to talk about. And they'd say a great deal more than that it was "unconventional" of her to have a young man in her house, with her alone there.

She hoped she would find that Rom had gone to bed and was sleeping soundly after his day in the open air. But, going into the kitchen, she saw an envelope on the table, addressed to her in Rom's fine handwriting.

"Now what?" she asked of the empty room. A terrible possibility slipped into her mind, and her hand shook as she tore open the flap of the envelope.

"My good friend,

I am walking to Canaan where I will take a bus to New York, to finish a matter on which I turned my back, a few days ago. I will return if you will permit it, and then I hope I may be given the opportunity to show myself more worthy of your unquestioning kindnesses.

Rom Barcek"

Deborah dropped down in a chair, frowning down at the lines. They told her nothing.

But, recalling his outburst of hatred of the whole female sex that first night he was here, she was certain his trouble was over some girl. She smiled a little. She wished she could tell Rom that hate was an armor you put on in instinctive self-protection—oh, she well knew —but it wore thin and thinner and then was gone. The hurt it was hiding gone, too.

CHAPTER XV

DIRECTLY AFTER breakfast, the next morning, Deborah found a spade in the shed and went out into the yard. If she were going to have an herb garden she'd better get to planting it. She needed a good workout, too, to clear her head of worry. Over Rom, over Willie's affairs and Susan's concern, Nell and her reckless, secret plans, young Bill who wanted to go camping—and why couldn't he?—John Wendell. Oh, if she made a list it would total to quite a column!

She already had staked off the space of ground for her herbs. Evidently Doctor Pryor had had a garden here for the soil was loose and very little grass had encroached upon it. She pushed the spade deeper into the earth, lifted it, turned the dark loam soil, then stood straight to breathe in the good smell of it. She laughed. "You're like an old soak, Deborah, sniffing up the fumes of alcohol!"

The sun on her was good, too. The quiet all around. She turned one spadeful of earth after another, loosened it with the edge of the spade, knelt, sometimes, to crumble a lump of earth with her fingers simply for the pleasure of feeling it.

As she worked, her thoughts slipped back to her first herb garden, back of the cabin in Twitchel.

Her baby was born in the April before that summer. While she was carrying him she had had to spend more time indoors and she had passed it in reading the magazines she had subscribed to a few months earlier. Among them was one entitled *The Amateur Gar-*

dener, which had been included with the others as a sort of bonus. It was made up of articles contributed by amateurs in gardening, telling of trial and error, others by experts offering advice. She never had had a garden, never had wanted one, but she read these simply because it was pleasant, when snow lay deep around the cabin, to think of sun and shade and things growing.

In the back of the magazine was a department given entirely to the growing of herbs. These columns intrigued her. She had known little more about herbs than the names of the commonest of them. She began to think of them as special, each with its different flavor and fragrance. "Plants with a purpose . . ." She decided she would have a garden of them in the summer. She sent to the address given in the magazine for seeds.

Then the baby, Waite, was born and she was too busy caring for him to think of a garden. Fighting to keep him. But in May he had died.

She would have said that she never again would feel happy about anything, yet when tiny pale green shoots of the different herbs she planted back of their cabin showed through the soil, sweet basil, rosemary, savory, others—she had the names on little wooden stakes in each plot—she enjoyed a wonder that was sheer happiness. How much greater the reward of her work was going to be she had no idea, then—it was enough that her seeds were going to grow.

She was anticipating such wonder, now, as she paused in her spading. "If I get them in tomorrow, in two, three weeks . . ." She had the seeds—she always had some on hand to plant in window boxes.

"Aunt Debbie, whatever are you doing?"

It was Susan, coming through the trellis. For a moment Deborah was sorry—it was nice to be alone with her spading and thinking. Then she remembered Susan's troubled face, the evening before, and called to her cheerily.

"Starting that herb garden I've had in mind."

159

"Should you be doing that? It's such heavy work—for you."

Deborah did not say she needed a workout. Susan might see that absurd in a woman of her age. She laid the spade on the ground. "I'll ache in every muscle tomorrow, without any doubt. But that won't kill me. Let's sit down here on the grass and talk—how is everything, my dear?"

"You mean—with Father? I don't know. He didn't say much to me—he was there all alone—he didn't seem busy but—terribly worried. He did tell me that a lot of orders he always has gotten have gone to that new plant over on the Flats. He's very bitter about that. And he doesn't know how he can go on paying the men—and he hates to lay them off. . . ." She stopped abruptly, with a shocked, stricken look. "Oh, I shouldn't be telling you all this!"

"Why not? Your father is my brother—whatever happens to him is a concern of mine."

"But . . ." Susan flushed deeply. "He told me I was not to speak of it to anyone—particularly . . ."

"Me," finished Deborah for her. She saw Susan's embarrassment, patted her hand. "Don't look so distressed, child!"

"But *why?*" asked Susan indignantly. "You'd think he'd feel . . ."

Tell her? She could, now—at least, a part of it; she was certain of the girl's fondness for her. She asked, "Do you remember your grandmother—your father's mother—my stepmother?"

"A little. I remember I was afraid of her."

Deborah laughed. "I can imagine that. Well, I wasn't when I was a girl. I guess I deliberately did everything I could think of to defy her. Not very nice in me to look back on, but—well, maybe one of these psychiatrists would say I did it to even a score between us." Debbie paused. She was not going to speak of the old hate between them, not here in the sunshine with the smell of the freshly turned earth sweet in the air.

"Then I eloped—that was the word then—with a boy she had

forbidden me to speak to. She had some qualities that might be called admirable but she was an un-understanding, unforgiving woman and strong-willed. After I ran away she pronounced me as dead to the family as though they'd buried me up there on the hillside. She wrote and told me that, in answer to a letter I wrote to my father telling him that Paul and I were married and where we were living. My father never answered my letter."

"Oh, how cruel!"

"Maybe I thought that at the time—yes, I did. Now the sad part of it is that my father was afraid of her, just as you were when you were small. Willie, too. With them afraid, she could impress her will upon them. Her opinions, her convictions. Maybe she thought she was always right. I remember that she was a steady churchgoer so she could not have had anything on her conscience!"

Susan was frowning. "But, Father—after she died . . ."

"I think I understand how Willie feels—he was fond of me when he was a boy, he looked to me to help him out of little jams with his mother. Perhaps he felt I'd let him down somehow when I ran off. So he was readier to accept his mother's opinion of me. That's the way I figure it out. I refuse to think he isn't fond of me now, down in some part of him, only he's lived so long with the other that he will not let himself feel it. He isn't the yielding sort."

"No, he isn't," affirmed Susan sadly. "That will make it harder for him if—if anything happens at the plant. He's so proud of it—of the generations that have run it!"

"So is an ostrich proud—and dumb," Deborah wanted to say. Instead she said, "Maybe it isn't healthy that in four generations there have been no changes. Maybe your father needs a jolt. . . ." She stopped, a little startled at hearing herself say almost what Mrs. Purdy had said, at the supper the evening before, of Sweethome.

She got up from the ground. "I'm talking too much, I guess. Let's go in and heat up the coffee."

Susan got to her feet, then hesitated. "Isn't—where's Mr. Barcek?"

Had Willie forbidden the girl to meet Rom, wondered Deborah. For an instant she was angry, then she smiled, a little wickedly. "He's in New York for a few days but he's coming back and then I want you and Nell to help me entertain him."

They went into the kitchen. "Put the pot over while I wash my hands."

While Susan was filling the cups with coffee she said, soberly, "You didn't talk too much, Aunt Debbie. What you said is going to help me understand Father better." She bent impulsively and kissed Deborah's cheek. "You don't know how glad I am you're here!"

Deborah put her fingers against her cheek, her eyes on Susan very warm. "Bless you, child, for telling me that. What's Nell doing today? Why don't the three of us go on a little bust—drive somewhere for lunch. Isn't there a Barn or something outside of Norfolk? I remember passing it. It looked inviting."

Susan had sat down across from her but she took only a sip of her coffee. "I'd love it—I've never been there—but I couldn't go today. I told Father I'd drive over to the plant this afternoon. He's giving Kate Briggs a vacation—he doesn't think she looks well and she is going to show me something about the books and things so I can take her place—for a while. I should be home now getting something ready for supper. Nell . . ." She stopped.

"Nell has a date?"

"She has a rehearsal, late this afternoon. But she *does* have a date nearly every afternoon with a boy. Aunt Debbie, I'm terribly worried about that, too." Tears showed in Susan's eyes for a moment. "She says she's terribly in love with him and she's so—sort of reckless. I don't know him—he may be all right. He lives over on the Flats but—that should not be against him. Only—I wish she would invite him to come to the house—that she wasn't going off and meeting him on the road somewhere and going nobody knows where.

If Father finds out . . . and he will, of course, someday . . . **Oh,** I'm dreadful to unload myself on you, this way!"

"Not at all. My muscles may be sore but my shoulders are strong. There isn't much you can do—Nell isn't a child—except *think* that it will turn out all right." Deborah spoke briskly over a desire to shed a few tears herself, but for Susan, too young to have all this responsibility put upon her, missing the good things of youth. She said, then, irrelevantly, though not so much so, considering the track her thought had taken, "John Wendell asked me why you were not at the supper. He was disappointed."

Susan's cheeks went hot and she covered them with her hands, her eyes shining for just an instant, then clouding. "If you're implying, Aunt Debbie, *please* don't! I haven't time to think of anything like that!" She got up from her chair. "I must go home now. Thanks— for everything. And I am going to send Bill over this evening **to** finish that spading for you."

"It'll be nice if he will," said Deborah, though it would be cheating her of that secret pleasure she got out of it. "I'll have him trim the shrubs, too. Clear out weeds. Pay him for it." To herself, "I'll bet the kid never has more than two nickels in his pocket."

She watched Susan cross the yards, hurrying back to her responsibilities. "You could have told her you'd make a meatloaf—there's that ground beef and Rom's gone—you could take it over hot and put it in their oven. Willie wouldn't know, to choke over it. Why *didn't* you tell her you would?"

It was a pity Susan did not have some of Nell's self-centeredness. *"I haven't time to think of anything like that!"* If she were not prevented, the girl would throw love right out of the window, along with everything of youth.

"Hang Willie," said Deborah Brent aloud. She had worked herself up to the point of indignation where she could say it with fervor. For his blindness—an ostrich, indeed. Saying he was giving that secretary of his a long vacation because he didn't think she was well.

163

He was laying her off for good, probably, and he would not face facts squarely enough to come out and say it. His pride was tighter on him than his skin.

Yet there was compassion in her little rage. "If it's money he needs right now . . ." But that impulse ran instantly against a wall. "He wouldn't take your money, Deborah. He'd think it was tainted!"

She turned away from the door. She could not go back to her spading—that must be left for Bill to do. But she could clean the back shed.

The afternoon of that day Father Duffy worked in his garden. He liked the feeling of the sun on him, as did Deborah Brent, and the smell of the earth as he cultivated it around his perennials. Now and then he paused to delight his eyes with the sweep of color before him. "Madonna and regal lilies among the delphinium, pyrethrums, stock, lupins . . ." To look upon the marvel of this blossoming always humbled him in some way, yet heartened his spirit, too.

Then, as he was hoeing along, he noticed a delphinium hanging limply toward the ground. It was one of his choice ones. He gave an exclamation of grief mixed with indignation, and with some difficulty, got down on his knees to examine it. It had been trodden down —by a dog, perhaps, going through the yard. He thought, hotly, "I will build a higher fence—a very high fence!" It appeased him to picture the fence, closely boarded, a barbed wire strung along its top, so that not even the thinnest dog or cat could get through. Even though he knew as he planned it that he would not build it, for a great part of the pleasure he took in his garden was that it was in full view of anyone passing by to enjoy as he did.

He ran his thick fingers along the bruised stalk with a great tenderness. It might be saved—stake it up, nurse it along. . . .

He was tying it to a stake with infinite care when a woman turned into the garden from the street. He recognized her, got to his feet, brushed earth from his hands by rubbing them down the old dungarees he wore. "Good afternoon, Mrs. DiVito. A very nice day to be out!"

The gloom on her heavy face did not alter at his cheery greeting. "I got to talk to you, Father!"

"We'll go inside, then."

He led the way to his study and motioned her to sit down in one of the hard chairs there. He saw her wipe perspiration from her forehead with a corner of the scarf she took from her head, and he went to the kitchen and filled a pitcher with cold water and brought it with a glass and set it down on the table within reach of her hand. He noticed, too, that she was big with child. She drank some water thirstily.

"It's about my Tony," she said then, bluntly.

"Tony, your son, yes." And Father Duffy was reminded of another afternoon when Mrs. Brent had sat in the same chair across the table from him. "It's been sometime since I have seen Tony."

Mrs. DiVito twisted the ends of the scarf in her fingers. "I scold him for that, Father—I talk to him until my tongue's tired! I weep over it! I pray to the Blessed Virgin to bring him back to the Church! But 'tisn't that, Father—it's that he could be giving me more money. I found out how much he makes—and I ask him and he turns away as if he had no ears to hear me! He buys himself a suit when I haven't a decent dress to wear to Mass. There's another baby coming. . . . His father's drunk more days than he's working. . . . I ask you— I ask Our Lady, what am I to do?"

Father Duffy had covered his eyes with his hand. He hoped she would think that *he* was asking the Blessed Mother but he wasn't. He was thinking, "It's the money that concerns her—not the boy slipping away from his faith!"

"Well?" she demanded sharply when he did not speak at once.

"If she handles Tony this way . . ." He remembered Tony from the days when he had served as an altar boy. Good-looking, smart but unreliable, a little sly—it was that impression he had recalled when Mrs. Brent spoke Tony's name. "Yet there must be good in the boy if he has been helping his mother at all!" He dropped his hand.

"Isn't it possible, Mrs. DiVito, that you are expecting too much of Tony when you ask him to give you more, maybe all of the money he earns? Naturally he thinks he has a right to spend some of it on himself. Isn't it possible, too, that you nag him? Young people do not like that!"

Mrs. DiVito twisted the scarf tighter. "I nag him, yes, I nag him—but it's because he's spending on a girl! I set Gio, the little one, to watch—Gio's seen them together in his car, twice, three times. He'd let his mother, his little brothers and sisters, starve and spend money on a slut!"

"Wait a moment, Mrs. DiVito—you are jumping to your own conclusions about the kind of a girl she is. It happens . . ." Father Duffy stopped. "How old is Tony?"

"Nineteen. He's old enough to marry. He could marry tomorrow—a nice girl I picked out for him. He could get a full-time job in the mills instead of in this place and that where he don't get ahead. He'd get enough to raise a family and help his mother, same time. But, no, he talks big—he's going away from here—he laughs at me when I tell him Florine Bouvais is the wife for him!"

Father Duffy smiled. "I am quite sure if I were in his place I would laugh, too." He went on, then, gravely, "Search yourself, Mrs. DiVito—are you not too possessive of this boy? You gave him life, true. A gift, but reaching adulthood, it is his to do with what he wills. You can only love him and pray that he may make it a good life. But he must do that for himself, learn by his own experiences. . . ."

Mrs. DiVito burst out, her cheeks purpling, *"That* kind of talk, Father, isn't going to feed my children!"

"No, it wouldn't," thought Father Duffy. And it was wasted on this woman; she was not like Mrs. Brent who had come to hear it.

He said, a little wearily, "If you are in immediate need . . ." He opened a drawer in the table, took out a tin box, drew two bills from it. "Here is twenty dollars." He had to look away from the way her hands reached out for it.

She got up and tied the scarf over her thick, black, untidy hair. "It'll help, Father, and God bless you for it."

His eye winked. "He'll have to bless Rudolph Petersen, who as far as I know is a man of no religious beliefs beyond helping his fellowmen. He brings me money now and then to use at my discretion. Very soon, thanks to him, we may have a health center here with a social service worker who can help you in your home problems."

This last was lost on her. She said, a cunning gleam coming into her eyes, "Maybe this Petersen would give Tony a good job in his plant. They pay bigger wages than the mills. Then, maybe, he'd settle down."

Father Duffy waited until she had gone, the bills clutched in her hands, then went back into his garden. But now he walked slowly up and down one of the narrow paths between the beds, without seeing the flowers. A sense of failure lay heavy upon him. She had gone away as confused, with every good instinct still as dwarfed by need, as when she came.

CHAPTER XVI

ON THE SATURDAY before Commemoration Sunday, the women met at the church to put it in readiness for this special service.

Two of them polished the wood of the pulpit until it shone. Others dusted the rails and the pewbacks of the pews, washed windows, swept corners which old Sam Sims had overlooked. They did it all gladly, with love and pride in this, their church.

They talked of the story of the Commemoration that had come out in the Hartford *Courant,* a few days before. A few thought it should have given the names of the women who were on these committees for the preparations. But in general they were satisfied and considerably set up by the publicity. They talked of the ministers from other Congregational churches who would be here, tomorrow; of Doctor Slade's coming. Now and then one or another glanced through a window toward the parsonage—would Mrs. Donnell have it spick and span for him? Had he come yet? Was there a car in the driveway?

While they worked and talked, Agnes Peely practiced her accompaniments on the organ, timidly, her wrists weak with nervousness. This evening the chorus would rehearse here in the church and two of her sopranos, Libby White and Carrie Stedman had called her this morning, *just this morning,* and told her that they were dropping out of the chorus and she *knew* it was because Nell Brent was singing that special part alone—but what could she *do?* And what if Nell Brent didn't appear?

"If Agnes doesn't play better than that tomorrow . . ." said Hattie Higgins in a low tone to Almira Coggin, who was helping her put the hymnals in orderly arrangement.

Quite a few of the women had brought their lunch with them and thermoses of coffee. They went down to the basement to eat, relax—and talk. . . .

Within a few minutes the talk was of Deborah Brent. Would she come to the service? Would she bring her young man? Would she sit in the Brent pew? "That'd be nerve—after her folks disowned her, the way they did!"

Then one of the women asked Almira Coggin, "What's this I hear about Will's secretary, Kate Briggs, taking a long vacation because she isn't well!"

Almira Coggin drew her lips together as though she were putting a clothespin over them. Then she opened them on a little burst of breath. "Coley said I wasn't to say a word about it but I'm going to! Kate's as well as I am! It was Will Brent who said she wasn't looking good, and that was just his way of laying her off!"

A stunned silence met this outburst. Then someone said, "You mean . . ."

At that moment the sound of a car came from the driveway outside the window. Agnes Peely cried, "He's come! Doctor Slade!"

The chairman of the flower committee sprang to her feet. "Goodness, let's clear up and get to fixing the flowers. He may come over to the church."

The flowers that had been contributed were waiting in a tub, borrowed from Mrs. Donnell, and filled with water. Their arrangement was a task to be done with reverence. Their loveliness—for gardens had been stripped of their best blooms—commanded a reverence, too. Those who had finished the work they had volunteered to do watched and praised. "They make the church seem holier," whispered Agnes Peely.

A boy appeared in the open doorway, stood there awkwardly, a great bunch of flowers clutched in his hands. Almira Coggin was near by. He made a rush toward her, thrust the flowers out at her, mumbled, "Father Duffy told me to bring 'em," turned and scuttled out.

"Well, look at *this!*" Almira advanced down the center aisle holding the flowers well away from her. "From that priest!" She read aloud from the card tied to the flowers. "To my good friend, John Wendell. With affection and my best wishes. Michael Duffy"

Hattie Higgins spoke behind Almira. "If they're to 'my good friend John,' take 'em over to the parsonage! Let him put them in his room to look at!"

But Martha Purdy took the flowers. "They're the loveliest we have! Look at these lilies! Let's put them where they show best!"

Almira Coggin and Hattie Higgins sat down on the edge of a pew, breathing fast, lips stiff with disapproval. Hattie whispered to Almira, "I'm going home and change and come back. If Doctor Slade comes over and I have a chance I'm going to tell him a few things! Someone should!"

"You're right—I'll go and come back, too," whispered Hattie. They walked out of the church, together.

Nell was late coming home to supper on that Saturday evening. To Susan's relief her father was too preoccupied or too tired to dwell on her absence or to speak of Bill's, for Bill had gone with the Purdy boys up the river to cook wieners over an open fire.

Her father scarcely tasted his food. "I think I may be coming down with a cold. It's possible I won't feel well enough to go to the service tomorrow."

Susan looked at him, startled. "Father! You're the Senior Deacon!"

"True, but it is not very considerate to expose others to a cold. . . ."

"Take some aspirin and go to bed. The bottle's in the cabinet in the bathroom. You *must* go tomorrow. Nell's going to sing. . . ."

He got up from the table. "I've heard her around the house. I will go to bed." He put his hand on Susan's head as he passed her chair. "Thanks for your concern, my dear."

"I'll bring you up some hot lemonade in a little while," said Susan. Her eyes followed him anxiously as he went out of the room. She never had heard him admit to not feeling well.

Nell came in, in a rush. "Gosh, I'm late! And there's rehearsal. . . . What's to eat?"

"It's in the oven."

Nell did not notice that her father was not at the table, and, if he had been there, her ears would have been deaf to anything he might have said, Susan knew, for her face had its look of rapt radiance which meant she was still with Tony.

Nell got her plate of food, came back with it.

"I pressed your white dress," said Susan.

"Thanks, darling, heaps!"

"It wasn't anything—I was pressing my own."

"Won't I look simply terrific in that purple robe?" Nell giggled.

"No one will see you in the loft."

Nell tossed her head, her eyes bright with triumph. "Tony will! I got him to promise he'd come. And I've told him to sit where, if he turns a little sideways and screws his head around, he could see me, for I'm going to tell Peely that I want to stand at the end of the loft to sing. I'll *make* her let me!"

"Everyone will see him there," thought Susan. "Say that Nell is showing off to him!" But this was only a fleeting concern; stronger was a moment's envy in her of Nell who was in love and did not care what anyone thought or said about it!

"Nell, why don't you invite Tony here for supper some evening, so that we can meet him."

"We being Father?" mocked Nell.

"Me, too. Bill. Aunt Debbie . . ."

Nell got up from her chair. "*That* went out with the horse and buggy." She took her half-emptied plate to the kitchen, then came back. "Got to run now. See you later!" She hurried off, singing as she went.

Susan longed to go across to Aunt Debbie's—the house seemed suddenly too empty. No, the emptiness was inside of her, in her heart. But she could not go, for her father might want something. . . .

The hot lemonade—she had forgotten it. She went to the kitchen, put the kettle over, got out a lemon.

Over in the other house Deborah Brent was pressing the blue dress, rather proud of herself for remembering to do it; usually she did not think of the possibility of wrinkles until she put a garment on. She had not gone to church since the Sundays when she went with Dale. She had not thought much, those times, about what she wore, or of the service—her heart had been too full of its own prayer, which was that Dale would find something of the help he so desperately needed in what he was listening to.

She was going tomorrow to hear John preach, Nell sing. "And, probably, I'll be worrying, every minute, over how well each one of them does it—instead of praying for my own soul!"

The catalogues which she had sent for had come, two from Boston, three from New York music schools. She would look them over, after she got into bed. It would not be "interfering" with Nell's life to know what each offered and at what price—she would have a talking point, then, if the need of one came up. She had not forgotten that little frown that had come above Father Duffy's eyes, for a moment, that afternoon.

Before she went upstairs she looked over at Willie's house, where one light was burning. "I *hope* Susan's out somewhere, having a good time!"

CHAPTER XVII

JOHN WENDELL AWAKENED early on this Sunday. He crossed the room to his window and stood there, looking out at the church beyond the intervening yards.

Two hundred years . . .

Two hundred years ago a half-hundred men and women had dedicated this spot to the worship of their God, in their chosen way. With their own hands they had built the first structure—there were in the office, torn, stained, almost indecipherable records of that slow building. One Timothy Pennyproud had come to be their pastor. John wondered what *he* had preached to his congregation—what the others who had followed him had preached. A long line of them . . . "Yet the Word is the same," he reflected.

He was conscious of the tightness which he always had felt during the war before moving into any action. Not fear so much as a waiting and not knowing. . . . What he would say today from the pulpit was ready in his mind, in his heart. It might mean nothing to his people—it might mean much. He had worked with desperate earnestness over it, too, writing pages of notes, discarding, deleting from them until, in the end, it was cut down to the bone. Not a sermon in any sense of the word but it might be more effective for its brevity.

From the adjoining bedroom which Doctor Slade was occupying came the sound of deep snoring. John found it pleasant to hear—the quiet of the house too often emphasized his solitary living. He was reminded, too, of the talk he and Doctor Slade had had before going to bed.

They had sat in the study, comfortably relaxed, each with a pipe. Doctor Slade had said, "Things seem to be in very good shape here, Wendell."

"Yes, they are. Our membership keeps its level. We have no real financial difficulties."

"And now—are you going on in Winfield Marcy's footsteps?"

Doctor Slade asked it quietly. He was a man in his sixties with a homely, lined face and thoughtful eyes which rested a little quizzically on John as John considered his answer.

"I am afraid I cannot do that, in any honesty."

"Are these people going to like that? In communities such as this they become pretty set in their pattern of thinking—they don't like to be disturbed in it."

It flashed into John's mind that someone had complained to Doctor Slade that his sermons were unorthodox, his ideas—perhaps even to speak of other things. There had been opportunity to do so for he had left the Superintendent to talk alone with the women in the church, during the afternoon, and with those of the trustees and deacons who had come to the parsonage during the evening, to meet him. Possibly Doctor Slade was leading up to a warning now.

He asked, "Are you suggesting that I'd better conform to their way of thinking? Or else . . ." John smiled.

"You said a moment ago that you couldn't—in any honesty. And honesty is not a thing to scrap."

"But you *are* thinking I might meet them halfway?" John got up from his chair, took a turn down the room and back. "I'm not sure I could do that. I already have disturbed some of the congregation—I am certain quite a few think that my ideas are unorthodox. . . . I shock their ideas of propriety. When I have any distance to go I ride an old motorcycle I happen to have. Saves buying a car which I cannot afford to do. . . ."

Doctor Slade lifted his hand. "Yes. I heard something of all that. And of some plan of yours to build a gymnasium, something of that

174

sort, here in the village, to be open to everyone in the community. A venture—I quote—'that would take money and time that should be spent on the church.'"

"This village badly needs such a place," asserted John. "Not only to give the young people here opportunities for recreation but to bring the older ones together in a community spirit that has no dividing lines. My plan goes as far as urging our neighbors, even of the colored race, over at the Flats, to use it—if it is ever built!"

He could not tell from the older man's face what he was thinking. Doctor Slade was emptying the burned-out tobacco from his pipe, taking a little time to it. "Choosing the kindest words for his warning to me," thought John, steeling himself to meet it.

Doctor Slade laid the pipe down on the table, got up from his chair, put his hand on John's shoulder.

"Well, good luck, my boy. And goodnight."

It had left John warmed, encouraged. He thought of the talk now, gratefully, as he stood looking out at his church. Slade's was no official "green light" for that was not his to give but John felt less alone and single-handed for it.

He began to dress. He would have time before breakfast to go over into the church—into a closet of stillness where thought was communion with God.

Before its bell stopped ringing every available seat in the church was occupied, everyone was expectant, sitting straighter than usually they did, proud of their participation of this hour as had been those men and women who had gathered here to lay the cornerstone two hundred years ago. A few turned their heads to see who were coming in, a few whispered together, a child whined and was reproved with a low hiss, but for the most part there was a hush over all.

Deborah Brent came in alone. She had not thought of coming with Will or Susan or Bill, at least not more than to think, "It would spoil the whole service for Willie, to have me walk in with him!"

Nor did she go to the pew which the Brents always used, had used back in her girlhood. She saw Clare and Fred and a space next to Clare and slipped into that. She had done this, more often than not, in those days. She knew by the way Clare squeezed her hand that she was thinking that, too.

She noticed then that Susan and Bill sat alone. Where was Willie? It was inconceivable, and worrying, that he should be absent from this service—or even late in coming. The Senior Deacon . . .

Just then a man's voice spoke low, with some hesitation, over her shoulder. "Excuse me—may I—if there's room . . . ?"

She nodded her head, moved closer to Clare, motioned to him with her hand to sit down. Then because he looked so self-conscious and uncertain, she smiled encouragingly at him.

She felt Clare's elbow dig hard into her ribs and knew by that or perhaps by a little vibration that quivered in the air that this stranger was the hated Rudolph Petersen. Whom she should hate, too . . . Though that would be difficult right now when she was crowded up against the man. She could feel the jerk of his arm muscles as he pushed back his cuffs, put a hand to his tie, straightened his coat, took a hymnal from the rack, put it back. From a corner of her eye she could see his face, still a little red.

"He hasn't been inside of a church for a long time," she thought. "A stray sheep for John." Impulsively she bent her head toward him and whispered, "Just do what everybody else does."

He gave her a surprised, grateful look, and Clare at her other side spoke another warning with her elbow.

Organ music, the first notes a little uncertain, floated out over their heads and John and Doctor Slade, followed by the guest ministers, walked up the aisle and took chairs back of the pulpit. Then John rose, stood behind the pulpit, his head bowed. Deborah thought he looked taller in his robe, older.

In simple words he offered thanks for the faith of those men and

176

women who had founded this congregation and a prayer that the faith might abide in the hearts of all gathered now within the walls of the church they had built.

Nell's clear sweet voice fell softly into the hush that followed John Wendell's prayer.

> "Spirit Divine, attend our prayers
> And make this House Thy Home . . ."

"She *can* sing!" Deborah almost spoke aloud in her excitement and pride. "And she sings as though she loves to!" But this was not the moment to dwell on plans. . . .

The service was going ahead in the order arranged by the deacons for this day. Doctor Slade read letters of congratulation from all over the state as well as from the Reverend Neal. The guest ministers offered brief prayers in turn. The congregation stood and sang a hymn, repeated the Lord's Prayer. John read from the Bible.

Deborah noticed with what concentration Rudolph Petersen was listening to it all, his eyes, fixed straight ahead, narrowed a little as if he were trying very hard to get something he wanted very much for himself from every word spoken.

Just so had Dale listened. . . .

"I think I'll start going to that church up at the corner, Deborah."

He had not asked her to go with him but she had gone, Sunday after Sunday, had sat beside him, had prayed her own special prayer. . . .

He had found something—he had gone for a stretch of months, that winter, without drinking. Then his brooding moods had come back to him, darker and darker, and then . . .

"Walk out on me, Deborah! I'm no good!"

But she hadn't—she never had even thought of it.

A considerable stir in the loft brought her out of that past. Four of the men of the congregation had gone forward for the collection plates. Clare pressed closer to her. "It's that chorus, now. Poor Agnes. You know, some of the sopranos dropped out, at the last minute— mad, about Nell. . . ."

But those who were left sang creditably, Nell's above the other voices, and then Nell's alone. *"Who is like unto the Lord our God . . ."*

Rudolph Petersen turned toward Deborah with a little smile. "You could think it was a bird, couldn't you?"

She nodded her head. No, she could not hate this man.

He had taken a bill from his pocket to put in the plate and was folding it into a small square but Deborah had seen the denomination before he hid it. Twenty dollars. Would they throw it out, she wondered, if they knew he had given it?

There was a general shifting and resettling of position as John moved to the pulpit to give his sermon. Deborah resettled herself as much as she could, wedged in between Clare and Rudolph Petersen. She was aware of a little nervousness in her expectancy, as if John, standing there looking out over the congregation, were in a way her own son on trial.

He did not begin at once to speak but stood for a moment tall and straight behind the pulpit rail and let his eyes go over the congregation. Then he repeated a verse of the chapter from the Bible he had read earlier in the service, slowly, a gravity in his voice. "But wilt thou know, O vain man, that faith without works is dead?"

"My goodness, he's going to question their good works," thought Deborah nervously.

"I am going to ask you to think with me for the next several minutes of the meaning of that particular verse, of the challenge in it. Think upon it, as I will, after we leave this service. Search your hearts as I will my own, to know if our Faith is a vital part of our daily lives or—no more than the sounding brass and tinkling cymbals against which the Apostle Paul warns us."

178

Irresistibly Deborah's glance went over the occupants of the pews in front of her. Some plainly had settled down to a quarter of an hour of not thinking about anything. Others appeared attentive. Hattie Higgins and Almira Coggin, side by side and flanked by their husbands, sat very straight. The thin, upright blue feather that adorned Hattie Higgins' hat looked to Deborah like a part of Hattie's upright spine, a sensitized finial. So absorbed was she in this idea and in watching the feather that she lost the thread of John's talk, but caught it again to hear him say:

"We may assert that the works of our Faith speak for themselves. That the evidence of them is all about us. In this church, in the generosity of time and money and effort given. In the sincere prayers we lift within these walls. In the example of Christian living we make to the others in our community. Evidence, yes. But, even so, may we not still be of the vain ones?"

Deborah looked at the feather. Definitely it was quivering.

". . . what of the works of our inner selves, where Faith lives. What of the evidence of that? 'Let your light so shine before men that they may see your good works and glorify your Father which is in heaven.' St. Matthew meant more than coming to service each Sunday, putting money in the collection plates, attending the weekly meetings and suppers, teaching in the Church School. These are good works but not what that admonition meant. Nor is it enough for me to preach to you from this pulpit each Sunday, lead you in prayer, meet in conference with your deacons, be ready at any hour day or night to give you the spiritual help you may seek. No. That light must come from within us. How strong it shines, how far, depends upon us."

Rudolph Petersen shifted his long legs. "He's got a cramp in them," thought Deborah and sympathetically because she felt a cramp in one of her own. Yet he was listening with interest.

"As good-principled law-abiding citizens of this community we obey the commandments we accept as God's, given to us. At least the letter of them . . . But do we, in thought and deed, obey the two 'greatest of these'? First, Love thy God; and second, Love thy neighbor? They are really one for one cannot live in obedience to the first if one does not live in obedience to the second."

Deborah straightened, sniffing the brimstone she had expected because of John's young anger in her kitchen, that June morning. Though the sternness had gone out of his voice; it was only quietly urgent now.

"This love of our neighbors is not the personal affection we know—for family, relatives, friends; rather, it is an outpouring of good will, God will, to all mankind. Its source is not apart from us where we would have to go and tap it, when we wanted to use it—it is within each one of us, nearer than breathing. . . . It is God, inseparable in us."

Clare was breathing audibly and her head was nodding toward Deborah's shoulder, to Deborah's discomfort and distraction. She nudged Clare gently, thinking it would be a pity if she missed any of John's talk when she had said she wanted so much to hear him. But it took a minute or so to rouse Clare and she herself missed what more John had to offer about loving one's neighbor.

When she gave her attention to him again, he was saying, "There is no God will without charity. We are apt to think of charity as the dole, food baskets to the needy, a coin dropped into a tin cup, contributions to institutions, such giving. But reread what Paul said of it in Chapter Thirteen, First Corinthians. Or look it up in the Webster Dictionary which uses fewer words than Paul. I quote it: Charity is the 'act of loving—all men as brothers because they are the sons of God.' Love, again, of which Jesus speaks so often through the Scriptures. The *act* of loving. What makes up that act? Oh, much more than giving food and clothes, a helping hand to the needy. I'd say kindness, kindness in every thought and in every word. Tolerance—a willingness to give to others the benefit of any doubt. Understanding—a seeking to know the real nature of a thing rather than being satisfied with what we think it is. Forgiveness—the forgiveness we ask for ourselves, never forgetting Christ's words spoken from the Cross: '. . . They know not what they do.' "

He paused, letting the echo of his last words sink into the hush of listening. Then he put his hands on the pulpit rail, leaned forward toward his congregation. "And do we—" he spoke sternly again— "do we practice all of that in our daily living? Let us ask that of ourselves. Do we sometimes speak unkindly of one or another? Do we pass judgment on others without knowing? Harbor grudges, rancor? Hold ourselves superior to those in our valley who seek God in ways different from ours? To those of another race, or color? If that is so, neither you nor I have any light to shine before all men. Our faith is but an outer garment we put on, our works but an outward show. We are, alas, of the vain. Again, I ask you to look into your hearts and know. As I will look into mine."

Here John stopped with some abruptness. Deborah saw his hands tighten on the pulpit rail, as if suddenly he needed its support.

Then he lifted them for the benediction. "I am borrowing this thought from a hymn that is in itself a prayer.

"God be in our understanding and in our speaking, in our hearts and in our knowing."

He turned from the pulpit.

As everyone rose and edged into the aisles, Rudolph Petersen spoke to Deborah. "You were very kind, madam. I hope I didn't crowd you too much."

Deborah ignored Clare's touch on her arm. She laughed. "We *were* a little like sardines, weren't we? Did you like the sermon?"

"Was it a sermon? Seemed more as if the man was just talking to us. Maybe that's the way, now. I haven't been to church since I was a youngster. Yes, I liked it. It was straight talk."

Now they were in the aisle, moving slowly, side by side, toward the wide doorway.

"Then tell John Wendell so. He'll be glad you came today. You're Rudolph Petersen, aren't you?"

"Yes. And you?"

"Deborah Brent."

"Brent? *Brent Nails?*" He gave her a startled, and oddly embarrassed look, and Deborah smiled to reassure him.

"I am Will Brent's half-sister. I've just recently come back to Sweethome after forty years away from it, so I don't know much of what's going on."

"I'd like to talk to you sometime, Miss Brent."

Even though she spoke low and there was a murmur of talk all around them, Deborah had no doubt that some had overheard him and would hear her prompt answer. "I'd like to talk to you. Come in some afternoon and we'll talk over coffee. I'm living in the old Brent home on Central Road. You'll know it by its fresh paint—white, of course. And it's Mrs. Brent."

"This week—say, Thursday?"

Treason, Deborah knew well. Yet she said, "Yes, Thursday." She was thinking that she might find out from Rudolph Petersen what Willie refused to tell her. She was thinking, too, that he was one in a million—to be concerned over a competitor he might be driving out of business. And he *had* looked troubled, that moment back. . . .

They reached the door, got outside where there appeared to be an informal reception going on under the tree. Though Deborah did not see Susan—she must have gone out through a side door. Nell —glancing about her, she saw Nell walking down the road with a black-haired boy beside her. Her Tony—had he come to hear her sing? Her own inclination was to slip away, but she must deliver John's sheep over to him, first. The man was looking awkward, again, a little uncomfortable. Perhaps he was aware of the hostile glances turned on him. No one moved to speak to him. Good heavens, she thought, with John's plea still in their ears!

Then John saw her over the shoulders of the men and women who were standing around him and Doctor Slade, gave her a quick smile, left the group and came to her. "Well, how did it go?" he asked boyishly, but with a real anxiety in his eyes.

"It was good, John. I've a lot to think about. I want you to meet Rudolph Petersen."

The two men shook hands. She could go now.

She felt cold glances leveled at her as she went down the walk. Agnes Peely caught her arm. "Wasn't it a *beautiful* service. Weren't you *proud* of Nell? And the sermon—it was simply inspiring. We can't help but be better for it! I'm waiting for a chance to tell John Wendell so!"

"I hope you will tell him," said Deborah.

Hattie Higgins was not waiting. Deborah saw the feather moving ahead of her down the walk, unbending, now.

"There'll be come-backs!" She added, thinking of her friendliness to Rudolph Petersen, "To me as well as John." But she felt no regret for her friendliness.

Susan *had* slipped out of the side door and was hurrying home, not so much because of any anxiety over her father, who had stayed in bed through the morning, as to be alone with this lovely stillness that was in her heart.

She could not have said how much of it was from a newly awakened sense of God in her or of John Wendell. For a fraction of a moment before he started his sermon his eyes had come to her—*her,* with something in them—as if he were giving her something. . . .

And that hymn he had used in his benediction—she had typed it on a card from his notes. Somehow that made it seem especially between the two of them.

She found no one about when she reached home and she stole up to her room and closed the door. For a little while longer she could be alone. Then she would go downstairs, tie on an apron, start dinner —then she would be telling herself that she was silly to think John had even *seen* her when his glance came her way. Reminding herself that, though he had said that evening in front of Agnes Peely's house that he was coming to call, he had not come. . . .

"Tony, it was simply thrilling! I just loved it! But where were you sitting? I looked and I couldn't see you."

"I wasn't in the church. I was hanging round under the window. I heard you, all right."

"Well?"

He let his hand touch hers, his fingers slip up her arm. "I've heard you sing before!"

"This was different! I mean, with all those people listening to me, I was panicky just for a moment and then I wasn't. I'd like to do it again. Tony, you were *sweet* to come!"

"I told you I would, didn't I? Say, can't we drive somewhere?"

They were walking toward the bridge, near which Tony had parked his car.

"Just a little ways . . ." Nell meant to some spot where he could kiss her. "There'd be a fuss if I didn't show up for dinner."

If she had been honest she would have said she would not miss showing up for dinner, to hear Susan, and perhaps Aunt Debbie, if she came over, tell her that she had sung well. Maybe they would say she had sung *beautifully!*

They drove up the hill road. Tony parked the car, kissed her. But there was restraint in his ardor and he held her only for a moment.

"What d'you think—I've a chance at a job at the Petersen plant. Pretty good one, too. Ran into Father Duffy the other afternoon and he tipped me off to it. Seems he's buddies with Petersen and Petersen'd told him, I guess, that he needed men and that he'd like to get them from here in the valley. I suppose Father Duffy's scouting round for

184

them. Petersen's is a good outfit to work for, everyone says—pays well, too."

Nell sat, stunned. *This* was not the future she had held in her mind for Tony—for Tony and herself. This would mean living on here in Sweethome, with everything just as it always had been. Or, worse, in the Flats . . .

But she said, though mechanically, "Wonderful, Tony!"

Tony was scowling. "Maybe I'll take it, maybe I won't."

He was not asking *her* which he should do! Nell felt chilled, left out. Instinctively she drew closer to him. "Whatever you decide, Tony—you love me, don't you?"

"I've told you I do." Tony said it almost irritably. Then his face changed, he took her hand and put it on the steering wheel, pressed his own hard down on it. "You're my girl. Now I'll drive you as near home as you want to go!"

CHAPTER XVIII

WHEN HER TELEPHONE rang before nine o'clock, the next morning, Deborah knew that it was Clare.

Clare wasted no words.

"Deb, how *could* you!"

"Hello, Clare. How could I what?"

"Be nice to that Swede! Even speak a word to him. I tried to warn you!"

"Why shouldn't I speak to him? I thought that was the approved thing to do when a stranger sits down next to you in church. Make him feel at home. . . ."

"But he's different. . . ."

"How?" Though her indignation was rising, Deborah found some pleasure in forcing Clare to say in what way Rudolph Petersen was different.

"You know perfectly well! He's a foreigner and he didn't have to move his plant here to this valley. He's likely to ruin the Brent Nail Works. I should think *you* of all people would feel the way everyone else here does about him!"

"This is a free country—he could move his plant to any place he chose. And it may not be entirely his fault if the Brent Nail Works is ruined."

"I just can't understand you, Deborah. Anyway, you didn't have to walk out of church with him. Everyone is going to talk about that. Yesterday afternoon . . . But I shouldn't say over the telephone what Almira said about it."

186

"Don't bother—I can imagine. What did you think of John Wendell's sermon—at least what you heard of it?" Deborah could not resist adding that.

"Wasn't it dreadful in me to go to sleep? Did I make any funny noises? Fred says I do, sometimes, when I go off in a chair. I *did* hear a little of it. He's got a good voice. But Hattie Higgins is furious! Says he was insulting to all of us, saying that our works were show. . . ."

"I think he asked us to ask ourselves—as he would ask himself—if our works were only an outer show."

"Well, some of the women work awfully hard for the church. Hattie's one. She's saying John Wendell ought to apologize to them. She's going to take it up with the deacons. And she's sort of a leader—gets the others to think the way she does."

"I can believe that. Clare, I've some ironing to do. Glad you called —I'll stop in some day soon."

"Poor John," thought Deborah as she set up the ironing board. It had taken courage on his part to say what he had said from the pulpit. And, after all, he only had urged the men and women listening to him to *think*. . . .

It was not easy to do that particular kind of thinking, Deborah knew, because, moved to it by John's plea, she had tried to. After supper, the evening before, she had composed herself in a chair in the parlor, shut her eyes, the better to summon up the inner self she was to search and question.

"Are you tolerant?"

"Well, you've had to put up with a lot!"

"Understanding?"

She dwelt a moment on that. "Are you? I don't know! Honestly, I don't know. . . ."

"Forgiving?"

Suddenly Nadine Petty had sprung into her mind. Nadine, whom she had vowed never, never to forgive. Nadine had come to Portland to spend several weeks with her sister, Mrs. Mulford, for whom Deborah was working. She was Deborah's age, pretty, gay, spoiled. Deborah had loved those times when she sauntered into the kitchen, perched herself atop of the small stepladder and talked to her. It was mostly about the fun she had in the college town which was her home, of the dates she was having in Portland, but it was friendly enough to warm Deborah's lonely heart. One of the dates was a dance. Mr. and Mrs. Mulford had gone out for the evening and Nadine had come to Deborah's room to show her the new dress she was wearing. Deborah saw the bracelet on her arm—Mrs. Mulford's, a circle of rhinestones and sapphires, too precious to wear often. Nadine had not had the time to put it back where she had found it the next morning before Mrs. Mulford missed it and began a frantic search for it. To Debbie's surprise, Nadine said nothing about having worn it and made a pretense of helping her sister search for it. Then she had come downstairs with it in her hand, said she had found it under the mattress in Debbie's room. Debbie could do no more than deny she had put it there for she knew Mrs. Mulford would not take her word against Nadine's. Mrs. Mulford had been very distressed. "I'm not going to call the police, Debbie. Until now, in these four years you've worked for us, I've never known you to be anything but honest. But you must pack your clothes and go, at once." Nadine had stood there, not speaking. *"I'll never, never forgive you!"*

She had had money enough saved to live on in a meager way for a few weeks. Then she had got the job with the Welcome Center. A temporary job at first and they had not asked for references. And after a few weeks they had put her on full time. Her work was calling on newcomers to the city, taking gifts to them of milk, butter, brands of cereals, other packaged foods, telling them about schools and churches, parks and such. "Make them feel the city's glad they've come here," she had been instructed. She had worked hard to do so, remembering the awful loneliness for her and Paul in Etna. And though she rarely saw any of them a second time, it had seemed as

188

if she were making friends. Soon Nadine was forgotten. Bringing it all back, now, seeing in her mind Nadine standing there and not speaking, it had no reality—no hurt.

"If I'd known at the time that it would be like that," she had reflected, settling her head more comfortably against the wing of the chair. Then, almost the next moment, she had dozed off.

Now, with the morning sun filling the homely old kitchen, the basket of ironing at her feet, she had to admit to herself that the inner Deborah she had tried to search was as little known to her as would be some woman down the street with whom she had never bothered to have more than a bowing acquaintance. Realizing that, why should she—or John—expect the Hattie Higginses and the Almira Coggins to find their inner selves in a twinkling?

Of more and immediate concern was the true nature of Willie's indisposition on Commemoration Sunday. She had gone over to the other house the afternoon before to ask Susan how he was and Susan had said no more than that he was staying in bed to fight off a cold. This morning she had seen him start off from the house, afoot, for the plant at the usual time. "There's something funny about it," she said aloud, frowning down at the cuff she was pressing.

She would know more about Willie's affairs, perhaps, after she talked to Rudolph Petersen on Thursday. "I'll make some of those Swedish cakes for him—the kind the jacks used to like so well!" At once she was aghast at herself—worrying about Willie and planning what she'd feed to his enemy, almost in the same breath! Clare had a point in what she had said. In all loyalty to Will she should feel toward this man as the others in Sweethome did—see him a foreigner and therefore suspect, an intruder, a serious threat to the Brent Works on which depended the livelihood of most in the community. Ally herself with them and their prejudices.

"I could write him a note and tell him not to come. I believe I will. Though I *did* like him yesterday . . ."

Her ironing finished, folded, put away, she was in the mood to find

189

other and strenuous things to do around the house. Even though most of what she did did not really need doing. Rom's empty room—she called it his—was in order, yet she dusted it, shook out the rag rugs, wiped up the floor boards. After lunch she baked some cupcakes to take over to Susan for their supper. "Young Bill will eat half of them!" Later in the afternoon, still disturbed in mind, she went out into the yard and began to dig weeds up from the border.

John Wendell swung into the driveway on his motorcycle. He looked tired, she thought, as he came up to her.

"Too busy to quit for a few minutes?"

"Indeed not. The weeds will keep. I was only working on them as an excuse to be out of doors. I'm glad to stop now. Let's sit down under the tree."

They sat down. The canvas chairs were in the shade and comfortable, and she noticed how he relaxed his long length tiredly into the ease of his chair.

"Well?" she asked, gently.

"You mean yesterday, I suppose. I don't know. Maybe I talked myself out of a job, maybe I didn't. Slade and the guest ministers spoke as if they approved what I said, but that may have been out of politeness. Lemuel Sims said I handed it to them pretty straight and whether that was approval or disapproval, I can't know—yet. He was the only one of the deacons who spoke to me after the service."

"Will had a cold," put in Deborah and then wondered why she had said it.

"I'm sorry, I noticed he wasn't there. Two or three of the women professed to be moved by my appeal. Others . . ." A slight smile twitched the corners of his mouth. "Mrs. Donnell wore her extra-severe look this morning which I know now is the kind she saves to give me after some particularly improper conduct on my part. As she was out through Sunday afternoon and evening I suspect she was sharing her opinions with others."

Yes, Hattie Higgins, Almira Coggin, no doubt. One or both of them had called on Clare—poor Clare, who could not get about! But Deborah did not say anything to confirm his suspicion. Instead she leaned toward him and patted his hand.

"If you've started only one or two thinking, John—you told me I should be satisfied with winning over only two. Be patient—give the others a chance. There're habits of thinking just as there are in living and it's not easy to break habits, you know!"

He gave her a quick smile. "You should be reminding me to practice what I preach. I'll try. . . . Anyway, I may have cornered two stray sheep—even three. I ran into your niece Nell this morning, and took the opportunity to tell her how much her singing added to the service. Then I had the sudden inspiration to ask her if she wouldn't sing a solo every Sunday. To my surprise she said she would—she appeared very pleased over it. Now I have to take it up with Mrs. Peely."

"You're thinking the girl may sing her way into salvation?"

John laughed. "There are many gates, you know."

Deborah was glad to hear him laugh, to see the tired lines on his face smooth out. She was touched by his coming to her in his discouraged mood; sharing with her, now, his pleasure in his three stray sheep. "And the others?" she asked.

"A Mrs. D'Arby from the Flats. Her husband runs a bar and grill. She came to the service yesterday and waited after it for a chance to speak to me. She spoke with surprising frankness. She belonged to a Congregational church in some Maine town where she grew up but after she married and moved to the Flats she never came across to this church—said that from things she heard she did not think she'd be welcome here. Then when she read in the paper about this particular service she decided to get up her nerve and come. Says she's coming again. There are other Protestants on the Flats whom I've wanted to reach and it may be I can through her. My third is Rudolph Petersen. Thanks for introducing him to me. Seems Father Duffy—they're good friends—had urged him to come and he says he is coming again. He's going to stop in at the parsonage some afternoon soon."

"He's half my sheep," thought Deborah, smiling. Then she sobered, reflecting quickly that Rudolph Petersen probably would have as cold a welcome into the congregation as the woman from the Flats whose husband ran a bar and grill. But she would not speak of this to dampen John's satisfaction. She said, warmly, "Good, John. Now let's go in and celebrate with something cold to drink. I'll call Susan over—she must be home from the plant by this time."

John got to his feet. "No. Don't call her over."

Deborah looked up at him, surprised, puzzled. "Why, John, what's this? I thought you liked Susan's company! You've seemed to . . ."

"I do. I've found that I more than like it. That's the trouble." His face flushed deeply as he made his blunt admission.

"What on earth are you trumping up in your mind?" demanded Deborah. "If you like Susan, more than like her—she's a fine girl . . ."

"Have it said through Sweethome that I am rushing a daughter of one of the deacons to further my own interests?"

"You haven't minded what anyone says about your old motor-cycle—and a few other things," countered Deborah with spirit.

"That talk does not involve Susan."

She saw the set of his chin. "I'd like to give you a good shaking, John Wendell! Truly I would. Here, help me up—we'll have our drinks by ourselves if you say we must." She spoke crossly, but there was amusement in her eyes, and fondness, too.

He gave her a hand, drew her up out of the canvas chair. "I'll take a rain-check on the celebration. I've some boys coming to the parsonage at five o'clock. We're going to organize a baseball team."

"Of which I suppose you will be the coach."

"That's the idea—if I can get them interested in it. We put the hour at five so that your nephew Bill could be in on it. Aunt Debbie . . ." He gave her an appealing look. "About Susan—can't you see that I must wait until I am reasonably secure in my position here?"

"And meanwhile?"

"I must take that chance."

"Well, go along to your boys. And come again."

He rode off and she went into the house. In the kitchen she gave a long sigh. Yesterday, after John's talk, she had felt such a calm in her and, now, it was gone—*nothing,* not even a nice love affair, promised to go as it should.

John was right, of course, there would be talk and plenty if he openly courted Susan before the deacons gave him any kind of a contract. *But would Susan understand?*

Thinking of Susan, she remembered the cupcakes, put them on a plate and went to the other house.

Susan was in the kitchen tying on an apron. "Oh, thanks, Aunt Debbie!" she cried when Deborah set the plate down on the table. "I was wondering what I could get together for dessert. You're grand to think of it!"

"Not grand at all—you know me, I'm happiest when I'm cooking. Where's Nell?" Nell should be getting supper, she thought. Susan looked tired, tears seemed just back of her eyes.

"Up in her room. She'll be down in a minute. I don't know where Bill is. Father hasn't come from the plant yet."

Deborah did not ask about his cold. She had a conviction that Susan thought of the cold as she did, and she did not want to put the girl to the pain of an answer.

She asked, "Had a busy day?"

Susan went to the refrigerator, came back with a pan of baked beans in her hands. "No. I wish—oh, I wish I were terribly busy but I'm not. Only—I'm there when Father does need me." Now the tears were in her eyes. "Aunt Debbie, I don't know what is going to happen! I heard Father and Coley Coggin talking—they're giving more of the men long vacations—and you know what that means. I don't care about myself, or Nell, or even Bill—*we* can get jobs doing something. It's Father, at his age. I mean—if he has to close the plant."

"Perhaps one has a courage of a different kind—at your father's age," said Deborah. It sounded well and it was all that came to her to say, but as she said it she wondered if it were true with Willie.

But Susan did not seem to hear her. Her eyes blazing back of their tears, she burst out, with a passion that startled Deborah. "I wish that horrible Petersen never had come to the valley. I hate him!"

Deborah said nothing for it was not a moment for her to speak in defense of the man or to argue with Susan that the Brent plant was run down, outdated, and well might go to ruin without any competitor near by.

Susan dashed a hand across her eyes. "I'm sorry I let go like that—it was terribly childish! You'll stay and have supper with us, Aunt Debbie?"

"Not tonight—I've some left-overs that would weigh on my conscience if I didn't eat them. Some other evening . . ."

She kissed Susan before she left her. She had again a strong desire to shake John Wendell. Susan, too. Susan minded talk too much. If the girl had a love affair to think about she would not be looking so strained, so worried. She would not be hating anyone. Like Nell, she'd be living in the clouds.

Back in her own kitchen she did not get the left-overs out at once. "No hurry!" It was a soothing thought. She sat down in the rocking chair she had brought down from one of the bedrooms and put by the window through which she could look out on the yard. "It'll be nice to have it here when I am tired," she had told Susan.

She was tired now, in her head as well as her bones. Too much was happening. No, not happening—for when things happened, there they were for you to know about. And all this with Willie was in the dark—you couldn't put your fingers on it.

"I *will* let Petersen come! Everyone—Susan may see it as terribly disloyal but I'll just have to take that."

Then she gave a small laugh. "You certainly never dreamed, Deborah, that you'd get into all this when you came back here."

She had thought she was contentedly settled for all time in the apartment into which she moved after her divorce from Roger—its anonymity, to open a door that was exactly like the seven other doors along the narrow ochre-walled hallway, close it on herself, was exactly what she wanted after living Roger's kind of life.

"But it wasn't really living," she declared to herself now. "Doing nothing more than look out for yourself! *Just thinking of yourself!*"

Young Bill came up the porch steps. She depended on him now to stop at Higgins' for her mail every day. He had letters in his hand, the New York *Times* for which she had subscribed.

"Come in, Bill. Thanks—put them on the table. Did you get a baseball nine lined up?"

His thin face which had worn a sullen look the few times she had seen him lately, lighted up. "Gee, yes! And it's going to be *good!* After we've practiced some we'll challenge the Norfolk Cubs, maybe."

"You've never had a team before?"

"We could've but no one bothered. Got to go now and eat chow quick. The Purdy fellows and I want to do some pitching over in their yard."

"Come in Saturday—I'll have some gardening for you to do."

Bill went out whistling and it was a good sound to Deborah's ears. "That's the way a boy should feel!"

She looked over her letters. Nothing of any interest—nothing from Rom. "You'd think he'd write me a line," she said aloud and realized that she was a little hurt, as well as worried, because she heard nothing from him. Well, that was part of living . . .

CHAPTER XIX

DEBORAH BAKED her coffee cake on Thursday morning, even though she was not certain in her mind, as she sifted and mixed and stirred, that she should be going to such lengths for this man; somehow it made her disloyalty—if it was that—the greater. But she went on, arguing with herself that as long as she was letting him come, she must feed him and feed him something he'd like.

"And, anyway, I like the smell of it baking!"

She was putting it in the oven when Martha Purdy came up the steps of the porch, a bunch of flowers in her hand.

"Come in, come in," Deborah called out. "Nice to see you."

Martha Purdy had come over before, as informally as she came now, stayed a few minutes, gone away. It was the kind of neighborliness Deborah liked, and it was the only neighborliness she had met as yet—she did not count Julia's and Win's call as such. She sensed a sort of championing in the younger woman's manner toward her which, though she felt no slightest need of it, warmed her.

"Pull up a chair. Are the flowers for me? They're lovely—thanks. Mind putting them in that pitcher? My hands are sticky with dough."

Martha filled the pitcher with water, put the flowers into it, sat down at the table. She sniffed at the air with a look of delight.

"Swedish coffee cake," said Deborah and instantly wondered if Martha might not guess why she was making it. But Martha only said, "H'm! If it tastes as good as it smells! I wish I could bake things like that—but I simply go dumb when I face a recipe. And you can imagine where it puts me when the women here talk about their pies and cakes!"

"But you can make a garden grow. By the way, have you ever seen Father Duffy's garden over on the Flats? It's beautiful."

"No, I haven't. But I saw the flowers he sent over to John Wendell for the service." She added, with a sudden flash of spirit, "I'm going to drive over there someday. Do you think he'd mind?"

"He'd be delighted. He's very proud of what he grows."

"I get downright mad sometimes, Mrs. Brent, at the feeling here toward the people on the Flats—oh, a lot of other prejudices. I suppose it's because I didn't grow up here. But *you* did—and I don't believe you have them!"

"Probably what were born in me were knocked out of me, living in other places."

"It's so *narrow!*" protested Martha. "I've been keeping my mouth shut when they go on, until just lately. . . . Walt says I might as well save my breath, but it makes me feel better to speak out!"

This spirit could be put to good use, thought Deborah, smiling. She looked in at her cake, came back to her chair. "A woman from the Flats came to church last Sunday. For the first time—she'd hesitated to come before, thought she might not be welcome over here. And she's promised to come again. John Wendell is very pleased about it, hopes to reach others through her. If . . ."

Martha Purdy leaned forward excitedly. "I know what you mean! If she isn't frozen out. I think I saw her—she was sitting way in the back. Walt and I were a little late and we sat in the back. I knew she wasn't from Sweethome. What's her name?"

"D'Arby."

"I'll look for her next Sunday—if she's there I'll speak to her, give her a welcome. I feel just like doing it!"

"Her husband runs a bar and grill over there," said Deborah.

"Whew!" breathed Martha Purdy. Then she laughed. "Well, that will make my crusade more exciting!"

197

She went away, in a few minutes. Deborah rearranged her flowers, took them into the parlor, put them on the cobbler's bench. She had tidied the room the day before but she looked it over carefully now for a sign of disorder or dust. She would keep this call of Rudolph Petersen's very formal—she would use the old fluted silver coffee service, the gold-banded plates and cups, which had been her grandmother's and which Mary had left here in the house. They'd talk of the weather and such—perhaps of last Sunday's service—until an opening came to speak of nails. She'd wear the new, lady-like dress. . . .

While she was eating some lunch she made a list of food with which to stock up for Rom's return. He'd need a lot of feeding after this ordeal he was going through. Steaks—she could keep two or three in the freezing compartment of the Frigidaire until he came. She would have to go to the bank for money, first, but she had time. . . .

She was standing at one of the narrow counters in the Winsted bank, writing out a check when she saw Willie. He was coming out of the president's office, shutting the door quietly behind him. There were only a few people in the outer room of the bank, yet he walked across it without seeing her. Walked stiffly, his eyes ahead, his head up. Yet Deborah was shocked, terribly moved. Never had she seen defeat so written on any human face, naked there in spite of his proud bearing.

"He's been asking Richard Prouet for a loan—and been refused!"

This conviction made her ashamed to take the roll of bills which the teller pushed toward her through the little opening of his cage. To buy beef steaks when Will needed money—desperately needed it. She turned on a sudden impulse and went to the door of the president's office.

She had come to him before to consult him on money matters of her own. The first time he had told her that he remembered her as a girl. There had been a twinkle in his eyes when he said it. "My folks lived on a farm three miles east of Sweethome." He had said, too, "I heard you'd come back, Miss Brent." "Even here in Winsted!" Deborah had thought. She had had to explain that she was "Mrs. Brent"—and divorced. But he had been friendly, approachable, not in the least like other bank presidents she had had to see.

He smiled at her now when she appeared in his door, pushed some papers away from in front of him. "Come in, Mrs. Brent. Sit down. What can I do for you?"

Deborah sat down. "Nothing for me—yes, some advice about an investment I have in mind. In the Brent Nail Works." She tried to keep her tone business-like, unworried.

His face sobered instantly. He gave her a quick look, then dropped his eyes to the paper cutter he picked up from the desk.

"You saw your brother just leave my office."

"Yes. I did."

"Does he know you have come to me?"

"No. He didn't see me when he went out."

"This investment—you call it that. It's really a loan of money?"

"I suppose so. The truth is, Mr. Prouet, I know very little of Will's business affairs; he isn't one to talk about them—to anyone. But I do know that he needs money and I have it to give him. And if it tides him over this crisis or whatever it is, isn't that an investment?"

Richard Prouet shook his head, with a slight smile.

"I took you for a harder businesswoman than that, Mrs. Brent. Guess blood-ties count."

He was silent for a moment, then said gravely, "I must tell you, Mrs. Brent, that to give your brother any amount of money as his situation is now would be throwing it away."

"I can spare it," said Deborah.

He ignored that. He leaned a little forward toward her in his chair. "I had to refuse Will a loan, just now. I hated to do it. We've been friends, good friends, for a long time. We've done his banking for a long time. I've—well, tried to give him some advice. I've been worried about his affairs, though they did not affect the bank or me personally. He's been going on too-thin ice. And at present . . ."

Deborah interrupted him. She had to ask it. "Is it this Petersen plant that has caused this present crisis?" If Richard Prouet said it was—well, there was time to telephone to Rudolph Petersen not to come.

"Yes and no. No, I'd say. Competition has been eating into Will's orders for some time. But he's refused to see it. To recognize that times have changed—that small plants like his have to fight the lower costs of production of the bigger plants. I'm talking frankly, Mrs. Brent, and I hope I don't offend you. If your brother has to close down, it will be his own fault—the result of his own short-sightedness. Some years back, in fact when the branch of the rail-road was built through the Flats, I advised him to move his plant over there—he could have gotten the land for next to nothing. Enlarge it—he wouldn't listen. Three generations—or is it four?—had run the plant where it is, as it is—that was in his mind, I think."

"Yes," said Deborah. Then she asked, "You think a shutdown is—inevitable?"

"Without money with which to carry on—pay the men. I am sorry to say that he has drawn out most of his savings account here. And even with money forthcoming—as long as he refuses to modernize his works . . ." The banker looked down at his hands. "This is very much out of order, Mrs. Brent, saying all of this to you. But if it will show you the folly of loaning or giving any money to your brother, just now. . . . You have your own future to take care of."

"I can take care of that," said Deborah. She got to her feet. "Perhaps Will can pull through—his way."

"We'll hope he can." The banker held out his hand. "Anything I can do for you, any time, don't hesitate to come to me."

"Thanks."

She did her marketing, though with little heart in it—it was worse with Willie than she had guessed, worse than he knew, himself, perhaps. She drove home, put her food away. She would not have time to change her dress, but she forgot that she had intended to do so.

On the minute of four, Rudolph Petersen's car turned into the driveway. Big, shining with chromium, pale gray—it seemed to flaunt its owner's importance.

Though he wore no such air—he had got out and was looking at the house with something of the shyness, the uncertainty, he had shown in church, the Sunday before.

"He doesn't know which door to go to," thought Deborah. She stepped out onto the porch and called to him. "This way—no one ever uses the front door. Come in."

He stood in the kitchen looking around it interestedly, a smile slowly breaking on his face. "Nice," he said, then. "I never have been in a kitchen like this—to remember, at least."

"I do have a parlor . . ." said Deborah.

"But couldn't we sit out here? I like the smell of it!"

"Swedish coffee cake."

"*You* made it?"

"Of course. I learned how from a jack in a lumber camp in northern California."

"You lived in a lumber camp?"

"Indeed I did. For seven years. I loved it!"

Deborah saw his slightly narrowed, very blue eyes center on her now in interest. "My father was foreman in a logging camp in northern Minnesota. I grew up in the woods there." He said it as though it gave them something in common.

She remembered the formality she had planned—and here they were, sitting at the kitchen table, talking about themselves.

He looked absurdly big in the small stiff-backed chair, but he was completely at ease. And Deborah felt completely at ease, too.

She put the coffee over, sat down across from him.

201

He asked, "You were born here?"

She liked the directness with which he satisfied his curiosity. But, no, it was interest. . . .

"Yes. My father before me. His father built the house."

"I was born in an old house like this. My mother's home—in Jämtton, Sweden. She was Hilda Johnson and there had been Hilda Johnsons before her back through several generations. I was only three when we came over here but sometimes I think I remember the place—the woods, a little lake near it. The water in the lake was very blue. There was a small island in the middle of it. My mother often took me there in a boat to picnic. . . . But perhaps I only remember it from the stories she always was telling me about it all. She was very homesick after we came here. Something vital was gone from her life. She could not adapt herself to a different way of living. She died within a few years."

"You never went back?" asked Deborah.

"No. The old place had been sold. I didn't want to see it with strangers living in it."

"You did not go on with lumbering." She did not make it a question for it was too obvious that he had not.

"The outfit failed. Good thing for me that it did. I was thrown on my own. I went to St. Paul and got a job of a sort. The only schooling I'd had was when I walked three miles to a district school, but it was enough to get me into a vocational school, of a sort. I went to night classes." He laughed. "All that was a very long time ago, Mrs. Brent."

But it had made him the man he was now, reflected Deborah, swiftly appraising the set of his shoulders, the strong lines of his face. A hard face, it could be, under certain circumstances, she acceded, but it wasn't now. . . .

She poured the coffee, cut the coffee cake, put a generous slice on his plate. He bit into it with boyish relish. "It *is* a treat. . . ." She had made the coffee strong and he liked that. He liked the pleasantness of the big kitchen, she knew, by the way his glance kept going over it, again and again. No, she could not think of him as the monster that Sweethome saw him.

"I'm looking for a home here in Sweethome," he told her presently.

"Yes, I've heard that you were."

"I want a place—to own it, live in it and know it's mine, die in it. I never have had one. I've lived in rooming houses and hotels ever since I walked away from the logging camp. It's been a lonely way to live. Cities are lonely—people all around you, yet you know no one. That was one thing that drew me to this valley—the thought that I could settle here, for the rest of my life, know real neighbors. Perhaps that was the effect on me of those stories of my mother's. To belong—in the way she belonged back in Jämtton."

Deborah cut another piece of cake and put it on his plate. "The poor man—he doesn't realize . . ."

She said, after a moment, "You don't know much about communities—such as Sweethome?"

He gave her a puzzled look. "No. Is there something I should know?"

She had got herself into this—she had to go on. "One thing—you can't *belong* to a place like this just by *wanting* to. Or by buying and settling into the biggest house here."

"You mean, I'd remain an outsider?"

"For a time—yes, I'm afraid you would. Maybe always. I don't think such an attitude is peculiar to this village or to New England villages—I daresay you'd find it in any small community. It may be some instinct of self-protection. I'm—I'm suspect. I ran away from here, a long time ago, and because of the circumstances of that and those which followed, I forfeited my belonging. I can't even claim this house in which I was born as really mine."

He looked astonished, and as if he did not want to believe her. She was spoiling this dream he'd been cherishing for some time, she knew. Well, she might as well go the whole way.

203

"You see, you've one big count against you right at the start. Over half of the men of Sweethome work at the Brent plant. Their fathers did before them. It's their security. Now, by the talk, it is seriously threatened and they lay that at your door. Unjustly, perhaps—but it's only human in them to do so."

He gave her the same troubled, regretful look he had given her as they walked out of the church and she marveled at it as she had then. He said, "I'm sorry about this situation, Mrs. Brent. Of course, there is competition—I've had that to deal with for the past fifteen years. It's part of manufacturing—you have to be alive to it every minute, if you are to keep going. . . ."

"And that's what Willie hasn't been," thought Deborah, grimly.

He went on. "I knew of the Brent plant before I settled over on the Flats. But I'd had competitors all around me, there in New Jersey. They're thick here in this state. But I did not know until a short time ago that your brother's business was pretty well shot— was that before I came. I was disturbed to hear it, but I can't, in any fairness to myself, take the whole blame for it. Though I can under-- stand how the people here—even you, perhaps . . ." He stopped, gave her a little smile. "No, I don't believe you are damning me."

"I'm not," said Deborah, simply.

He emptied his coffee cup before he went on.

"Has your brother told you that I went to him and suggested a merger?"

Deborah's face glowed. "A merger? Petersen and Brent?"

Rudolph Petersen laughed. "We didn't get as far as that. In fact, we didn't get off to any start on it. Your brother squashed it by a look even before he spoke a word."

"He would," said Deborah. Yet she was wishing she knew what to say to make this man understand that Willie's refusal was all part of living in a place like Sweethome.

"I got out of his office before he threw me out."

Deborah crossed to the stove, thinking, "He doesn't need to worry about Willie's business—he could just not care. And he *does* care. . . ."

She came back to the table, filled their cups. "There *is* a house you can buy—the old Hurrell place. It's not right in the village, on the hill road back, but near enough. The old furniture is still in it. You could settle right in—at least after some cleaning. I heard Ham Higgins say at the church supper that he has the key now."

Rudolph Petersen gave her a broad smile. "You're suggesting that I dare to settle here?"

Deborah laughed. "If you want to." She remembered what Clare had said about her own return. "I dared to come back!"

"We'd be rather in the same boat, then, wouldn't we? That gives me courage. I'll stop in at Higgins' store someday."

At the door, he turned and looked back over the kitchen. "This has been the pleasantest afternoon I've had in a long time. May I come again?"

Deborah said, "Yes," and felt like saying, "Whew," in Martha Purdy's manner, as she watched the big car back out of the driveway. It was well after five—Susan might see it; the neighbors across the road. . . . It would be known all through the village by tomorrow. Yet she could summon not the slightest compunction for spending the afternoon with him. For jumping within two hours into an intimacy which, with others, would take months or more to reach.

Late, the next afternoon, Susan came over with her newspaper.

"Bill forgot to stop in with it and he's gone off with the Purdy boys." She put it down on the table without looking at Deborah, and Deborah knew by her manner that she knew. . . .

"Susan . . ."

For Susan had moved to go. She turned. "Aunt Debbie, how *could* you!" Her voice shook with feeling.

"You mean—let Rudolph Petersen come here."

"Yes. When you know . . ."

"Susan, have you forgotten what John Wendell said last Sunday? About trying to know the real nature of a thing rather than accepting it as what we think it is? Or something like that . . ."

"But we *do* know this," said Susan. "Everyone does! And you're one of the family! It's—it's awfully hard for me to understand."

It came to Deborah's lips to tell Susan, word for word, what Richard Prouet had said, then she remembered it had been said in confidence. She controlled her voice to a quiet tone. "Perhaps sometime you'll see it differently, Susan. Until then I wish you would trust my judgment about what is loyal and what isn't. Thanks for bringing me my paper. Can't you stay and eat supper with me? Isn't Nell home?"

"Not yet. No, I must go back. Father . . . Some other time, thanks." Susan went quickly out of the kitchen.

Deborah watched her cross the yards, saddened that this had come between them—she realized how fond she had grown of Susan. "And there isn't anything I can do!"

Though a few days later an idea sprang, full size, into her head. She was coming back to the house from Higgins' store—where Ham Higgins had inquired, with overinterest, after Willie's cold—and paused, as she almost always did, on the walk in front of it, to look at it in its fresh paint. Then . . . "I'll ask Willie to sell the old house to me. He'll have the money he needs—and I'll have the house."

She should give it a little sober thought, of course, so, the next day, she spent quite a bit of time in the rocking chair, trying to think practically about it. At the old desk in the parlor, going over bank statements, putting down figures. But most of the time in the rocking chair and at the desk she found her thoughts dwelling on the pleasantness of spending the rest of her life right here. Settled— Rudolph Petersen would understand how she felt! *A place that's your own, to live in, to die in.*

She knew nothing of the value of the house; she would have to accept the price Willie put on it. Wait, too, until Willie appeared to be in a talking mood.

Young Bill precipitated the moment. So that he could earn pocket money and she could see a little of him without his father around Deborah saved small jobs for him to do evenings and Saturdays, some of which he did and some of which he didn't do, and most of which she would have enjoyed doing herself. He came in after supper, an evening or so later, to tell her he would not be over the next day, which was Saturday.

His face was glum. "I got to stay at the plant, Father says. And we fellows were going fishing!"

"That's tough luck, Bill."

"And why does he make me stick round over there? He's given most of the men vacations. And they don't have to go to any old school in a few weeks! You should hear 'em talk, Aunt Debbie. Guess they think I haven't any ears or maybe they don't care but if my father heard 'em—well, he'd know what they think he is!"

"Bill, you must not listen. . . ."

"I'd have to be deaf. Anyway, you hear it outside. The Purdy boys hear it and they ask me questions. . . . Aunt Debbie, do y'know what I'm going to do if the old plant fails?" His gloom lightened. "I'm going out West to some ranch, get a job as a cowboy. . . ."

She was shocked at his lack of concern for his father. She said, to say something, "They're not like they are in the movies, Bill. They're mostly hoboes."

"Well, I'll go somewhere. . . . And it won't be back to school."

"Is he talking that way, to Susan, adding to her worry?" Deborah wondered as the boy went off. Fifteen years old . . .

After supper she phoned over to the other house, asked Susan to call her father. "Willie, can you come over for a few minutes? There's something I want to talk over with you."

Let him think it was something about the old house. "Well, it is."

He came very soon, though there was some unwillingness in his approach, in his brief greeting. He looked as he had when he walked out of the bank. "Let's sit here in the kitchen, Willie. I think it's the nicest room in the whole house. I like this big table—see, I gave it a good sandpapering. Think of the meals that we've eaten off it!"

He made a slight move of his hand that said he had no intention of thinking of them. "What did you want to talk over?" His tone was brusque.

"I want to buy this old house, Willie. At your price . . ." She sat back. That was enough to say.

She saw a look of swift calculation touch his expression. "He's thinking that it will bring in the money he needs." Then it went away, his lips tightened, the little vein in his temple stood out.

He said, cuttingly, "To bring your men to. To cause more talk here in the village. Heaven knows there's enough about you, as it is! No, I have more respect for my father's wishes where you were concerned than to consider such a thing!"

At the moment Deborah was more startled than angered or hurt, for he had looked just like Sarah Brent when he spoke, had spoken in Sarah Brent's voice.

"Well, that's that," she said without knowing she said it.

Will Brent got to his feet. "Is there anything more?"

"No, I guess there's nothing more."

"I'll say goodnight, then."

"Goodnight, Willie."

She sat on at the table, her eyes on the chair in which Willie had been sitting. As if he—no, Sarah Brent—were still there. She felt terribly cold, though the night was warm. "My father's wishes where you were concerned . . ." It was that, not what Willie had said about the talk or that the village might be wishing her away, that made her shiver. Disowned—the loneliness of it closed in on her, more acute now than she had felt it, in Etna, those years ago, when, day after day, she had looked for a letter from her father, or even when she was informed of his will.

She roused, looked over the kitchen which she had come to love. "Well, you've paid rent up to the middle of September, Debbie. Willie can't put you out before then!" She said it aloud and a little loudly, to push the lonely feeling away from her.

CHAPTER XX

"NELL, YOU WILL clean the kitchen floor today?"

Nell had just come down from her room. Susan was ready to start for the plant. The breakfast dishes were washed and put away.

Nell took that as a reproach because several times she had let them wait until close to suppertime. Susan's tone, too, as a reproach that she had not mopped up the kitchen floor yesterday.

"Maybe," she answered and reached up into a cupboard for a box of dry cereal.

As Susan went off, Nell shut the cupboard door with a little bang.

"She needn't *nag* me! She ought to know I'll do things when I get ready to!" She threw a dark look over the kitchen floor. Susan thought it had to be mopped on Tuesdays and Fridays of every week, else the house would tumble down! Today was Tuesday. "I'll just let it go—to show her!"

Though Nell, sitting at the table with a frown on her face, her breakfast untouched as yet, knew that it was not the household tasks she had had to take over from Susan that depressed her. Nor was it the feeling of some change hanging over the house, suggested by Susan's troubled face, by her father's preoccupation when he was home—these last few weeks he had had nothing to say when she came in late for supper. Perversely, she had missed it—it took something away from being with Tony, left her a little flattened. She knew it was because things were bad at the plant but she was too engrossed in Nell Brent to share Susan's worry or feel concern for her father.

She missed going to the old house on the hill—missed it terribly. Oh, Tony was darling, but it wasn't the same, driving around. . . . She never felt now, after she had been with Tony, as if she were living in the clouds; nor, on her bed, her lights out, could she bring him close as she always had before.

"I'll go to you wherever you are" had lost something of its music. Tony had not taken a job with Petersen's—"Tie up with any eight-hour day? Not me"—but he never said anything now about going away. Rather he appeared satisfied with things as they were.

"And I'm just stuck here," thought Nell, now. With the ironing and the dishwashing, the sweeping and dusting . . .

The only break in this disagreeable routine—except her times with Tony—was when she went to Mrs. Peely's to practice her solo for the next Sunday. John Wendell almost always came in, listened, made suggestions. Mrs. Peely was a silly old woman and he was a preacher, but it was exciting to sing her best and see them both look as if she were wonderful. It was exciting, too, to stand up in the service and sing, even though no one could see her up in the choir loft. Even though Tony had not come a second time to stand under the windows.

But today was not a practice day. Tony had told her he could not meet her today—he had to take his mother to Canaan to look at some old stove that was advertised for sale. Long empty hours stretched ahead of her.

Back, before everything was different, she had never minded being alone, but this morning, the house was intolerably quiet, empty. She walked out of it, across the yards, to Debbie's.

She had not seen Aunt Debbie for some time, for Aunt Debbie did not come over for supper, any more, and she had not bothered to go to see her. But to talk to *any*one would—would keep her from thinking.

Deborah was out in the yard doing something with a hoe. She put it down at once, and came to meet her. "How are you this warm day, Nell?"

"All right. I thought Bill was taking care of your yard." Nell had heard that talked about at the table. Bill had said, "Gee, Aunt Debbie's going to pay me three dollars a week doing things in her yard!" His father had said, "You see that you save it, son." She had thought with some envy, "I could use the money!"

Deborah laughed. "I was just puttering about. Nell—why don't we drive somewhere for lunch, you and I? I haven't seen nearly as much of you as I'd like, and the summer's going."

Nell hesitated, thinking of her outburst in which she had told Aunt Debbie she was going to run away with Tony. She had not run away, and somehow now it did not seem so definite. Aunt Debbie might speak of it. But, as if she had jumped at the suggestion, Aunt Debbie finished, "Go and change your dress and I'll change mine."

Dressed, Nell surveyed herself in her mirror with a little excitement. It was silly of course to feel excited over just riding around with anyone as old as Aunt Debbie but—it was something to do!

She went across to the other house. Aunt Debbie was backing the car out.

"Do you drive?" she asked Nell.

"I learned—I took my test. But Father won't let me drive our car very often—says I'd waste gas."

"I'd love it if you'd drive. Then I can sit back and enjoy myself."

This did warrant a lift of spirit. "She's a good egg," thought Nell as she slid in under the wheel.

At Deborah's suggestion they took side roads, up hills, down hills. "This is what I like," said Deborah. "You may know where we'll come to, but I don't. It's sort of adventuring."

Nell drove carefully—Aunt Debbie must think she was a good driver. Every now and then she glanced at Aunt Debbie to see if she looked nervous. She didn't—she was sitting comfortably back on the seat, with an expression on her face of complete enjoyment in the moment. She was not talking much and when she did it was not about anything that might lead to Tony.

Nell relaxed, gave herself over wholly to the thrill of driving. "Maybe she'll let me use her car sometimes!" As she hugged that possibility, without knowing, she hummed a bit of the hymn she was practicing with Mrs. Peely for the next Sunday.

"That's nice—go on," said Deborah, when she broke off.

"I didn't know I was singing! I do that, sometimes."

"Nell, why don't you study voice? Susan told me you did think of it at one time."

"You think of a lot of things that are crazy."

"Crazy?"

"Oh, well, things you can't do."

"Wild Goose Inn," read Deborah from a road sign. "Next road— two miles—turn right. Let's see what it's like, Nell. I'm getting hungry."

Nell turned into the crossroad. Deborah did not say more about the singing lessons. "Why should she?" thought Nell. "She knows I'm going to marry Tony!"

The inn was an old white house set back from the road behind ancient maples. "Looks clean and nice," approved Deborah.

Nell thought it looked dead but she drove in under the maples, parked expertly next to two other cars on the grass at the side of the house.

These cars belonged to a party of young people, three girls and three young men, sitting around a table in the dining room. Nell and Deborah sat close enough to them to overhear their lively talk and soon gathered that they were students in a near-by art school. One had sold a painting and there was considerable bantering over that. They were dressed casually, two of the girls in slacks and their hair in pigtails; their camaraderie was young and casual.

"They're nice youngsters," thought Deborah of them. Particularly the lad at the end of the table with the tow-colored hair and very blue eyes. She liked a cleanness about his looks. She noticed that his eyes came to Nell quite frequently. Why not? Nell, with her blaze of hair . . . Then, meeting Nell's glance, he gave her an engaging grin. And again he grinned at her, when a burst of hilarity over something broke around the table. Deborah saw nothing forward in it—he only wanted to include Nell in the fun, because she was young, like they were.

She saw Nell smile back at him.

But Nell kept her eyes on her plate when the little party went out of the dining room. The friendly boy gave his smile to Deborah as he passed their table, which she thought very sweet of him. In a moment they were gone; the room seemed dull and empty.

"Thanks a lot for the lunch, Aunt Debbie," said Nell, when they went back to the car. But she said it in a perfunctory way—not as if she really had enjoyed it. And Deborah did not think her preoccupation, as they drove back toward home in the circuitous way they had come, was wholly in her driving. Her face had a brooding, rebellious look.

"If the girl had more chances to meet other boys—boys like that nice one . . . Get together like those young people were today . . .

"If I had had . . ."

She let her thoughts slip back to her own girlhood. Sweethome, then, had had no more to offer in the way of good times for young people than it did now. The same boys, the same girls, doing the same things over and over . . . Then she'd met Paul. But hadn't Paul seemed different to her, exciting, only because he was forbidden? Because he meant a defiance of Sarah Brent, of the stupid old village? Escape?

It had been so easy, so very easy to believe in the future that they had talked over together. "And we wouldn't have had it, even if Paul had lived." She knew enough, now, about life and men to know that Paul had had nothing in himself to mature on.

Then, as if some sudden honesty were driving her thoughts to further admissions, she recalled personal habits of Paul's that had offended her, even shocked her, of which she had not known until she lived with him. She had spoken once of something he did and he had been angry, had told her she was just stuck up because she came from Sweethome. She had not tried after that to change him.

"Shall we go on home?" asked Nell, slowing down at a crossroad.

"Might as well." Deborah looked at her wrist watch. "It's near four. It's been a nice ride but perhaps stupid for you, my dear."

"It's fun to get my hands on a steering wheel!"

"No reason you can't drive the car whenever you want to, Nell. It just stands there in the barn most of the time."

"Oh, I'd love that, Aunt Debbie! Just to get out . . ."

"You can drive me over town when I have marketing to do." She was ready to go to any lengths, for some animation had come into the girl's face.

"I could do errands for Susan," Nell said.

"We'll go off for lunch again someday."

They came to the Flats. Deborah straightened. "Nell, turn along the next road. I'd like to see the old Bouvais place—I think I can locate it. One of Paul's brothers is living in it, Father Duffy told me. It'll only take a few minutes." She leaned forward, searching the road ahead. She could not understand this sudden impulse of hers—knew only that it was impelling. "There—I think that's it just on beyond."

They came to it, an old one-story frame house, badly needing paint, its narrow porch sagging, leaning sheds flanking it, weeds high around it where the earth was not trodden down to a dull brown. Children of all sizes, and chickens swarmed over the place. An older girl was taking a wash down from a line, stopping, as Nell and Deborah came along, to slap a child out of her way. It was all as Deborah remembered it from that time she had come here with Paul —she half-expected to see his mother appear in the door. Just beyond

215

and close to the road, a man, stripped to the waist, sweat glistening on his dark skin, was straightening a post in the tumbled-down fence. As the car came opposite him he lowered his sledge hammer to look at them, then turned back to his work.

Nell said, "They're related to you, aren't they, Aunt Debbie?"

"Yes, I guess you could say they are. In-laws."

"How awful!"

Deborah heard some horror in Nell's voice. Then the girl burst into tears. Angry tears . . . "That's why you wanted to drive around this way—so that I'd *see!"*

"Nell, I wasn't thinking of you at all. I've been thinking of Paul, some, as we drove along."

"Well, it doesn't make any difference! Tony hates it, the way he has to live! He *hates* it. As soon as ever we can get away . . ."

"Nell, pull yourself together or we'll land in the ditch."

They had come to some traffic. Nell gave her attention to her driving. Until they reached the bridge . . .

"Different backgrounds *don't* matter," she asserted, defiantly.

"Not if you are sure in your own heart that they don't."

Nell thanked her for the drive a little briefly and went through the trellis to the other house. Deborah went into the kitchen. "You spoiled it for her—going around to see where Paul had lived." Though maybe . . . Maybe now was the time to put those catalogues where the girl would see them, next time she came over.

Susan came home early from the plant. "You might as well go home, Susan—I've nothing more for you to do," her father had said to her.

She called, "Nell," as she went into the house. There was no answer. "Perhaps she's at Mrs. Peely's." She went into the kitchen, saw that the floor had not been mopped. She made a little sound, half of indignation, half of despair. Now she must do it herself, and quickly, so as to start supper. And she ached in every bit of her

216

from the strain of the day. Not that she had done anything, a few letters was all; it was seeing her father at his desk going over and over columns of figures, with that white look on his face. . . .

Suddenly she said aloud, "I won't do it! It can go—supper can be late!" To throw to the winds a long-fixed habit of routine was startling but even so she resolutely turned her back on the kitchen and its unmopped floor.

She needed bread and cereal for breakfast. She had planned to send Bill to Higgins' for it after supper but she decided suddenly to go herself and go now. She'd walk—she needed the exercise after sitting most of the day in her father's office.

She washed, changed into a fresh cotton dress, brushed her hair. That all this and her decision to walk had anything to do with the possibility of running into John Wendell, she would have stoutly denied. She had had too much else to think about to cherish that silly idea of hers that she meant anything to him. The few times she had met him lately he had said no more than a few words to her—of course there had been others around but he could have *looked* at her. . . .

Yet, for all her discipline of her heart, when she saw him coming out of the parsonage, turning up the walk toward her, she felt her breath catch in her throat.

He stopped, held out his hand.

"Hello, Susan. Very warm day, isn't it?"

"Yes. Smothering . . ."

"How's your father?"

"He's well, thank you."

"You're helping him at the plant, someone said. . . ."

"Yes, while Kate Briggs takes a vacation."

"Sorry you're not going my way."

That was all—*all*. Not a word more than he'd say to anyone. The color was high on Susan's cheeks as she walked on. Just for a moment, that moment when he put out his hand, she thought she had seen something in his eyes, warm, as if he were especially glad to meet her, but she had only imagined it—"The way a starved old maid thinks things that aren't so!"

She found Hattie Higgins keeping store and Almira Coggin visiting with her over the counter.

"Why, we were just talking about you, Susan," said Almira Coggin. "Saying we didn't see much of you nowadays. I suppose you're awfully busy doing Kate's work. . . ."

"She knows I'm not," thought Susan, while she answered, "Yes, I am quite busy."

Hattie Higgins spoke. "Everyone's wondering if Deborah Brent's taking up with the Swede has anything to do with the plant here." Her eyes bored into Susan as she said it.

Almira saved Susan an answer. She laughed. "I think more likely Deborah's just looking out for Number One!"

"Well, *something*'s got to happen," said Hattie, pushing Almira's bag of purchases toward her. "What can I do for you, Susan?"

"All I want is a loaf of bread and a box of Wheaties."

"The bakery bread, I suppose. Not the homemade . . ."

The homemade bread was five cents more than the bakery loaf. Susan always had bought it until two weeks ago when her father told her they must cut corners on food. But she said, quickly, with a slight lift of her head, "The homemade, please."

To her dismay, Almira Coggin waited to walk away from the store with her. "Hattie's upset," she told Susan outside. "Says business in the store has fallen off a lot this summer. But what can she and Ham expect with so many of the men laid off like they are?" Her tone said, "You and I can call a spade a spade—we're in the know." "Hattie's always been one to say what comes to her tongue." She put her free hand under Susan's elbow. "Like that about your Aunt Deborah . . . But, tell *me,* Susan, *has* Petersen fallen for her?"

"I don't know—and even if I did, I wouldn't say. It's Aunt Debbie's affair."

218

It was the first time in her life Susan had ever deliberately spoken rudely and, just as when she decided to let the kitchen floor go and the start of supper, she felt some release in herself from it. For defending Aunt Debbie, too.

They had come to the Peely house. Almira stopped. "I think I'll run in and see Agnes for a minute. If she isn't busy . . ." She gave Susan an arch look. "Maybe you don't know that the Reverend Wendell comes here whenever Agnes is coaching Nell—we thought it was you he had his eye on but looks like it's your little sister! 'By, my dear. It was nice to see you!"

So strong was Susan's revulsion to the woman that it was several moments before the full implication of what she had said struck home to her heart. *Nell!*

Well, why not? Nell was prettier, younger, livelier. She could see in how many ways Nell would be more attractive to a man than she, herself, was. She told herself all this very sensibly, her heartbeat as steady as her footstep.

Reaching home, she found Nell mopping the kitchen floor. She cried out, "You don't have to do it at this hour! When it's time to start supper . . ." She stopped, shocked at the way it had come out, at her voice. "Oh, *Nell* . . ."

But Nell had thrown the mop to a corner, was stalking out of the room.

CHAPTER XXI

On Thursday evening of the next week Rom Barcek came back, appearing in the door at a moment when Deborah, in the rocking chair by the window, was feeling very much alone.

The day had dawned, hotter than the several days before it, with an oppressive sultriness in the air, a continuous threat of storm. Ordinarily excessive heat did not affect Deborah but she wakened to this morning, tired and depressed and at breakfast decided to keep inside all day, doing next to nothing.

Then her telephone rang. She hoped it was Susan or Nell; she had not seen Susan since the evening Susan had reproached her for disloyalty, nor had Nell come over to use the car. But it was Clare.

"Deb, can you come over? I've got to talk to you! It's—it's awfully important."

Deborah heard despair in Clare's voice. "Yes, soon as I put something on."

Clare was waiting for her on the side porch. "You were *good* to come so quickly! We'll have to sit out here—I can't get up the gumption to move. Isn't this heat awful?"

Deborah sat down on the glider beside Clare. "What is it, Clare?" If she could get Clare to the matter that was important, hold her to it . . .

"I wouldn't mind if we had a terrible thunderstorm. It'd clear the air. Did you hear that Mrs. Carr had a stroke the other day? They took her to the hospital in Winsted. Agnes Peely's got that girl Minnie Carr had living with her—she couldn't be left alone up there. And the girl had two cats she had to bring along with her and poor Agnes hates cats! Most think it's up to the Methodists to do something about the girl, but no one did anything. Between you and me I think they haven't liked it that John Wendell has been going up there to see Mrs. Carr—you remember he went there when Silas died. . . ."

"Oh, I'm sure they recognize plain kindness!"

"Well, in a place like this—you've forgotten, Deb. No one tries to get a person to leave one church and join the other and there are some who see John Wendell doing just that. Oh, did you know that Hattie Higgins has vowed she won't set foot inside church until he apologizes for what he said in that sermon? They say she hasn't been these last two Sundays so I guess she means it."

Deborah folded her hands firmly. It was too hot to let herself get mad. But she must stop this babble . . .

"It'd be just right for me to take the girl—I'm of neither the one church nor the other. But I can't—I'm going away the middle of September."

Clare's mouth hung open for a moment. Then she cried, "Oh, *no,* Deb!" There was genuine regret in her voice but a little excitement, too. "It's a crumb of news for her to serve out," thought Deborah.

"Someone—Almira it was—asked just the other day if you were staying and I said I was sure you were—you've seemed so settled here in spite of—well, you know, the talk. I'll miss you terribly."

"Clare, you said there was something important. . . ."

Clare's hands fluttered, caught, twisted together. Tears gushed to her eyes. "I hate to speak of it, I just *hate* to, but I don't see anything else to do. It's Fred. His trucking. We've lived for years—we haven't had much but it's been enough—on what he got from trucking for the nail works and now he isn't getting anything. He's so glum he won't speak a word and I don't know what's going to happen. And I thought maybe you'd ask that Rudolph Petersen to give him some kind of work over at his plant—you know him pretty well. . . ."

"I've talked to him twice. But—yes, I know him pretty well."

"Fred's funny—he wouldn't go and ask for work himself. He's done what he's been doing too long. But if you'd ask Mr. Petersen to call him up—tell him he had a job for him—Fred wouldn't know you and I had anything to do with it. Oh, Deb, *will* you?"

Deborah heard desperation again in Clare's pleading, fright, too. The shell within which Clare had lived was threatened.

"But may not Fred refuse any such offer of work?"

"He *can't!* No one here would—they're talking that way now, Deb. The men all think Will's going to shut down for good. It's awful, after all these years. And they're willing to take any work they can get. Even if it is with Petersen."

"I'll talk to him—about Fred."

"I knew you would if I asked you to!" Clare's warm, moist hand closed over Deborah's. "You're my best friend, just as you used to be. I can't bear to think of your going away! Where will you go? Out West again?"

"No. I'll stay in the East—in a hotel somewhere until I decide where I want to live."

"Deb, you have enough to live on? You've never told me."

On a sudden decision, Deborah said, "I have my soup."

"Your *soup?*"

"I thought you knew." Deborah was smiling. Yes, tell Clare—let Clare tell the women here that she was not living on alimony. She should have done it when she first came, despite her feeling that it was no one's affair but her own. As she told briefly the story of the soup, she saw Clare's eyes widen with excitement.

"Deborah Brent, you're the smartest thing! Imagine getting money for just a recipe, of all things!"

Her half-giggle, her tone, implied some clever maneuvering in the deal. The implication would go with her story of it, Deborah knew. She smothered a half-sigh, got to her feet. "I must drive along

222

home, Clare. And I'll get in touch with Mr. Petersen right away."

She telephoned to his office, as soon as she reached home. She made her call very business-like. "This is Mrs. Deborah Brent, speaking. If Mr. Petersen is not too busy I would like to talk to him for a few minutes." Evidently Mr. Petersen was not too busy to take up his telephone at once. "Hello, Mrs. Brent!"

Deborah went straight to the point. "I have a favor to ask of you. But I can't, over the phone. Could you stop in at the house sometime —rather soon?" She smiled, wondering how many might be listening in.

"Delighted to. This afternoon? About four-thirty?"

"That will be fine."

She thought, "I'll have iced coffee and some of that cheddar cheese and chives spread on crackers. . . ."

Today he parked at the side of the house and came directly in through the kitchen door without even the formality of a knock. He shook Deborah's hand, sniffed the air. "What? No coffee cake?"

"Too hot today to use the oven. Another time . . ."

"Nice and cool in here." He looked over the room as he had the first afternoon he had come. Deborah put the pitcher of iced coffee on the table, the plate of spread crackers, motioned to him to pull out a chair, sat down herself, and filled their glasses.

"Tell me, now—what's the favor?"

His directness made it easier to tell him. "It's to give a job to Fred Hersey. He's done trucking mostly for the Brent Nail Works and now that seems to be finished and he is left with no livelihood."

Rudolph Petersen interrupted her. "Why do *you* have to ask for it? Why doesn't the fellow come over to my plant and apply himself?" When Deborah hesitated he answered himself. "I get it—this prejudice against me."

"That—and more. Fred's never done but the one thing; he doesn't know how to start out to find something different to do. I know it's irregular and all that for me to appeal to you but I'm doing it be-

223

cause Fred's mother gave me mothering when I was a girl here and needed it badly. His sister was my closest friend and their home was more home to me than my own. So, you see why I have to ask this, now."

"Not everyone remembers that particular kind of a debt," said Rudolph Petersen with warmth in his eyes. "I'll find a job for him!"

"Will you have someone phone to him? Tell him there's work for him? And don't speak of me?"

Now Rudolph Petersen threw back his head with a hearty laugh. "I've heard of women's influence behind big business, but this is the first time I've run into it. It's rather nice! Shows up what I've missed in my life. I'll tell Bogart to phone him—he's head of employment. Here, write down his name and phone number. But, no, give it to me and I'll write it. Bogart must not suspect any petticoats in this."

Deborah found herself warming to him for his amusement over it, which made it all so unembarrassing.

She gave him Fred's name and telephone number and he wrote it down in the memorandum book he had taken out of his pocket. "Thanks," she said and drew a breath of relief.

"Don't thank me—I'm in your debt, Mrs. Brent."

"Mine?"

"For your kindness to me that Sunday in church. One doesn't meet up with that often, these days. By the way, I haven't seen you there since!"

"So you've gone? And I haven't. . . ." She did not tell him that she had hesitated to go because she thought her presence there would embarrass Willie.

"I like young Wendell—I've had some good talks with him. I'd like to help him in that plan of his for a gymnasium and playground for the young people here." He smiled a little dryly. "Though I must remember that you warned me I could not buy my way into this community."

Deborah thought of Clare, importuning her to ask this man's help

224

for Fred. "If they get desperate enough they may turn to you."

Rudolph Petersen put down his glass, got up, walked across the room and back. "A merger would solve this unemployment situation here—why can't Brent see that? Save his own skin." He spoke brusquely. "I've been going over the terms of it in my head. I'm not being generous—it's to my advantage, as much as to his. I can use him and the men who've been working for him—that space in his place. I'm going into the manufacturing of cutlery. No one would lose anything on it—except Brent his pride."

"Why don't you put it all in black and white and send it to Willie? He'd read it, when he wouldn't listen."

"I'll do that." Rudolph Petersen sat down, picked up his glass.

He told her, before he went away, that he had stopped at the Higgins' store to talk to Ham Higgins about the Hurrell house. "Didn't get far—but I'm finding out that with you Yankees there has to be so much talk before you're down to business. One-sided talk—about all Higgins said was, 'Mebbe.' Though that was better than a flat 'no' and I don't think he'd be averse to receiving a commission on the sale. I drove by the place the other day and it rather appeals to me. Needs a lot done to it but that would make me feel more that it belonged to me. I may be asking your advice, Deborah."

It was pleasant to hear him use her given name, to think that she might be able to help him in small ways. It was so, what she had said to Clare, "Yes, I know him pretty well." He had said he was coming again, soon.

But, after he had gone, she remembered that she had very little time to enjoy this pleasant friendship. She looked slowly over the room and saw it as not hers but Sarah Brent's. It had been Sarah Brent speaking through Willie's voice, that evening, denying her a home here.

Bill banged in, dropped her newspaper in a chair, banged out. "Want t'get some baseball in before it rains." Neither Susan nor Nell came over. She ate some bread and milk, washed the bowl and spoon, put them away. Thunder was rumbling, closer now, and there was a stir of storm in the air. She sat down in the rocking chair, let her lonesome feeling have its way. Soon she would be one of those women, living alone in one dreary hotel or another.

Then Rom came up the steps.

Deborah sprang to her feet.

"Rom!"

He stood still a moment, in the door.

She crossed the room to him. "I've been looking for you every day!" She saw his thinness, his face, emptied-looking, like an old man's. She wanted to put her arms around him but instead she said briskly, "Go, wash up, and I'll fix some food for you."

Without a word, perhaps too tired to trust himself to speak a word, he went upstairs to his room.

Deborah got out one of the small steaks she had bought, cold potatoes to fry, bread, butter, milk. The storm broke with thunder that crashed overhead but she felt snug, happy. Rom was back. "Why—" she held her knife still over the potato in her hand—"It's as if it were my son, Waite—come home, after being away. . . ."

Rom came down, washed, shaven. Deborah was bending down to turn the steak. He put his hand under her arm, drew her up straight. "Let me do that."

Deborah yielded her fork to him, smiling. Yes, let him do it—as Waite would, in his place.

With his supper before him Rom only looked down at his plate. "I think I should tell you . . ."

Deborah said quickly, "You don't have to tell me a thing, Rom, unless you want to!"

"I do want to. . . ." Though he paused as if it were not easy to go on.

"It was a girl, wasn't it?" asked Deborah helpfully.

"Yes, a girl. I knew her before I came to the States. She was one of my father's pupils. She got to Paris, managed to get a letter to me—I joined her there and we went together back to Poland. I tried to persuade her to return to the States with me but she said her work was there—mine here. We didn't marry—it did not seem necessary. We were as much one as though a dozen marriage services had been spoken over us!" He finished, harshly, "I've believed that, these last few years, but I found it was not so!"

"That was hard on you, Rom, but wasn't it—understandable? All this time and the distance between you . . ."

He looked up at her, his eyes blazing with anger. "If that had been all! But it wasn't. The money I've entrusted to her to use as we planned it—it's gone, yes, into the rebuilding of my father's school, but the school is not used for the teaching of the principles of liberty my father taught! She laughs at them now! It is that betrayal I will never forgive!"

No, no use to say to the boy that he'd forget it, someday. So Deborah said, gently, "You've got it told now, Rom, and you're home, so eat your dinner." She crossed to the stove. "I'll keep you company with a cup of coffee."

CHAPTER XXII

"Can't make it today, baby. Got to work. . . ."

Tony had just said that over the telephone and Nell kept hearing it, even after she put the receiver back on its hook. He hadn't said he was sorry and it had been three days since she had seen him. He had said, "Tomorrow—same time?" but that did not help her hurt. Or hold back the doubts that, lately, crouched just outside her mind, ready to spring into it. Was Tony tired of her?

"No. *No!*" she cried aloud, walking away from the telephone. "You're just imagining it! Because things are going wrong here at home you think everything is going wrong!" Yet in spite of that logic, tears filled her eyes as she looked at the dress she had washed and ironed to wear when she met Tony this afternoon.

And now what was there to do? The lonesomeness that was somehow mixed with the dark doubts settled over her. If she liked any of the girls here in Sweethome—but she didn't; they pried so—they bored her. She had done all the things Susan had asked her to do today—all but cleaning out the refrigerator and that could go until another day. Go over and ask Aunt Debbie if she could use the car? No—she had not forgiven Aunt Debbie for taking her around there in the Flats; she refused to believe it was just to see the Bouvais place.

"I'll walk up to the Hurrell house—I'll go there alone!" It was a faintly comforting decision and it seemed the proper place to take her heavy heart. Sit under the tree at the back door and think of that last afternoon when she and Tony had sat there and she had felt so close to him.

She did not change from the old plaid blouse and dungarees she was wearing or brush out her hair. Tony would not be seeing her. . . .

And she did not go by the road over which she and Tony always drove; she took an old overgrown trail left from lumbering days that climbed the side of the hill and came out on the upper road near the Carr farm. She would meet no one on it, for few frequented it after the blackberry picking was over.

The Hurrell house looked different, approached from this direction. The old trees hid its gables, its fine façade. But not the back yard . . . Suddenly her step stopped short. For in plain sight, back of the house, was Tony's car.

She stood still, frozen with shock, fighting desperately not to believe her eyes. But it was—oh, it *was!* She knew his car as well as she knew the color of her hair. *And Tony wouldn't go there alone!* She knew that from a knowledge of him she had refused to admit before. She wheeled around, ran, stumbling a little, back along the road toward the trail. To hide herself there—to let her heart break there. She sobbed as she ran, queer sobs, that broke with her panting breath. Safe on the trail she threw herself down on the ground beside it, pressed her hot face into the cool green and gave way to a passion of weeping. It was the end—the end of everything.

She felt all her flesh burning as her face burned. "I hate him! I *hate* him!" The last time—three days ago—he had kissed her and now, now . . . "I *despise* him! He's loathsome!" she sobbed into the grass.

"Nell."

She threw back her head to see John Wendell standing near her. He wore soft shoes and his step approaching on the trail had made no sound. For all she knew he might have been there for several minutes, watching her. She turned the fury that was consuming her on him. "Go *away!*" she cried.

Instead he sat down on the grass a little away from her. "Would it help you, child, if you told me something of what has upset you?" He spoke gently.

She sat up, glared at him. "I'm not a child! And it isn't any of your affair! And anyway, *you* wouldn't know anything about the way I'm feeling. . . ."

He broke off a long blade of grass, drew it slowly through his fingers, looking down at it. "Maybe I wouldn't but—can I make a guess? You've been hurt by someone you trusted."

"Hurt!" Nell flung the word at him. Calling it just hurt—when her heart was *broken* . . .

"It's a tough thing to take," continued John Wendell as if she had confirmed his guess, and continuing to smooth out the blade of grass, keeping his eyes on it. "One of the toughest. It seems to shatter everything. But it's better to know. . . ."

"Oh, skip the preaching! No one asked you to," put in Nell rudely, strangling back a sob at the same time.

"Okay. I won't say any more about it."

"And *go!* Why are you here anyway? Were you spying on me—to—to tell Susan?"

The corners of John Wendell's lips twitched as if he were repressing a smile. But his voice kept its quiet, sympathetic tone. "No, I wasn't spying on you. I was coming from the Carr house—I was asked to go and look for any papers left there. I happened to see you turn into the trail. You appeared terribly distraught—I was concerned."

"I'm not and you can go. Where's your old motorcycle?"

"Broken down and, I'm afraid, beyond repair." He got to his feet. "I'll go a little way along and wait until you're ready—then I'll follow you down."

Nell caught her knees in her arms. "I can go by myself, thank you!"

230

"Well, it happens I don't like to leave you alone in this isolated spot."

Nell gave a contemptuous snort at that. "You're wasting your precious time. I'm going to sit here for hours!"

Ignoring that, John Wendell went on, disappeared out of sight around a turn in the trail. Alone, Nell put her face down against her knees. But her eyes were dry, now, and mixed with her anguish of heart was a lively curiosity over whether the fool was really waiting. "I *will* just sit here for ages!"

But after a little she grew conscious of a slightly frightening aloneness in the spot. Though years ago, she had come here herself often, after blackberries, now it seemed strange. The trees closed in on her too much. She sprang up, started quickly down the trail.

There he was, waiting. She stalked past him, her head high, but she knew that he got to his feet, and was following her, a little way behind.

She walked faster, a hysterical giggle breaking her breath. If she ran, would he run, too? She was tempted to try it. The interfering old busybody. He'd see—she wouldn't sing another Sunday for him!

Reaching the level of the village, turning into Central Road, she looked back over her shoulder and saw that he had gone in the opposite direction. And with the little excitement of his pursuit so abruptly over, the fact of Tony's betrayal rushed back into her. Sobs choked up in her throat, again, but forlorn now, rather than angry. "I wish I could *die*." For there was nothing, *nothing* to live for . . .

She could not go into the house, face Susan. Susan'd know, with just one glance at her, that Tony had—that Tony had . . . Susan would look sorry and she could not bear that; she was not going to have anyone pitying her. She turned, a little desperately, toward Aunt Debbie's house.

Deborah was in the kitchen doing something at the stove. She exclaimed, "Nell! What is it, child? Come right in—stay to supper. I've made a black-raspberry pie!"

But Nell hesitated just inside the door. She realized that she made a sorry figure, bits of grass on her dungarees, staining her blouse, streaks of tears on her face. She avoided Deborah's eyes. "I look awful!"

She crossed the room to her. "Not a bit! You can go up to my room and tidy up." She lowered her voice. "I'm particularly glad you came in, Nell. Rom Barcek's back—maybe you know. He's up in his room working on something he's writing. He sticks at it all day long and way into the night. It isn't good for him. You see—" now she whispered—"he came back all broken up—he'd found out that a girl he was awfully fond of wasn't what he thought she was. He'll get over it but he needs diversion, someone young around. Now go along and get ready for supper."

"She *knows*," thought Nell, as she climbed the stairs. Yet she had not looked pitying, as Susan would have—she had not asked one question. Intensely grateful for that, as she passed the closed door behind which she heard the click-click of a typewriter, Nell thought, "I suppose I've got to be decent to that Pole—at least just tonight."

So she washed her face vigorously, brushed her hair with Aunt Deborah's brush until it stood out alive around her head and, lacking lipstick, bit her lips hard to bring color into them, then went downstairs.

It was about half-past four when Nell ran stumbling into the lumbering trail. At five o'clock Rudolph Petersen turned his car in between the broken wooden pillars of the driveway at the old Hurrell house. Ham Higgins sat, a little stiffly, beside him. He had consented to at least give the Swede a look over the place.

Rudolph Petersen stopped his car in the drive, but he let the engine run. "How many acres did you say?"

"Didn't say. A hundred—though most of it's timber, back. Good pasture here to the left—Hurrell kept cows. Ain't good land for truck farming—too stony."

"Nice view," commented Rudolph Petersen, looking about him.

"These fool folks who want a view!" thought Higgins. Then he drew forward. "Who's here? Who owns that car back there?"

At that moment a girl darted past the car, around the barn. But not so swiftly that the two men did not see her lithe figure, the picnic basket over her arm. At the same time they saw a young man jump into the car.

"Go ahead, Petersen. I got to see about this! I'm responsible for trespassing on these premises!"

As Rudolph Petersen drove ahead, Ham Higgins shouted, "Hey there, young fellar, you stop!" Though there was no choice about that for Rudolph Petersen's bigger car blocked the smaller one.

Ham Higgins got out nimbly, advanced on the trespasser. "What're you doing here? I know you—you're that young Eyetalian, Tony DiVito, from the Flats! You just come back into the house with us and we'll see what's been going on!"

His face dark and sullen, Tony went ahead of Ham Higgins to the door which still swung open.

"Using a key, eh? How long's this been going on? Making yourself pretty much at home, I see."

They were in the kitchen. A bottle of wine, half-emptied, and two glasses stood in sight on the drainboard of the sink.

Ham Higgins turned to Tony. "You go along but I'll be picking you up, soon's as I swear out a warrant. I can find out easy where you live. And mind you're on hand—it'll go worse for you if you try to skip out."

As Tony went out Ham Higgins picked up the bottle, sniffed at it. "Poison," he pronounced sternly. "What're these young people coming to? And Will Brent's girl's goin' to be dragged into this!"

"Brent—Deborah Brent's niece?" Rudolph Petersen's tone was startled.

233

"Same. A piece off the old block as they say. Wildish, like Debbie was . . . But I got to do my duty." There was importance in his statement, and relish, too.

"Are you certain that this girl . . . ?"

"Who else? She's been runnin' round with the fellow for months. Meetin' him down by the bridge. Everybody's seen her. Everybody, guess, except Will Brent himself and he's too busy sittin' in his office waitin' for his works to fall down on his head. Goin' to go hard on him—he's more pride than most."

Rudolph Petersen walked over to a window, stood there staring out, frowning, troubled not only over Nell Brent but because this boy was the one in whom Father Duffy had expressed a special interest. He wished it were left with Father Duffy to handle this present situation. He did not like Higgins' harshness . . . or his obvious enjoyment in it all. Suddenly he wheeled around.

"If I should close this sale with you here and now—will you leave this matter of trespassing with me?"

Ham Higgins' mouth gaped. "Why, you ain't seen over the place yet!"

"Enough. What I've seen I like. I happen to know the price the Watertown bank has put on it. Twenty thousand—I'll write you a check for ten thousand. That should cover your commission."

At the mention of that, he could see yielding come to the other man's face. He drew his checkbook from his pocket. "This is with the understanding between us that you will take no action against this young man!"

" 'Tain't right to let him off," said Ham Higgins, but his eyes went to the checkbook and fountain pen in Rudolph Petersen's hands. "Though the bank'll be mighty glad to get rid of this place."

Rudolph Petersen wrote the check, handed it over. His eyes were cold and very blue. "I'll make a bet with you, too, Higgins. A hundred dollars that that girl we saw wasn't Deborah Brent's niece."

Ham Higgins pulled himself out of the shock of seeing another

234

man write off ten thousand as easily as if it were ten dollars, said piously, "I'm not a betting man, Petersen." Then he added, with a grin that showed a gap in his teeth, "Set on Debbie, are you?"

"I happen to know her as a woman of fine character—and you said the niece was like her. Shall we go now?"

Higgins stared at him. "You mean you don't want to see the rest of the house?"

"Not now. You might give me the key and I'll go over it some other day. Get in touch with the bank and we'll drive there and close the sale." Rudolph Petersen turned with some abruptness toward the door.

After he dropped Ham Higgins at his store he drove on to the Flats and directly to Father Duffy's. He found the priest eating his supper at the kitchen table.

"Ha, Petersen! Glad to see you! Have you eaten?"

"Not yet. I've something on my mind and I want to unload it on you."

"Well, sit down, sit down. Have some of this brown bread—fresh-baked." The priest's eye crinkled. "Baked it myself!"

Rudolph Petersen spread a slice of it but he put it down before him and let it stay there while he told his story.

The priest shook his head sadly. "Tony, Tony! I've failed somewhere, somehow!"

"It's in my hands now," went on Rudolph Petersen though he did not tell how it had got there. "I am not certain the boy should be let off scotfree. That's why I've come to you. You'd know best how to deal with it."

Father Duffy dropped his chin into his hands, thoughtful for a moment. "Glad you did—I don't like the usual processes of law where young people are concerned."

"It must not go to the police," put in Rudolph Petersen quickly. He had not intended to bring Nell Brent's name into it but now he had to. "Higgins is certain it was Mrs. Brent's niece with the boy—

235

it's bad enough that he will insist that it was she, but it must not come up in any police charges!"

The priest looked startled, more troubled. "The little Brent girl . . . There *has* been something between them; Mrs. Brent came to me one day . . ." He pushed his plate away. "I don't want to believe it. Alas, if it *is* so, I must have it on my conscience that I might possibly have prevented it. I gave the wrong advice to Debbie Brent that day she came to me." He lifted himself to his feet. "Drive me over to the boy's house—let me talk to him. By the way, would you still give him a job? It may be, shown kindness in this thing, he'd take it, settle down. I'll be ready in a few moments."

The priest went into his study, closed the door. Praying, perhaps, thought Rudolph Petersen. He was aware of a sudden envy. If it helped, he'd missed that help all his life.

The doorstep of the DiVito house seemed swarming with children but Father Duffy made a way through them to the door, touching the heads of the ones nearest the path. "Ma's takin' on awful," shouted a boy after them.

Mrs. DiVito answered the priest's knock, her face swollen with weeping, but with anger, too, as her flashing eyes betrayed. At sight of Father Duffy she threw her apron up over her face. "He's gone. You don't need to come after him. He come home and piled his things into his car—everything he owns to his back. He's gone for good! And he didn't leave so much as a penny. . . ."

Father Duffy put his hand on her arm, pushed her back from the door, walked on into the room. "Mrs. DiVito, we have not come after Tony—only to talk to him. Did he tell you where he was going?"

"*Him,* tell me? Has he ever? No. All he said was if the police came, to thumb my nose at them! What's he done? But how can anyone tell? He's bad—it could be anything. . . ."

"*Stop,*" thundered Father Duffy at her. "If you were a good mother you'd defend him! We're not the police—we came only to talk

236

to Tony, to help him. Tell Tony that. Tell him to come to me—that I am a friend."

Mrs. DiVito had dropped her apron. Now, her eyes black, she blazed at the priest, "That isn't going to feed all those children out there! They're hungry now. And another one coming! All your talk isn't going to put food in their mouths!"

Instinctively Rudolph Petersen's hand went into his pocket. But Father Duffy shook his head at him, and advanced on the woman, a threatening figure for all his plain, shabby suit. "What are *you* doing to feed them? Go into your kitchen—come, I'll go with you. We'll find something, I am certain."

Rudolph Petersen remained standing just inside the door. He looked over the crowded room with the revulsion that any orderly person feels for untidiness, uncleanness. He had known poverty— but not this. . . . From the kitchen came only the sounds of cupboard doors opening, closing, Father Duffy's heavy footsteps, an occasional angry sob from Tony's mother.

Presently Father Duffy came back into the living room. "We'll go now," he said.

In the car he humped forward on the seat, his face dark with wrath. "There *was* food," he growled. "Enough . . . That's been a stranglehold she's kept on that boy. What chance has he had? Or her man—I've checked up on him. He drinks, yes—but may he not be driven to it? He's a steady enough worker when there's work for him." The priest broke off with some abruptness, settled back, eyes closed.

Then he spoke, low, now, sorrowfully. "God forgive that woman! She doesn't know what she has done!"

Rudolph Petersen remembered that John Wendell had repeated that plea in almost the same words in his Commemoration Service. He reflected, "It belongs to all men, beyond all differences in creed." But, alas, so did the stupid, blind not-knowing. Might not that be the great sin of the human race—back to the first man? He frowned into the space of road ahead, recalling Ham Higgins' relish over this afternoon's affair. Higgins was in all probability a good citizen of the community—something or other in Wendell's church. He would without doubt stoutly deny that he had found any satisfaction in that situation—yet it had been there, on his face. . . .

"It's all beyond me," muttered Rudolph Petersen aloud.

"What's beyond you?"

"Human instincts . . ."

Father Duffy's eye gave its wink but there was a sigh in his voice when he answered. "It's beyond me, too, Petersen, very often."

Hattie Higgins was alone in the store when Ham came in.

"Lock the door and come with me," he said, passing her and going on to the rooms back of the store.

Hattie stared at him. It was not like him to suggest such a thing—anyone coming in, if it were for no more than a package of gum, was a customer—but she closed the doors, drew the bolt across them and hurried to join him.

He stood, holding the check in his hand.

"What's that?" she demanded to know.

"For ten thousand—look at the figgers, Hat! The bugger wrote it as if it weren't nothing. For that old house up there. Didn't even go over it. I'll get my commission out of this. We won't starve right away!"

Hattie Higgins took the check from him, ran her finger over it. "There'll be a lot who'll say you shouldn't have sold to that foreigner."

"They will, eh? Let 'em—they've cut down their trading here—how about that? Anyways, Petersen seems a good sort. Though how he got where he has with no more business sense than he shown today beats me!"

Both heard a rap on the store door. Hattie returned the check to him. "Someone wants to get in."

"Wait, Hat. Let 'em go. I got more to tell you!"

238

She sat down in a chair, her face, her stiff back, disapproving. With trade poor, like it was lately . . .

"Who d'you think we caught up at the Hurrell house? Nell Brent and that Italian boy! Leastways we caught him—the girl ran like a rabbit round the barn and out of sight. And they were doing more'n trespassing or I wasn't born fifty-seven years ago. Mebbe Petersen'll bring charges against them—mebbe not. I don't know."

"*Nell Brent,*" breathed Hattie. "Though it's no more than we might have expected to happen."

"It'll go hard on Will when he knows." Ham Higgins folded the check, put it in his pocket. "It'll bring him down off his high horse, mebbe."

The knock at the door was repeated. Hattie got up briskly from her chair. "You open, Ham. As long as you're home I'll take a few minutes to run over and see Almira. We've got to line up the committees for the Bazaar—should have done it before this. Supper's ready just to heat up. I'll be gone only a few minutes."

CHAPTER XXIII

THE COMMITTEE for the Congregational Church Bazaar, held annually in October, was organized by the next afternoon and in accomplishing this with each telephone call, each brief visit, went the story of Nell Brent being caught, or as good as caught, up there in the old Hurrell house with that Italian boy from the Flats.

It reached Susan through Libby White's mother who had volunteered to ask Susan to serve on the refreshment committee. She approached the Brent house just as Susan drove in, returning from the office.

"Susan, I'm so glad I caught you! I'll just take a minute—I know you're tired. And you have supper to get, don't you? It's the Bazaar—will you be on the refreshment committee? We want the young people on that and you were so good on it, two years ago. Just tea and coffee and cake, you know."

Susan pushed her hair back from her face and forced a smile. "Thanks, Mrs. White. But—I'm awfully busy."

"I know it, my dear. But we think, we were saying, it would be *good* for you to get into things outside. You haven't, lately."

A flush ran up Susan's face. Did Mrs. White and the other women think she was staying out of what she called "things" because of John Wendell's interest in Nell?

"You see I'm doing my father's office work now," she explained, with a faint defiance.

"Yes, we know Kate isn't well. How is your father?"

240

"He's fine, thank you."

"Susan . . ." Mrs. White put her hand over Susan's. "I'm so *terribly* sorry over this about Nell!"

"*Nell?*" Susan echoed the name in a startled voice. She had not seen Nell this morning and for only a few minutes the evening before when Nell came home from Aunt Debbie's. "What has happened to her?"

"Oh, Susan, I thought, of *course,* you knew! How dreadful of me to speak of it! Oh, I'm embarrassed! Still, someone would . . . Ham Higgins took that Swede up to show him the old Hurrell house —he's *bought* it—and they caught Nell there with that Indian boy. . . ."

"I don't believe it was Nell!" cried Susan, hotly.

Mrs. White said, "I only know what Ham said and he said he saw her. But probably they weren't doing anything wrong. Only it's too bad to have the talk going round, account of your father. I must go along. Susan, come in some day and see Libby—you haven't been over once, this summer."

Susan barely waited for Mrs. White to turn before she ran into the house. She called, "Nell! Nell!" But there was no answer.

She wanted to hear Nell deny that she was the girl Ham Higgins had seen. But she was remembering the lunches Nell had packed so often to take with her when she met Tony—where had they gone to eat them?

Nell might be over at Aunt Debbie's; Susan ran through the yards, into the kitchen of the other house. She stopped short just inside the door, as Nell had, the afternoon before.

"Why, Susan, *hello!*" said Deborah. "Come on in!"

Susan did not move. "Is—is Nell here?" she asked, her voice breaking.

Deborah put an arm over the girl's shoulder, drew her to the table, pushed her gently down into a chair. "No. She drove over to Winsted. . . ."

"In your car?"

"Yes. I told her she could use it any time she wanted to—it just stands there in the barn. And she's doing some shopping for me. Rom went with her. . . ." Deborah smiled over Susan's head, remembering the strong reluctance on Rom's face, on Nell's too, when she suggested that he go. Nell did not know and there was no reason to tell Susan that she had seized an opportunity to whisper to Rom, "Be nice to Nell—something's upset her terribly."

"Aunt Debbie . . ." Susan stopped, flung her arms out over the table, dropped her face down against them.

"I know, Susan—it's this story about Nell that's started." She said it with grimness. Clare had called her a half-hour earlier, all shock and sympathy. She put her hand on Susan's shoulder and said, "We're not going to believe it was Nell—until we know. And, Susan, if it *was* she—we've got to give her understanding. She's young—heedless."

Susan lifted her head, an unaccustomed flash of rebellion in her eyes. "I wish *I* could be heedless for a change—about everything!"

Deborah sat down across from her. "I wish you could—you've carried too much, this last year. But you're not made that way."

"Aunt Debbie, if Father hears about it—I don't know what it will do to him! I'm terribly worried about him. Lately he's acted—as if he were ill, yet not in his body. He doesn't talk, even at home. At the office he sits at his desk—he doesn't know I am there until I speak. He stays there—he's staying this evening, and there's nothing for him to do, I know. Today—Coley Coggin came in but they didn't talk much and that was worse, their not having something to say. Coley's working without any pay. Oh, why doesn't Father *do* something?"

"Yes, why not?" Deborah's tone was hard. "He could . . ." Tell Susan now about the merger Rudolph Petersen had suggested to Willie and was going to suggest to him again.

Susan listened, her eyes on her tightly clasped hands. "Father'd hate it," she said when Deborah finished. "But he ought to do it, even so."

She got to her feet. "Aunt Debbie, you don't know how much good it always does me to talk to you about *anything*! I'm sorry about that other evening. . . . And Nell—no matter what, I'm going to understand!"

She kissed Deborah on the cheek and hurried out of the kitchen.

There was a half-hour before she had to do anything about supper, so Deborah sat down in the rocking chair. She felt confused—the happenings were taking shape now, too many and all at the same time.

Though the problem of where she would go from here was partly off her mind. Two evenings ago she had found an advertisement in the *Times* of the sale of an old farm three miles out of Waterbury, Vermont. The house was furnished, its plumbing modernized. "Ideal for an elderly couple who wish to spend the remaining years of their lives in the quiet and seclusion of the Vermont countryside." Though she did not particularly hanker after seclusion, it would be a good place for Rom to work in. She had written at once to the realtor whose name and address had been given in the advertisement asking for more information.

Rom had talked to her about his work. "It isn't what we planned, Aunt Debbie," he had said a little apologetically. "I had to write this first—it's of my father's life, of what he believed in, what he tried to make others believe in. I must do what I can to keep it alive."

"Put everything you've got into it," said Deborah. "The other can wait until I'm through living and I'm not through yet."

He had put some bills down before her.

"Rom!" she had protested.

"You must take it. It isn't enough—any amount of money is not enough to repay you for what you are doing for me. This is an advance on my royalties—what better way can I use it?"

Yes, that farm was the place for Rom just now—where he could lose himself in his special work. "And I'll be busy feeding him up." Come spring, she could plant an herb garden. *Why not bottle the salad dressing she made with her herbs for a base?* Her soup might not sell forever. . . .

She wished, absurdly, that she could take John Wendell to that farm. She was troubled about him. He had stopped in yesterday for a few minutes. She had told him that she was going away from Sweethome. "I may be going myself," he had said and his smile had not altered the hard set of his jaw. "I've had two anonymous letters. One protesting the sermon I preached at the Commemoration Service, the other charging me with bringing undesirable people into the church. That refers to Mrs. D'Arby—and possibly Rudolph Petersen. Also that I am wasting time I should give to the church in playing baseball."

"But, John! *Anonymous letters* . . ."

"Oh, I tore both up. But some of it all is certain to go to the deacons—I smell it in the air!"

"Seen Susan lately?" She had asked it to divert him but had known at once by his face that it was the wrong moment to put the question.

"No." The flatness of his tone was to remind her that Susan was the daughter of the Senior Deacon.

"And maybe he isn't as much interested in Susan as he said"— Deborah thought, now, with a small sigh, because it would be so good for Susan, just now, to have his interest. And this reflection sent her full thought to Willie. Susan had said he looked and acted ill, and he was ill in his mind, of course. His crash probably was close and he was afraid to face it. If he'd only have sense enough to consider a merger. . . . "I'd like to *shake* him into it," she said aloud, crossly.

Then suddenly she remembered a time when she *had* shaken him. She drew up straight in the rocker, the better to bring the occasion back in detail. He'd refused to admit his part in some prank—oh,

244

more than a prank for they had painted someone's calf in stripes like a zebra and tied it to old Mrs. Sharp's door. She had almost died from heart failure and the calf *had* died from licking the paint. Willie had been afraid to admit his share in the blame—afraid, of course, of Sarah Brent. She had lost patience with him, had caught him by his shoulders, thin, like young Bill's, shaken him good and hard. "You face this, Willie Brent!"

She did not smile at the memory. Her hands moved as if they reached out now for his shoulders.

Then she heard the car in the drive. Nell and Rom.

Rom and Nell came in, their arms full of packages. By their faces Deborah would have said they had not spoken to each other throughout the whole trip. But she greeted them cheerily.

"Did you get everything? Thanks. Put that bag there, Rom. I'll empty it later. Nell, stay to supper?"

When Nell hesitated, Deborah suspected that she was as reluctant to stay as she was to go home. "Guess I will, if you don't mind." She said it dully and Deborah saw how all its young vividness was gone from her face.

"Go and tell Susan you're staying. Or, no, I'll tell Bill when he brings in my paper. Car run all right?"

"Yes! Thanks, Aunt Debbie. I love driving it."

"Make some lemonade while I heat up supper—it'll taste good."

Susan was wrong, for Will Brent did have something with which to occupy himself, these evenings when he stayed at his office.

On shelves in a small closet off the office were old files and boxes of papers dating back to his father's and grandfather's time. Of no value, yet Will Brent had kept them out of respect for those past generations. Now he was destroying them—each evening taking down a box or a file, wiping the thick dust from it, carefully looking over each paper, then putting all in the stove and touching a match to them. A somber task—the beginning of the end.

Only one box was left and this he intended to look through tonight. That done it remained only to bolt the doors, some day, take down the old sign, walk away.

With the box on his desk before him he waited until certain that Coley Coggin had left the plant. Lately Coley had hung about, unnecessarily, for there was nothing for him to do, then had come into the office for a word or two before going home. Often Will Brent caught Coley looking at him with the same concern Susan showed and was irritated by it, but at the same time he saw in Coley a faithful friend—his only friend, probably, now.

As he expected, Coley opened the door. "Why don't you come along with me, Will?"

"Not now. I've work to do tonight."

Coley Coggin crossed to the desk, stood looking down at the box. He knew what Will Brent had been doing, these evenings.

"Sort o' sad, Will, ain't it?" He paused, shifting his weight from one foot to the other. "I suppose you'll be closing the plant any day now?"

Will Brent said coldly, "When I have made up my mind on what course to follow, I'll tell you."

"Only asked it because Almira keeps at me about it. I guess a lot in the village are asking her. They don't know what to do." Coley Coggin was not a man of easy speech and he reddened a little under the burden of saying what he had said. He went on, "Heard last night that Fred Hersey's took a job with Petersen's. Petersen's called him on the phone and offered him it."

Will Brent half sprang up from his chair, then sat back in it, his hands gripping its arms. "Damn you, Coggin, are you hinting that *I* turn to Petersen?" He shouted it.

"Now, Will, keep your shirt on. I've no say about what you should or shouldn't do. Just happened to speak of what I'd heard. I'll go along—see you tomorrow. Don't stay too late without some supper in you."

For several minutes Will Brent sat, tense, in his chair, his anger pounding against his temples. It was not so much anger at Coley, as a fresh wave of fury at Rudolph Petersen, from whom had come a letter this morning, suggesting a merger. Aware from its first line of what it was about he had torn it into pieces without reading it through. He had had time to burn the scraps before Susan came. That the letter remained unanswered would be his answer to the fellow. The upstart . . .

He opened the box. Because it was marked personal he had left it to the last to look over. Certificates of stocks, sold long ago, old tax receipts, old receipts from house painters, carpenters, seed and feed stores . . . Coming upon one of the latter, he recalled Dolly, the horse his father had driven when he was a little boy. His father had allowed him to hold the reins sometimes, though his mother hadn't. . . . He remembered the vacation he had started in to work here at the plant. Sixteen. "You're a Brent man now, son. See that you live up to it," his mother had said. He thought, suddenly, unwillingly, of young Bill, who would have no such heritage. But the fact of that must wait. . . .

He came upon the deed to some woodlots his father had bought. His father had lost money in the venture—he remembered that for a long time it had been a subject of much talk on his mother's part— that it was at such times that his father withdrew into himself, became silent, self-effacing. As he had after Debbie ran away.

He folded the old deeds, started to put them back in the envelope, when he noticed a thin sheet of paper caught under the inside of the flap. He drew it out, recognized his father's squarish handwriting on it, then read at the top of the sheet, "I hereby make my last will and testament." The date followed. A sound escaped Will Brent's lips as he read it. September 18, 1910. His father had died suddenly on September 20, two days later.

He stared at the paper—this was his father's last will, not the one his mother had produced from the locked tin box she kept in a drawer of the chest in the kitchen. His hands stiff on the paper he read on, forcing his eyes from word to word. "To my wife, Sarah, I leave my life insurance, what government bonds I own and the savings which are in the bank in Winsted. Also the use of the Brent house through her lifetime. After her death the house is to go to my very beloved daughter, Deborah Brent Bouvais. The interests in the Brent Nail Works I wish to be divided between my son Will and my daughter Deborah, with the exception of a twenty percent share in aforesaid interests which I bequeath to my good and faithful friend, Elmer Coggin. I have come to believe that in matters of importance three heads are better able to come to wise decisions than one. . . ."

Stunned, Will Brent dropped the sheet. "My very beloved daughter Deborah." This had been his father's unspoken answer to his mother's edict that Debbie be as one dead, forgotten. He had regretted writing the other will, had written this, here at the office, left it here.

"Mercy!" He clapped a hand to his head. Were not a part of the profits of all these years due to Deborah?—to Elmer's son, Coley, who legally had inherited his father's twenty percent share in interest in the plant? The Brent house had been Deborah's all this time. He felt beads of cold sweat under his hand. "Ha! The best they'll get is a share in my failure!" His laugh rang harsh.

He read the signatures of the witnesses. Jonathan Seegar. Harry Stock. Cory Bond. He remembered them as friends of his father's, who had lived, not in Sweethome, but about the countryside. All dead now.

Suddenly with both hands he caught up the paper. Coley knew nothing about this will, no one knew of it. Why not—why not . . . ? The other papers which he was going to burn lay on the desk before him. His hands moved to put the thin sheet with them.

Then a sick shaking horror stayed them. "You haven't come to *this!*" he cried aloud. And at that moment Susan opened the door.

"I drove over to take you home— *Father!*" She cried out in alarm, ran across the room to him. "Are you ill? You're shaking so. . . . What is it? Oh, what is it?"

He put his hand across his eyes. "I—*was* ill, for a moment. It's over now."

"Father, I wish . . . Coley Coggin stopped in—he told me what you were doing. He's worried about you. *Are* these papers so important that you have to go without your supper?"

"I have found one that is. Read it." Will Brent's voice was grim. He thrust the paper into her hands.

Susan read it, lifted a bewildered face to her father. "Why, in this— and everyone's always thought . . ."

"My father wrote it two days before he died, left it here with his papers. No one ever found it."

"Then it is his last will!" Susan read it again, swiftly now, cried out, "Aunt Debbie *owns* the old house! And as much of the plant as you do! And Coley—wouldn't he have his father's share of interest? Father, this changes everything, doesn't it?"

Will Brent stiffened in his chair, drew his lips into a grim line. "There is nothing that can be changed."

"I mean—just as Grandfather wrote—that perhaps three of you . . ."

He took the paper from her, folded it, put it in his pocket. "I can scarcely look for wisdom from my half-sister Deborah and Coley Coggin has accepted my thinking for a long time." He shoved the other papers back in the box, got up from his chair. "I'll dispose of these some other evening. We'll go, now."

Susan did not move. "You're going to tell Aunt Debbie—tell her right away?"

"I'll take this paper to Jed Weaver—he'll tell me whether it holds legally after all these years. If he says it does he will inform her."

"Father—not that way! You must tell her yourself! It's going to make her so happy, to know that Grandfather really wanted it that way. She's told me—she wrote a letter to him after she went away

249

and he never answered it. It'll make it all up to her. Father," now there was a flash in Susan's quiet eyes, a faint scorn in her voice, "you've always been so particular about paying up bills as soon as they came in—you've said the Brents always were—this is a debt— can't you pay *it?*"

Will Brent was on his feet but, startled, he took hold of the back of his chair for support. For sometimes Mary had spoken to him in that same voice, with that same look. He remembered that usually it was when she was trying to get him to stand with her against his mother about something. For the moment Susan was Mary and his mother was in the room with them, stern-lipped, dominating. He felt himself shaking again.

"If you will put this box back in the closet, Susan . . ." He gave the box to Susan without looking at her. "I think you are right— I should not go so long without food."

CHAPTER XXIV

A SENSE of failure was beginning to weigh on John Wendell, heavier with each day. Though he refused to feel any regret for any word he had spoken from the pulpit, anything he had done in his parish work. On the contrary he felt a deep satisfaction in seeing Rudolph Petersen in his congregation each Sunday, Mrs. D'Arby in the last pew. In the baseball team he had organized among the boys of the village—two from the Flats—and in their interest and enthusiasm. He had found an old barn on the outskirts of the village that could be bought and built over into a gymnasium and recreation hall, the barnyard into a playground. It would take money, of course, but if the parents in the community were shown what it would mean to these youngsters here, might they not contribute to it? He had made acquaintance with the farmers and their families around about outside the valley, going about his calls on foot, since his old motorcycle had failed him. He had very recently formed a Bible study group among the women in Sweethome, to meet with him once a week—five had come last week. But all this measured nowhere near to the earnest hopes he had cherished when he took over the church.

In spite of himself and prayer he could not dismiss the anonymous letters from his mind. Or the suspicion of who it was who had written them. The t's had not been crossed—nor were they on some of the checks that had come in with the provisions Mrs. Donnell brought from the Higgins' store and which she always made him look over that he might know she was thrifty in her providing. He was aware, too, that Mrs. Higgins had not been to a service since Commemoration Sunday. She was prominent in the church affairs—without any doubt she would influence others to share her antagonism.

But the bitter edge to his feeling of failure was that he might never be able to seek out Susan Brent. A man who appeared to be unacceptable to this, his first parish . . .

His failure was in his thoughts as he walked back to the parsonage from a call at a farm two miles out of the valley, late one afternoon of the next week. Agnes Peely had told him of a Mrs. Hunter there who was dying. "She used to come to our church, years and years ago. And maybe she'd like to hear you say a prayer." But Mrs. Hunter had not wanted him to—she had turned her head with its pitifully scant white hair away from him, not in scorn of him as a preacher, but simply not needing him. He had put his hand over the bony one that lay still on the coverlet, then had gone away—his prayer for the dying unuttered.

Mrs. Donnell met him in the hall. "Your supper's waiting. And I suppose you're in a hurry to go out and play with those boys."

This was much more than she had said to him in some time and there was an unwonted liveliness in her face, both of which, if he had not been tired, would have put him on his guard.

"I'll wash up—be down in a minute."

To his surprise she had set his place at the table in the dining room. She put a plate of stew with dumplings down before him. He had not had as hearty a dinner as this for some time.

She did not leave the room when he began to eat. She sat down on the edge of a chair and waited for him to speak a few words of grace. That done, he picked up his fork but at once he put it down, for she was folding her hands on the table and now he knew that something was coming.

She said, "After Monday, Mr. Wendell, you'll have to do for yourself. I'm going to my cousin's in Hartford. She's written me—

she takes roomers and she needs me."

Before he could speak John Wendell had to control a surge of relief. He thought swiftly of Father Duffy's simple, peaceful home-living. When he said nothing, she added, "I don't doubt the ladies here will find someone for you—if you'll be needing anyone."

She meant, he thought, that he would not be here. He looked down at his plate. He must say something. . . . "This is a very good dinner, Mrs. Donnell!"

"We had that meat left over and I don't waste things. I made the dumplings extra. And I baked a cake."

"Good. I'll enjoy it."

But she had not unfolded her hands. There was more. . . . She began, "I thought I ought to say, before I go, that I think you used good judgment in not letting Nell Brent sing in church, last Sunday."

"Not *letting* her . . ." He stopped. He had had nothing to do with it—Nell simply had not appeared.

"After what she'd done. You know about it, don't you? It's the talk of the village. . . ."

John steeled himself now against a surge of feeling that was not relief. "I have not heard of anything she has done that would prohibit her from singing in the service."

"Maybe your ideas are different! But when a girl is caught with a boy up in that empty Hurrell house, caught running away half-naked—Ham Higgins saw her when he took the Swede up to look over the house. It was that Italian boy from the Flats—Ham got ahold of him. Even if she is a Brent, it don't make any difference!"

John remembered Nell's agitation, that afternoon of last week when he had encountered her on the old trail. He remembered her incoherent outburst that had suggested some shattered faith—definitely not what Mrs. Donnell was implying.

"When was all this?" he asked, quickly.

"Last week, one day. Wednesday, it was. Wednesday afternoon."

"At what time?"

Mrs. Donnell's face expressed annoyance at this questioning. "Ham Higgins'll tell you! Though it happens I know about what time it was for I went into the store just as Ham rode away with that Swede to go up and show him the house and Hattie wanted me to stay a while and I looked at their clock and saw it was five and said I couldn't—so I figure it'd be soon after five that Ham caught them."

John got to his feet, pushed the chair back with such force that it fell over. "You are wrong, Mrs. Donnell. On Wednesday afternoon, at that time, *I* was walking with Nell Brent down the old lumber trail. I had been with her for the last half-hour. I wear a wrist watch, so I happen to be certain of the time."

He started toward the door.

"Where're you going? You haven't touched the dinner I cooked!"

But he did not answer her. He was out of the house, going down the walk toward the Higgins' store. Mrs. Donnell sniffed and picked up his plates. "It'll be his word against Ham's, he'll find."

John did not go into the store but went around to the side door which he knew led into the living quarters back of the store. His face was still stern, white with anger. This story on these women's tongues must be stopped, even if it meant more enmity toward him.

Ham Higgins answered his knock. " 'Evening, Reverend. Didn't look for it to be you outside the door. Anything wrong? You look palish."

"It's Mrs. Higgins I must see."

"Well, come in. We're just finishing supper. Hattie, here's the Reverend Wendell. Pull up a chair, Reverend. Have some of Hattie's berry pie."

John refused both the chair and the pie with a quick shake of his head. "I've come to ask you, Mrs. Higgins, to go out, go out this evening, and tell every woman you meet that the girl caught up at the Hurrell house last week was *not* Nell Brent!"

Hattie Higgins sucked in her thin lips. "And why should decent people cover up what the girl's done?"

"I am not asking you to cover it up—I am telling you that it was *not* Nell Brent and it is a cruel thing to let the girl suffer for a mistake in identity!"

"It happens Ham saw her."

Ham Higgins drew forward in his chair, embarrassed. "Wait a minute, Hat. Mebbe I was hasty. I just took it for granted the girl was the Brent girl. Come to think of it, I didn't see she had red hair like Nell Brent's, and hers would show a mile away. Guess it is up to you, Hat, to say mebbe there's a mistake—just drop in on Almira, like you did before."

Hattie glared at him. "Make me look like a fool, because you're one, Ham Higgins! Who's going to believe you guess maybe you made a mistake—a week afterwards!"

"Mrs. Higgins, you may tell everyone that Nell Brent was with me at half-past four of that day up on the lumbering trail. At five we walked down it—we separated when we reached Central Road, she went on home and I returned to the parsonage. You will not appear foolish in giving such evidence that Nell could not possibly have been at the old Hurrell house, that afternoon!"

As John spoke the indignation on Hattie Higgins' face changed slowly to a smug satisfaction. "This will finish the young man with our congregation," it said. Admitting, as cool as brass, to taking girls up on that old lumbering trail . . .

Ham said, humbly, "I did wrong—should've remembered that sermon you gave us, Reverend! When you told us to know what we were talking about before we talked. Now it's all squared up, have your pie!"

"Thanks, no. Sorry I had to interrupt your supper but it was too urgent a matter to let it wait."

"It certainly was," agreed Ham. "Well, another time. Goodnight, Reverend. And Hattie'll run over to Almira's." He chuckled. "Don't know any quicker way of unsaying what's been said."

As he walked back to the parsonage, John went over in his mind those of the circumstances of his encounter with Nell, that afternoon, which he had not told to Mrs. Higgins. He had no doubt now but that Nell had seen the boy's car at the Hurrell house, knew that he was not alone there. Though he felt far from smiling he did smile, remembering that there had been more fury in her tears than real anguish of heart, remembering the toss of her head as she walked past him down the trail. Then his smile stiffened as the realization came sharply in on him that from what he *had* told Mrs. Higgins the talk now would be that he was courting Nell Brent. It would come in that light to Susan's ears. . . .

He found Mrs. Donnell gone from the house, his plate, with his dinner still on it, on the kitchen table. He looked down at it, picked it up, scraped the congealed food into the garbage receptacle, got a bottle of milk from the refrigerator. But he had no appetite even for that.

On this same evening Will Brent, coming home from Winsted, where he had been for most of the afternoon in conference with Jed Weaver and Richard Prouet, found Susan the only one in the house.

"Where's Nell?" he demanded as they sat down to supper. Even though the question had an automatic sound, as if his lips, from long practice, shaped it by themselves.

"I don't know—maybe over at Aunt Debbie's."

"I don't like it. That Polish fellow is there now."

"Father, he barely speaks to anyone! He's all wrapped up in something he's writing, Aunt Debbie says."

Will Brent frowned down darkly at his plate, remembering the memoirs of which Deborah had spoken when she first came. Also that Debbie would not be going away from Sweethome in ten days or so, unless she chose to go. . . .

"It's quite possible you might get a court to nullify this will you've found, Brent," Jed Weaver had said to him at the end of their talk. Then he had added, "But, knowing you, I rather think you'll want to carry out your father's last wishes, to the letter."

Susan had not spoken of the will since that evening in his office. But her eyes, when she looked at him, asked him, "When are you going to tell Aunt Debbie?" with a quiet insistence in them that was like Mary's. Indeed, these last few days, Mary, through Susan, had haunted him.

"Even so," he answered Susan, finding a vent for this feeling in a show of irritability. "There'll be talk. I daresay there has been plenty as it is over Nell and that Italian fellow. I hope you put a stop to that."

He saw Susan's lips part on a quick-drawn breath but he did not give it any significance for he suddenly realized young Bill was nowhere about.

"Where's Bill?"

"He ate something and went to play ball."

"I don't like that," said Will Brent. "He's getting out of hand!"

"Father!" Susan's voice was sharp. "You can't deny Bill *some* good times! You must have had them at his age! Or—maybe you didn't— your mother didn't let you and that's why you don't want him to— or Nell. . . ."

He looked up, startled. This, from Susan! "And you, yourself?" he asked coldly.

He had every reason to expect quick denial from this dutiful daughter, an apology for what she had said, yet he felt a curious sinking at his heart as he waited for her to answer.

"Yes, me, too, sometimes." Susan said it quietly and began to eat her supper.

He tried to be angry—he *should* be angry—but he was too shaken. It was as if some prop on which he long had depended suddenly had failed him. Mary, before Susan, Mary standing between him and his

257

mother. Deborah, before Mary . . . *His father never had had anyone.* The drumming was beating at his temples, Jed Weaver's last words running through it.

"Susan." He spoke stiffly, "I have asked Coley Coggin to go with me to your Aunt Deborah's this evening. I will inform them both at the same time of the contents of the will I found."

Susan's head came up, her eyes warm. "Oh, I'm so *glad* that at last you're going to tell her! I was afraid. . . . Then it's legal and all that?"

"Weaver says it can be probated as long as there was no distribution of the estate at the time of my father's death."

Susan sprang up from her chair, ran around the table to him, kissed him swiftly, warmly on his cheek. "You're going to feel better, now, Father, about everything!"

He drew up his shoulders. "An assumption, my dear, in which I doubt I can share." Despite his words the sinking feeling was gone. He began to eat his supper.

In the other house Deborah Brent and Nell were washing and wiping the supper dishes. In silence mostly, for Nell was shut up in her own thoughts and Deborah respected her right to this preoccupation too much to try to force her out of it. The girl'd talk when she got ready to. . . .

She was glad Nell came here to do her brooding—she couldn't in front of Susan and her father. She wasn't hiding away, disgraced, because each day she had driven off somewhere in the car. Deborah had trumped up endless errands for her to do and sometimes just had said, "Drive off somewhere, Nell! Get the air. . . ." The mileage was piling up fast but Deborah did not care, for Nell, on her return, for just a few minutes, was more like her former self.

Still she wished the girl would say something—it was not good for her to lock it all up in herself, whether it was remorse or rebellion.

Deborah had troubling thoughts of her own to dwell on. A letter

258

had come from the realtor about that farm. The place needed some repairs, the realtor admitted, but he wrote at length of its beautiful view, of the creek that ran through the property, of an acre of good growing soil for a garden. There it was and all she had to do was to buy it and pack her things and go with Rom. But—*might she not be lonely there?*

Rudolph Petersen had told her he had had no word from Willie in answer to his written suggestion of a merger.

"I can't do much more."

"No, you can't."

He had come in yesterday, unexpectedly. Just to let her know, he had said, that he had found a good couple in Winsted who were moving in a few days into the old house up on the hill, and would get it cleaned up, ready for him, and would stay on with him. "They're Swedish," he had added with a broad smile. "As soon as I'm settled in, you're coming to dinner. You're going to be my first guest."

He was so pleased about it all—he was so friendly in dropping in, as he had, to tell her, to want her to be his first company, that she could not bring herself to tell him she would not be here.

Nell hung up her tea towel, went to the window, stood there a moment, her back to Deborah, then wheeled around.

"Aunt Debbie—how do you *know* when you're really in love?" She demanded it, almost angrily.

The girl was saying something at last—but *this!* Deborah dropped down in the nearest chair, startled. She must think for a moment. When she did not speak at once, Nell said, "You should know—you've been married so often!"

"Yes, I suppose I should know. But—it's different, as one grows older. . . ."

Nell gave a quick, impatient sound. "I don't mean when you're older! I mean—my age. If—if *you'd* found out that Paul Bouvais wasn't true to you—that's before you ran away with him—would you have been just *mad* or utterly crushed?"

So Nell *wasn't* that girl they'd caught! And she knew about her, some way. . . .

Debbie said warmly, "I'd be mad—just plain *mad!*"

"That's what's worried me, Aunt Debbie. I tried to be heartbroken —I could make myself believe I was for a little while—and then I'd just be furious again. So I couldn't have been truly in love!"

The girl looked so young, so puzzled and unhappy—Deborah longed for reassuring, wise words to come to her tongue about love— that it was friendship, too, and companionship and partnership, a sharing of fortune and misfortune, of happiness and grief—oh, she knew it all so well but the knowledge was too intimate to speak of it. And when she hesitated Nell drew a long, sad sigh. "It was so wonderful! Now I suppose I'll never fall in love again!"

Deborah had words to answer this. "Nonsense, child! It'll come! You forget this boy and how he's hurt you! Think of something else— your singing. . . ."

The telephone rang. Deborah left Nell to answer it.

It was Clare Hersey. "Deb! I had to call you!" So breathless was Clare's voice that Deborah, except for knowing it was impossible, would have thought she had been running. "Almira Coggin and Hattie Higgins have just been here. And they told me that that girl with the Italian boy *wasn't* Nell! I am *so* happy to know it—I had to call you right off for I knew how you must have been feeling about it. . . ."

"Did you?" Deborah could not resist asking it, or her tone of doubt. But Clare did not hear it. She went on, still breathlessly. "And the way the truth came out—John Wendell heard the story from Mrs. Donnell and went straight to Hattie and he asked Hattie to tell everyone that he was with Nell that afternoon, *all* afternoon—they were up in the woods. Of course Hattie's glad to tell everyone—it was dreadful, a mistake like that and about a girl like Nell. And I think it's quite exciting, don't you?"

"What?" demanded Deborah.

"Why, about John Wendell and Nell. Though probably you suspected something!"

"Clare, some other time we'll talk about it!

"And it will not be over a party line of a telephone," Deborah muttered as she hung the receiver on its hook.

She did not go back to the kitchen at once but stood by the telephone, fitting what Clare had told her into the whole happening. John must have met Nell up on that road—the girl probably was upset and he had stayed with her, walked down the hill with her. Honest in him to go straight to Hattie Higgins and tell her so, but— "You've started something more, John!"

She found Nell on the porch. "I'm going home, Aunt Debbie. Thanks for supper. . . ."

"Come over any time, Nell. Use the car whenever you want to. Wait!" Deborah went into the kitchen, caught up the catalogues, put them into Nell's hands. "Here, look over these. It'll keep you from thinking of other things."

Nell glanced down at them. "What's the use? The nail works is going to crack up any day, Bill says. He says he's going to skip out West—crazy kid. I suppose I'll just be a clerk in some store in Winsted. . . ."

"Maybe not," said Deborah.

Going back into the kitchen she wondered why she had said it. She would not be here to do anything for Nell, to help Susan or Bill or Willie himself through the threatened crack-up.

She went into the parlor. She might as well get a letter off to that real-estate man—send a deposit on the purchase price, too. She drew out paper, picked up her pen. However, she only held it in her hand, thinking, "How many different places have you lived, Debbie?" Checking them off on her fingers, "Etna—St. Louis, with the Mulfords, Portland, Twitchel, San Francisco . . ." She looked down at the blank sheet of paper, the old fear of loneliness growing in her. "I guess it's meant for you to have no roots anywhere."

Then she heard men's steps on the side porch, put down the pen, went out to the kitchen, saw Will Brent and Coley Coggin at the door, Will standing stiffly straight, one hand raised to knock, Coley Coggin a little behind him, his face puzzled and uncertain.

"Hello, Willie. Good evening, Coley. Come in." Its usual heartiness was not in her voice: a sudden weariness deadened the curiosity she normally would have felt. Whatever more Willie had to say to her— it was too late, wasn't it?

She stepped aside to let them come in.

"Will you sit here in the kitchen—or would you rather go into the parlor?"

"Wherever we are the least likely to be interrupted," said Will Brent.

"If you mean by Rom—he is up in his room and horses wouldn't drag him out of it."

Deborah sat down at the table. Coley sat down, looking over the kitchen with a slow, reminiscent smile. "Been a long time since I've come in here!" But Will Brent remained on his feet.

"He probably feels more authoritative like that," thought Deborah and she did not urge him to take a chair.

He drew a paper from his pocket, cleared his throat as if some obstruction in it made it difficult to speak. Then he said, stiffly, "I have asked Coley to come here with me tonight because the contents of this paper are of interest to him as well as to you, Deborah. It is a will of my father's which I found the other evening among his personal papers—written and signed before witnesses two days before he died."

Instinctively Deborah hardened herself to meet what was to come, though . . . "My father couldn't cut me off any more than he did!"

Will Brent continued, "I will read it and then you both can look it over, if you wish." He coughed again, then read what was written on the paper. Then he folded it, held it in his fingers. "I have been in consultation with Weaver and Prouet—both agree that, after all

262

these years, a court might set it aside. But I have no idea of going to court. I have too much respect for my father's wishes not to carry them out to the letter—as far as I am able." He sat down, then, with some abruptness.

Coley was scratching his head, bewildered. And Deborah's immediate thought, to the exclusion of all that the will revealed, was that Willie had said just those same words to her about living in this house. Then, with a quick, glad sound she moved forward on her chair. *"Willie,* that means—Father *did* go on loving me!" She was too moved to care that Coley Coggin was with them. "If I'd known that all these years . . ." She stopped, to control her voice, then she shook her head. "No, I wouldn't want my life to have been any different!"

Coley Coggin put out his hand. "Let me look at it, Will. Funny thing, isn't it? That paper in the office all this time! Yes, that's your father's handwriting, all right. I remember it—it was sort of different. My father'd kind o' liked to have known about this—showed your father put trust in him. How long's it been?"

"Thirty-eight years."

Enlightenment slowly dawned on Coley. "I'd o' got it, wouldn't I?" He looked pleased. "I got everything my father had, though 'twasn't much."

Will Brent rose to his feet again, stiffened his shoulders. "I regret to say, Coley, that this you come into now is—nothing. My half-sister gets this house but as to the nail works and her and your interest in it—within a few days the plant will be worth no more than what a junk dealer may pay for the machines." He spoke in a strained, cold voice but Deborah saw red running up his face, his hands opening and closing nervously.

Just so had he stood before her when she charged him with having something to do with painting that calf! Her thought came as quickly back to the present. Be hard on him now as she had been, then?

She stood up. "It needn't be, Will Brent. You know perfectly well

263

what you can do—you can go into a merger with Rudolph Petersen. He's suggested it twice—his terms are more than acceptable. . . ."

"Sell over to him an industry that has been in my family for three . . ."

Deborah did not let him finish. She flew around the table, caught him by the shoulders, shook him hard. "You make me *sick,* Willie Brent!" She heard the sound of a suppressed chuckle from Coley but she did not let it silence her. "You think of *that,* with more than half of the men in Sweethome thrown out of work! With your own children . . . young Bill, who isn't through school. You'd rather take that sign down and frame it and hang it in your room, maybe keep pansies under it for remembrance. You're *afraid!* The trouble with you is that you don't see when times change, and change your way of thinking with it!"

Will Brent drew out of her hold, his face white with outrage. "You will find Coley agrees with me," he said thickly.

Deborah turned to Coley, thinking swiftly, "Yes, Coley can speak up now, same as I can!" "Do you?" she demanded of Coley. "Which do you think is the saner thing to do—listen to what Petersen has to offer—or close up?"

Coley moved uneasily in his chair, looked from her to Will, then down at his hands. "I don't know—I sort of understand how Will feels about it—and I've always thought he knew what was right to do. But there's something in what you said about times changing— mebbe we ought t' see that and hear what Petersen offers. Our neighbors here—they'd like to be sure of their jobs. . . ." His voice trailed off as embarrassment overcame him.

"And now, what, Willie?" asked Deborah.

She felt her breath holding, waiting. He could, of course, ignore what both she and Coley had said—this last will had not gone to probate. He could close the plant tomorrow. . . . He was shaking, she could see, and his hands were tight on the edges of his coat. He swung around and moved toward the door but not with his usual stiff erectness, Deborah noticed, too.

Near the door he turned. "Call your fool Petersen in!" He shouted it. Then he said, "If you're ready to go, Coggin . . ."

Coley Coggin got to his feet, still looking embarrassed. After an instant of hesitation he held his hand out to Deborah. "Good night, Mrs. Brent." A very slight twinkle was in his eyes for an instant, then was gone as he followed Will Brent out of the kitchen.

Deborah stood still, one hand on the table. *Poor Willie*—how it hurt him to yield up his pride—how it *hurt!* But, he'd broken through it! Give him time to get used to it and he'd be a different man.

She went to the refrigerator, feeling suddenly spent. Some food—after all, she had eaten very little for supper because neither Rom nor Nell had eaten much. "I'll make some cheese sandwiches—call Rom down."

She got out the cheese, turned, looked over the kitchen. "Why, it's mine!" she cried, aloud. "It's *mine!*" She wanted to laugh, to cry. She dropped the cheese on the table, went around the room, touching one thing and another, knowing it was silly—"a woman my age"—yet loving the feel of each thing her fingers touched. "It's mine, now—not *yours,* Sarah Brent! It's *my* home."

She longed to tell someone—Rom? No, he was too remote in his work. Susan, or John Wendell . . . *Rudolph Petersen* . . .

"I'll tell him tomorrow. I have to call him anyway." She laughed. "Petticoats in business!"

CHAPTER XXV

It was Hattie Higgins' idea, to call a joint meeting of the different committees for the Bazaar. "And right away," she said to Almira Coggin. "It'll start everyone working harder for it."

Almira agreed quickly that it was the thing to do.

But each had a thought in mind of which she did not speak. Hattie's was that she would use this meeting to start some definite action where John Wendell was concerned. The time was ripe for it, she considered. His taking young girls up into the woods! That would stir up the women. Almira Coggin saw the occasion as an opportunity to enjoy a recognition of her new status in Sweethome, wife of as-good-as-a-partner in the Brent Nail Works. Why, all these years she and Coley could have been holding their heads as high as Will Brent did! That the Brent works might fold up on any tomorrow did not lessen her new pride.

Coley had told her of the will that had been found when she pressed him to tell her why Will Brent had asked him to stop in at the house, that evening of the past week. "We went over to Debbie's. . . ."

"To *Deborah Brent's house?* Why'd you have to do that?"

"Well, Will wanted us both to hear it, same time." He had finished, "She's some girl."

"What do you mean, Coley Coggin? Some Girl! Why, she must be way in her sixties!"

"Not as I recollect from past years. She wasn't no more'n three years older'n Will, then, so she can't be now. And he was fifty-six last birthday. She must be getting close to fifty-nine, if she isn't that al-

266

ready. And I say again she's some girl."

Almira let a look of scorn for "you men" take care of that, for the time at least. She had to digest what else he had told her.

He had said the will would go to probate at once. Yes, it would be in the newspaper. So, talking to Hattie, she had thought, "Everyone will know it by next Friday."

"At Clare Hersey's?" she suggested.

"Clare would like that. She's on the apron committee."

When Friday came, there was a full attendance, with nearly every woman arriving at the appointed hour, eleven o'clock. Martha Purdy was among these. "Something tells me I should be there at the first gun and stay," she had said to Walter.

There was the usual immediate chatter. "I've found some of the sweetest chintz for aprons. . . ." "Miss Crawford, over on Storm Hill, is going to give us two of her grandmother's pieced quilts to sell. . . ." The chairman of the baby booth put in, "I'm promised some jackets and bootees, if they're done in time!" But the talk was hurried, as if it were automatic. Then the chairman of the foods booth, which usually sold only cakes and pies, said, "What about this I hear—that Deborah Brent makes some kind of special soup and sells it?"

She put the question to Clare. Clare said, obligingly and proudly, "She doesn't make it—she sold the recipe for it. *That's* what she lives on!"

One of the committee members cried, "My goodness! Really? Why didn't I think to sell that recipe of mine for lemon cake!"

"Maybe she'd donate some of her soup for my booth. Martha, will you ask her if she will? You see something of her, don't you? Living right across the road."

"I run over sometimes. . . ." Martha Purdy hesitated. She wanted to say, "Why should she donate *any*thing to us?" But she remembered that Walter had warned her to watch her tongue. "Yes, I'll ask her."

Agnes Peely spoke up, nervously, yet with some urgency. "Why don't we ask her to help—you know, pour the coffee or something like that?"

There was a moment of silence, which Clare broke on a quick breath. "I think that'd be nice—as long as she's going to live here!"

All eyes went to Clare, tongues waited. Almira straightened expectantly in her chair. Those who didn't know about the will would know now. She had been let down considerably because no one had spoken of it.

"She really *is* going to stay?" asked one of the women, after a moment.

Someone answered for Clare. "It was in the paper—about that old will that was found. Deborah gets the Brent house—it's been hers all these years, only she didn't know it. And here everyone's thought her father didn't leave her so much as a penny account of her running away."

Hattie Higgins was going on with her work, plying her needle, with little jabs into the dish towel she was hemming, cut from a bolt of cloth Ham had found slightly damaged. She wasn't interested in this will—let Deborah Brent stay! She'd probably be spending some of the money she got from that soup in the store. Hattie was content to wait until this topic was exhausted, then her moment would come. . . .

"She's had the same interest in the nail works as Will Brent's had, all these years," put in Clare. Now Almira, like Hattie, waited.

Someone laughed, with a little bitterness. "A lot that means, now!"

"I don't know. Maybe . . ." Clare stopped, uncertain whether she should speak of Rudolph Petersen who had, at Deborah's request, given Fred a job. She finished, "Maybe Deb'll think of something."

Now several of the women laughed. "Clare!" expostulated one. "What could *she* think of?"

Clare reddened in embarrassment. "What I meant—she knows Rudolph Petersen so well!"

The name had the effect of bringing to their attention the escapade

268

up at the old Hurrell house, which had not yet been touched upon. They fell into it immediately. Had that Italian boy been arrested? No. And wasn't it dreadful that everyone had thought at first that the girl was Nell Brent? Hattie Higgins held her needle over the toweling but she did not speak—no use defending Ham for making that mistake, or herself for telling it. Just wait. . . .

"And all that afternoon Nell was with John Wendell! He came right out and said so, didn't he?"

"You'd say there were older girls who'd attract him more," said Julia White. "If he's looking for a Brent there's Susan. . . ."

Hattie Higgins folded her towel, put it in her knitting bag, snapped the handles together, at the same time drawing forward in her chair.

"We're all here together—we women who work for the church— *care* about it. It's same as a meeting and it's time we did something. It's my opinion and I think you'll all agree with me that we've had just about enough of John Wendell. It gets worse the longer it goes on. I won't speak of some things like his motorcycle and his baseball playing. More serious is that sermon of his, that Sunday—an insult to every one of us! Now he's bringing in that woman from the Flats— and, mark my words, there'll be others like her. And this *last*—taking our young girls up into the woods. I haven't a girl but it's just as shocking to me as though I had. How do we know how many before Nell Brent or how many since?" Hattie had to pause to moisten her lips but no one spoke for surprise held every tongue. "So *I* say, today, right *now,* let's sign our names to a letter to the deacons, demanding that he be sent away, as unfitting to be our minister. I've it written out. . . ." She opened her knitting bag, took out a sheet of paper. She took the silence in the room for agreement. "Here it is, all ready."

But Agnes Peely protested in a distressed voice, "Oh, *no!*"

It gave others courage to voice protests.

"I didn't think that sermon was an insult, Hattie. I've thought of it often, since. I think he *said* something we needed to hear."

"How do we *know* that he takes girls up into the woods? Maybe Nell Brent but if it's that way between them . . ."

"He scarcely could court her on Central Road!"

"I like his ideas about starting our youngsters doing things right here in Sweethome, instead of going off other places."

"We've been critical of him because he's different from Winfield Marcy—but maybe it's good for us to have someone with new ideas. . . ."

One after another spoke in John Wendell's defense, some timidly, others with a spirit of conviction.

Hattie Higgins, sitting straighter, bridling, gave Almira Coggin a commanding look which told *her* to speak up. But Almira lowered her eyes from it to the work in her lap. When no one else spoke of Coley's part in that old will Hattie might have said something. . . .

Martha Purdy had brought no sewing with her but her hands moved as if she were putting some away. She was going to open her mouth, and in spite of Walter's warning, go the limit. She drew forward on her chair, as Hattie had.

She did control her voice and managed a smile which she turned around the room. "It *is* true that this is much like a meeting and while we're all here I'd like to have you vote on a suggestion of *mine!* And that is that we write a letter—I just thought of it this minute so I haven't the letter written out but I have a pen in my bag and I am sure Clare has paper—and ask the deacons to give John Wendell a three-year contract." She drew a quick breath, went on over an audible snort from Hattie Higgins, "It is so that John Wendell has different ideas from those we're used to. But he's awfully earnest in his work, he *cares* about it—about us! He wants the young people to have normal, healthy recreation—he's talked about his plans with Walter and me and they're *good,* only they're something new here. He wants to bring more people into the church—people who don't go to any other. But isn't that part of his work? Mrs. D'Arby—I spent the afternoon with her a week or so ago—she said she'd loan me some of her hooked rug patterns. She's just like any one of us! She was lonely for a church to go to—and aren't we being pretty choosey to say she isn't welcome in ours? Others, too—from anywhere. Rudolph Petersen—let's make him welcome. Let's build up our congregation, help John Wendell—and not be smug and—and intolerant about it. If we are, our works *are* just an outward show!"

She stopped, a little frightened but glad she had spoken her mind at last.

Hattie Higgins was too furious to speak, others too astounded. Almira was weighing the moment swiftly. Then Agnes Peely said, a little unsteadily, "I really do think we're smug—or have been! Martha, I vote that you write the letter right now and if that's a motion or you'll make it one, I second it!"

"I do move that we write such a letter," said Martha Purdy, firmly.

Even though only hands moved here and there, there seemed a stir in the room, much like a gust of wind blowing through it. Julia White said, with a little laugh, "If you want a minister with a flibbertigibbet wife . . ." but somehow it was lost. Then Clare said, on a pant of breath, "I second it, too."

"I think my suggestion comes first," put in Hattie Higgins belligerently.

Agnes Peely said quickly, "Martha made hers a motion first—we have to vote on that—Hattie, you're chairman of the Bazaar committee—you ask for the ayes." There was a twinkling in Agnes Peely's eyes that no one ever had seen before. In Martha Purdy's, too.

Hattie Higgins' face purpled and she had difficulty unlocking her lips. "The noes, too," she said tartly. Then, "Those who are in favor of this motion—and it's ridiculous—you don't know what you're doing to the community—say aye."

Ayes came, some all at once, others more hesitantly. Several did not speak.

"Hattie, please ask those in favor of it to stand up," said Martha Purdy.

271

"Can't they speak without being on their feet? All right. The ayes stand up, then."

A few stood quickly, others more slowly. "I simply can't get up out of this chair," said Clare. "But I vote aye."

Only Julia White and Almira Coggin remained seated. Then with a slight lift of her shoulders Julia White got to her feet. Agnes Peely looked at Almira. "It'd be nice if it were unanimous, Almira!"

Hattie Higgins bored Almira with her eyes, her lips pressed hard together. Almira moved uneasily. "I don't know *really* what I ought to say! I do think as Hattie does about a lot of those things—only, you see . . ." She was on her feet now, her head high. "All these years Coley's really been a sort of partner of Will Brent's and his father was of Will's father—and if John Wendell is going to marry one of the Brent girls—I suppose I ought to vote aye!"

"You fool," muttered Hattie Higgins.

Agnes Peely said quickly, "Then you can write, Martha, that it's unanimous. The chair doesn't vote, unless there's a tie, does it? I'd make three copies, one for each one of the deacons, so they can think it over before they act on it."

The women sat down again in their chairs, but Hattie Higgins, who had remained seated, got up. "I came here today to sew for the Bazaar. But I can use these towels myself, so I'll go home and hem on them."

"Hattie, there's coffee . . ." protested Clare. But Hattie was going through the door.

CHAPTER XXVI

THE NEXT WEEK brought another meeting, different from that of the women of the Bazaar committees, yet as momentous in the life of the valley.

To Deborah they appeared an oddly assorted group, these five men who sat in the office of the Brent Nail Works on this afternoon of September fifteenth. Will, stiffly erect at his desk, his back half turned to the others, his eyes wholly averted from them. Jed Weaver, across the desk from him, his arms folded around the shabby brief-case he held. Near by, Rudolph Petersen and his lawyer, the latter's chair drawn up within whispering distance of the others'. In a dark suit, obviously new, and a stiff collar, Coley Coggin sat in a corner, uncomfortably on the edge of his chair, his eyes on Will Brent's back. Debbie, like Coley, sat a little apart from the others.

Rudolph Petersen was reading the terms of the merger he was proposing but she was not listening—probably they were what he had outlined to her before and if he had added others she would know about them later. She was watching Willie with anxiety and sympathy. His face, as much of it as she could see, looked as if it had turned into gray stone in his effort to keep it from betraying his feelings. Like the faces of the closest-of-kin, standing beside an open grave. This *was* the same as death to Willie, she thought. This, now, the last service . . .

She had arranged the day and hour of the meeting but it had been Rudolph Petersen who had suggested some formality to it. "I'll send for Reggie Nicholsen, one of my lawyers, to come up from New York; and tell Brent to have his lawyer there, too. Don't know as we need them but it might make it easier for your brother. Think we should have a few bankers standing around backstage?"

She had not laughed, or indeed answered, for she was thinking how *kind* this man was—to want to make it easier for Willie!

Perhaps it did, she reflected, now. Made Willie, for all the death agonies of his pride, feel important—this big manufacturer coming to him for something, bringing the sleek little man from New York, asking that Jed Weaver be here to listen in, too. Coley's new suit— if Willie noticed it—added somehow to the formality. She had put on the dress and hat she had bought that day with Susan.

Rudolph Petersen finished, folded the paper. For an instant his glance met Deborah's, then went to Will Brent's bent head. "I wish to add this, that, if this merger goes through, I'd like to see the old sign left over the door, out of respect to the years it has hung there and the honorable industry it has stood for. Also, that no alterations be made on this particular building itself."

Deborah saw Willie's head lift at that. She gave Rudolph Petersen a warm smile which he missed but which his lawyer caught and answered with a slightly contemptuous glance over the old room.

Rudolph Petersen put the paper down before Will Brent. "You and Mrs. Brent and Mr. Coggin will want to go over this with your lawyer but I'd like some word or two of your feeling about it, Brent. Yours and your sister's . . ."

Will Brent got to his feet, one hand holding to the edge of his desk. The vein bulged dark on his temple. He opened his lips but it was a moment before he could force any sound through them. Then he said, icily, "I have no doubt but that you are fully informed as to my half-sister's answer—Coley Coggin will think as I do. And I am given no choice. Circumstances beyond my control force me to accept any terms of a merger you may make."

He dropped down, then, into his chair, as if all his strength suddenly had failed him.

"Poor Willie. *Poor* Willie." Deborah blinked tears from her eyes.

Rudolph Petersen was holding out his hand to Will Brent. "Between us, Brent, we'll turn out a product of cutlery that will have the reputation your nails have had for so long. Shake on that!"

Will Brent's right hand jerked back against his body, then stiffly moved out to meet Rudolph Petersen's.

"Dear God, *thanks!*" breathed Deborah.

She got up from her chair. She had to get outside where she could let a few tears run. "If there isn't anything I should do . . ." Her voice was not quite steady.

Rudolph Petersen crossed the room to her, put his hand under her arm. "Not now—later there'll be papers to sign. Weaver will tell you when. Let me take you out to your car."

She gave a nod to the others that passed as a word of parting, went with him out of the office, to the yard where her car was parked. His hand stayed on her arm.

"You're shaking, Deborah!"

"Yes, and I want to cry, too. Isn't it silly? I used to be like this whenever Willie had to give in—I'd be glad he did and sorry for him at the same time."

"He stayed in character to the finish, didn't he? Is that your New England backbone?"

"Perhaps . . ."

He opened the door of her car, helped her in, closed it. But he stood outside it, one hand on the open window.

"I suppose you realize, Deborah, that we're partners in industry now?"

"I hadn't thought of it that way—I won't. You know very well that you don't need petticoats to help you run things!"

Rudolph Petersen threw a quick look over the yard, leaned through

the window toward her. "Maybe I do—when it's a woman like you."
A sudden red ran up over his cheekbones. "I'm not good at this but
I've been thinking—wishing that we could be more than part-
ners. . . ."

Deborah broke in quickly, "Why, we *are!*" She put her hand over
his. "We're *friends.* Good friends! We'll always be!"

He stepped back. His smile, though warm, was a little forced and
did not hide the deep disappointment in his eyes. "That's a promise?"

"Yes."

He lifted his hand and she lifted hers and drove out of the yard.

Rom was in his room, writing, but she was glad to be alone for
a little while. She changed her dress, went out and sat in one of the
canvas chairs under the cherry tree. She felt tired. The meeting at
the plant had been more of an emotional strain than she had realized.
Perhaps, somewhere in her, *she* had a little of the Brent pride! She
kept seeing Willie's stony face. But he wasn't too old to adapt himself
to a different order of things. And there were all these men in Sweethome—they'd go back on a payroll on the day the merger was signed.
That was one of the terms of the proposition. Their families would
be relieved of worry. They all must appreciate Rudolph Petersen's
generosity. . . .

She had not intended to let herself think of Rudolph Petersen
until she was rested, but now her thought went of itself from his
generosity to that look in his eyes when he stepped back from the
car window. "A nice way to reward him!" But he had not asked
it as reward—he was not looking even for thanks: he had told her
that this merger was as much to his advantage as to Will's and he
wasn't a man to say things he did not mean. She drew straighter in
her chair. "You were *right* to stop him! At our ages we'll be better
friends for just being good friends!"

But, in spite of this stout assertion, a sigh escaped her lips, lifting
from a sudden queer ache in her heart, and she felt tears in her eyes
again.

She was glad to hear Martha Purdy's voice behind her.

"Hello, Mrs. Brent! Looks as though you are resting, but mind if I disturb it?"

"Not a bit—I'll like it. Sit down here with me."

Martha Purdy sat down.

"I can only stay a moment—I've a pie in the oven. Mrs. Brent, I was commissioned at the meeting of the Bazaar committees last week to ask you if you'd contribute some of your soup to the foods booth. I didn't want to—I've kept putting it off for it seemed nervy to ask you, considering—well, everything. But . . ." Martha gave her quick, short laugh. "Maybe it's a gesture that shouldn't be overlooked!"

Deborah laughed. "Maybe it is! I'll send for a case—tell them I'll donate it to the Bazaar."

"Oh, Mrs. Brent, you make it so *easy!* And I was dreading so to ask you!"

She got up from her chair, stood over Deborah, a twinkle in her eyes. "I wouldn't be a bit surprised if you were invited to pour coffee, the afternoon of the Bazaar! And you know *that* is a distinct honor!"

"My goodness—what's happening here?"

"A lot . . ." Then Martha shook her head. "My pie'll burn if I go into it. But before I run back home—Mrs. Brent, Walter told me about that will, that this house is yours. I hope awfully that you intend to stay here!"

"I do, until I die."

She dwelt on her words, after Martha had gone. The peace of heart they brought. . . . She glanced at the side wall of the old house, what of the garden she could see from where she sat. She did not think of this home as belonging to her but rather of herself belonging to it. To the valley. She saw the valley swiftly in its succeeding seasons— white with snow, copper and russet and red, pale green, lustily leaved in summer. . . . "Why, that's what you've hungered for and didn't know it, all these years!"

She belonged to these people. An overture, Martha Purdy had

said of the request for a donation of her soup. "That concoction you got up to fill the boys' stomachs has served you pretty well, Debbie Brent!"

Nell came through the trellis. She had the catalogues in her hand. She dropped them into Deborah's lap. "May I use your car for a half-hour or so? I've no place in particular I want to go—just drive!"

Deborah saw a restless look on her face. "Of course you may. It's full of gas." She lifted one of the catalogues. "Did you look these over?"

"No. Yes—one of them. The Boston one. But—it's silly even to read it! I haven't a penny to my name and I don't think Father has much more." Nell turned to go to the garage.

"Wait, Nell. Listen to me a minute. I've had it in mind to stake you, if you showed a real interest in studying voice. I haven't been certain that you wanted to. I've the money and it's the particular kind of investment I like to make. I can talk your father around to letting you go. But it's for you to say . . ."

"Oh, *Aunt Debbie!*" The words came on a high breath. "It's what I'd like to do most in the world—now. I'll work—I'll work terribly hard! I'll pay you back, someday!" Suddenly a shamed expression came over the glow on her face. "I haven't been as nice to you as—as Sue has! It's Sue you ought to be doing it for!"

"Sue can't sing! But I'll find something to do for her. Now go along for your drive, child."

But Nell did not move in the direction of the garage. She asked, "Is Rom upstairs? Can I tell him?" She did not wait for Deborah to answer but ran into the house. Deborah heard her calling Rom from the foot of the stairs.

Of all things, *the girl had to tell Rom!*

They came out of the house together. "Rom's going with me," Nell said to Deborah as they walked on toward the garage.

Deborah stared after them, perplexed. "What's been going on that

278

you've missed, Debbie?" She had not heard either one speak with more than bare civility to the other and now, this . . . "It just means you never can tell, with young people." But each would be good for the other, she reflected, her pleasure mounting. "Each may learn from the other to trust, again."

She knew a sudden deeper contentment. This was what staying here meant, too. She would be close to these young people for the rest of her years, share with them whatever came to them of happiness or unhappiness. She had a family, at last. Young Bill . . . Like Nell, he needed an understanding beyond Willie's; she'd try always to have it ready for him—as if he were her own boy. Susan . . .

Here some sadness shadowed her mood. What *was* there in prospect for Susan? Might not these sacrifices of hers, since her mother died, of good times with other young people set her in a pattern of living she could never break? Drab threads in it, growing drabber as the years went along. She was close to thirty years old. . . . John Wendell was going away, maybe, and what other man was there here in the valley? For quite simply, it was a man and a man's love she wanted for Susan.

She sat erect in her chair. "I believe I'll go to John, tell him if he leaves Sweethome to take Susan with him, even if she is a deacon's daughter! Shake him, if I have to, out of his pride, like I did Willie. Love's more important! Only . . ." Suddenly her erectness sagged. "You don't know if it's that way, now, between them. After all these weeks—and that matter of Nell!" No, she did not know. . . .

So intent was she on this concern that she did not hear steps on the gravel of the drive or realize anyone was near until she felt John Wendell's arm around her shoulders and his hearty kiss against her cheek.

"John, are you *crazy?* If your anonymous letter-writer saw that!"

"Impelled to it, by affection and the state of my mind."

"Funny, I was just making up my mind to go to talk with you.

279

Whatever's happened?" She knew something had, by his voice, his face. On this day to be memorable for its happenings, she could expect anything.

He pulled a chair close to hers. "Your new estate, Aunt Debbie! I haven't had a chance since I heard of it to tell you how deeply pleased I am over it. My ball team beat the Norfolk Cubs yesterday. Two friends of Mrs. D'Arby's are joining the church. I've three more good prospects, back country. . . ."

"John, there's more—get to it!"

His face sobered. "Yes, there's more. Lemuel Sims stopped at the parsonage two hours ago, to speak for the deacons. They are offering me a three-year contract to preach here in their church."

"John, my *boy!*" Deborah caught his hand, squeezed it. "All your worry was for nothing!"

"My worry, maybe—my prayers not. To be thought worthy of this field here. I am told that the deacons received a letter signed by a considerable group of the women of the church asking that this contract be offered to me." His smile came back. "It's not for me to question how it came about—only to be grateful that I am accepted."

Deborah smiled, remembering that Martha Purdy had said a lot had happened at that last meeting of the church women. A free-for-all, perhaps, between those who were for John Wendell and those against him. As well as for and against Deborah Brent. Well, it was a good thing to have happened—it cleared the air somehow. Then she remembered that she was planning to give John some sound advice and this was her opportunity. She said briskly, "And now, John . . ."

But he forestalled her. He got up from his chair. "And I'm on my way to ask Susan if she'll marry me. Aunt Debbie, what do you think she'll say? These last weeks I've deliberately avoided her—you know why. But she may not know." His uncertainty was in every line of his face.

"And maybe she's thinking you got interested in Nell."

"Nell!" His astonishment denied it flatly.

"Well, there's talk of that. But you can tell Susan there's nothing to it. Now go along—you're wasting time here with me. Oh, no, a minute—if she says she has to stay with her father and the boy, and she probably will, you tell her I'm here to look after them!"

She smiled after him, yet saw his tall figure in a blur, for, for the third time in this afternoon, tears filled her eyes.

She wiped them away with the back of her hand, got to her feet, went into the kitchen. She did not feel tired now; she felt very alive. "You'd better be starting some supper," she said aloud to the room. "Make some biscuits—they'll go good with that left-over gravy. A lot of them—Nell likely will stay—Susan and John may come in— I must feed them up well."

She laughed, realizing that for the greatest part of her life, she had been feeding people up. And she wasn't through. . . . But now they'd be her own. These young people would be coming in. Rudolph Petersen. "I'll tell him to bring Father Duffy to supper some evening." Martha Purdy and her husband, Clare and Fred—Fred could get Clare over in his truck. Maybe—yes, maybe Willie some day. It was going to be *nice*—

"Debbie, you need never be afraid of lonesomeness, again!"